Also by Jill Shalvis

White Heat

BLUE FLAME

JILL SHALVIS

AN ONYX BOOK

ONYX
Published by New American Library, a division of
Penguin Group (USA) Inc., 375 Hudson Street,
New York, New York 10014, USA
Penguin Group (Canada), 10 Alcorn Avenue, Toronto,
Ontario M4V 3B2, Canada (a division of Pearson Penguin Canada Inc.)
Penguin Books Ltd., 80 Strand, London WC2R 0RL, England
Penguin Ireland, 25 St. Stephen's Green, Dublin 2,
Ireland (a division of Penguin Books Ltd.)
Penguin Group (Australia), 250 Camberwell Road, Camberwell, Victoria 3124,
Australia (a division of Pearson Australia Group Pty. Ltd.)
Penguin Books India Pvt. Ltd., 11 Community Centre, Panchsheel Park,
New Delhi - 110 017, India
Penguin Group (NZ), Cnr Airborne and Rosedale Roads, Albany,
Auckland 1310, New Zealand (a division of Pearson New Zealand Ltd.)
Penguin Books (South Africa) (Pty.) Ltd., 24 Sturdee Avenue,
Rosebank, Johannesburg 2196, South Africa

Penguin Books Ltd., Registered Offices:
80 Strand, London WC2R 0RL, England

First published by Onyx, an imprint of New American Library,
a division of Penguin Group (USA) Inc.

First Printing, December 2004
10 9 8 7 6 5 4 3 2

To David, Kelsey, Megan, and Courtney,
who happily lived on fast food for the duration
it took me to write this book.
Love you bunches.

PROLOGUE

Dangling from a third-story window ledge wasn't a good thing. Dangling from a third-story window ledge by the tips of his fingers, with fire blazing all around him was even worse, and though Jake Rawlins had been in tougher situations, at the moment he couldn't remember one.

"Go away!" cried the young teen, trembling on the very corner of the flaming roof above him. "Go away!"

Jake adjusted his precarious perch, and eyed the kid. "I'm a firefighter, I'm here to help you. Just don't—"

The boy scrambled out of Jake's reach.

"—move." Damn it. Apparently nothing about this call would be easy tonight. So far, he had a mansion of a house on fire in the dead of the night; occupants caught unawares on a rural street, with the fire hydrant just far enough away to create a sea of hoses at his crew's feet, all on hilly, uneven land in the outskirts of San Diego county. Oh, and a terrified teen sitting above the inferno, on a roof, holding one arm against his chest as if he'd injured it.

The winds whipped right at Jake, stirred by the fire itself, trying to tear him from the house. It'd only been two minutes since the ladder engine had malfunctioned, trapping him up there, but it felt like a lifetime. He had at least eight minutes before another ladder engine would arrive. Only problem, the roof wasn't going to last another eight minutes.

"Billy! Somebody get my Billy!" screamed the kid's mother from three stories below. Her terror stabbed at Jake, and fueled him on. Adjusting his grip on the ledge, he reached for the rain gutter, which was thankfully anchored to the house, and began to climb.

The house itself was nothing but a bright ball of flame around him. No one could get through the inferno to get inside, not until they tamed the fire, which his crew was working on from below. Long streams of forced water flew through the air toward the flames, which only seemed to enrage them all the more.

"*Mom!*" Above Jake, Billy's voice sounded weak and smoke-ravaged.

Jake got high enough to see him again, and his heart nearly stopped. Shaking in terror, Billy sat about three feet back from the ledge, completely surrounded by flames, cradling his arm and screaming. "*Mom!*"

"She can't hear you from there, buddy."

"I didn't mean for this to happen, I didn't!"

Had he started the fire? At the moment it didn't matter. Neither did the fact that as captain of the malfunctioned engine, Jake was usually on the ground, strategizing and organizing the crew, not straddling a rickety rain gutter thirty feet above ground. Christ, he hated heights. "Hang on, now." Jake kept his face averted from the heat and flames blasting toward him, but then the kid shifted to bolt away.

The roof was a goner. A wrong move now, and he could fall through. With no ladder and nothing to brace his foot on, Jake had to use sheer strength to pull himself up, and he felt every one of his hundred and eighty pounds, not to mention the additional sixty-five pounds of gear.

The kid stared at the flames engulfing the roof, flinching as areas began to cave in. *"Mom!"*

"Your mom's safe. Let's do the same for us." With the flames leaping far too close for comfort, Jake reached out for him.

"No!" Whimpering, Billy crawled backward, out of Jake's reach and straight into the danger zone. "I don't wanna go over the edge!"

Jake could hear more sirens coming closer now. He could feel the mist of the spray his crew were frantically sending around them, trying to keep them safe. "Billy, we need to go."

"I want to go through the attic door, the way I came!" Dropping to his knees, Billy scooted away from Jake and the feared edge, and directly toward the flames.

Jake understood the height issue, and sympathized more than the kid could know, but there was no help for that. They had to get off the roof, and fast, and they had to go the way Jake had come—via the ledge.

From far below, new swirling lights joined the others, and he knew the other ladder engine had arrived. Relief was cut short by a thundering crash directly on his left. Whipping around, he watched a good part of the roof cave in, including the attic door and stairs.

Billy stared at the gaping hole in horror. Flames immediately filled it, but unbelievably, the kid took a step toward it.

"No." Jake reached out, and got a hold of Billy's shoe, which promptly came off. *Shit.* With his other hand, he caught the kid's ankle, but lost in his fear, Billy thrashed around.

"It's okay," Jake tried to soothe. "I've got you—" He took a well-placed kick to his chest, which nearly sent them both over the edge of the three-story house.

"I want to get down!"

"Yeah, but not the way the stairs and attic door just went, okay?"

Another crash, and only three feet away this time, and more of the roof vanished. Jake's stomach dropped to his toes. It was now or never. With the hot, unforgiving wind whipping his face and the smoke clogging his lungs, he got a better grip on Billy, trying to be careful with the injured arm. "Hold it tight to you." Jake spread a protective hand over the limb as best he could. "The ladder's here."

"We're going down on a fire engine ladder?"

"Yep." Holding on to Billy, Jake leaned slightly over the edge to take a look. Indeed, the malfunctioned engine had been moved, and the new one was in position, the ladder inching its way up.

It felt like slow motion. Another roaring boom came directly behind them, and Billy cried out, clinging to Jake.

Jake's gaze met Steve's, the firefighter on the end of the ladder. The silent urgency passed between them as more of the roof dissolved around them. They were running out of time.

Steve reached out but was still too far away. It was going to be too damn late. Jake could feel the immense heat beneath him, all around him. He figured he had less than a minute to get them down before there wasn't a square foot to stand on.

The ladder bumped the building, and Steve reached

for Billy, whose one good thin arm was wrapped so tightly around Jake's neck that he could hardly breathe. "Billy, Steve's going to take you down."

"I want you to do it!"

Again Jake's gaze met Steve's. They didn't have time to switch positions, not with fire raining down over them, the ladder slick from the hose. Jake pulled free of Billy's grip and shoved him at Steve.

An ominous rumble came from beneath Jake's feet. Steve was still right there with Billy, trying to get out of the way for Jake, but the flames whipped up from below, taking over the ledge, forcing Jake back another step, separating him from Steve and Billy by a wall of fire.

Who would miss him? came the inane thought. His mother? Nope. His brother? Double nope. Cici, the beautiful brunette he'd seen twice and who'd been so hot just last night? Yeah, maybe *she'd* miss him—

The roof gave beneath his feet, and he fell.

And fell.

Jake opened his eyes to find himself still in the hospital, where he'd been for two days. He lay there and listened to his pretty little nurse kick some serious reporter ass.

"No, you can't talk to him," she said furiously into the telephone by his bed. Candy—or was it Cindy?— was the quintessential California girl—blond, tanned, five foot two tops, with a sweet curvy little bod that Jake watched quiver indignantly.

"I have no idea how you people got this room number but you have to stop calling," she said. "Firefighter Rawlins doesn't want to talk to the *Times*, the *Gazette*, *People*, or *US Weekly*. Nobody. Got that?" She slammed

down the phone, gave an incensed little huff, then shot
Jake a smile of pure gold as she blew her too long bangs
out of her eyes. "There. That should buy you five minutes of peace. Want me to take the phone out of here?"

"Nah, they'll give up eventually."

"I doubt that." Moving to his IV, she skimmed a con-
soling hand up his arm before she shot him up with the
morphine he'd required since his reconstructive shoulder surgery the day before. Amazingly enough, other
than his crushed shoulder, he had only a concussion
and a few second-degree burns on his back. Not bad,
considering. The euphoria from the drugs kicked in,
and he began floating happily. In and out . . .

He came to sometime later, apparently in the middle
of a conversation with his good friend, fire inspector
Joe Walker. He was leaning over Jake's hospital bed
with a look in his eyes that Jake hadn't seen since
they'd lost Danny in that horrific building fire six
months ago. "I'm not dead," Jake said quickly, craning
his neck to catch the welcome sight of his monitors,
and the equally welcome movement on the screen in-
dicating he was indeed breathing.

A shadow of a smile crossed Joe's face. "No. Apparently you have nine lives."

"Well then, stop looking at me like that."

Joe's expression didn't change, and Jake's heart
started a heavy drumming. Ah, shit. What was the matter? What hadn't they told him? What had he missed
while in la-la land? He could see his toes, could even
wriggle them—

"Look, Jake. I know firefighting is everything to
you." Joe's eyes looked suspiciously shiny. "Jesus, how
can I not know that? I've watched you risk life and limb
on this job for years. I saw how you hated being injured

last year, having to work on the hiring board instead of fighting fires, but . . ."

Jake closed his eyes to the torment in Joe's voice. Now all he could hear was the steady bleep bleep of his monitors, no longer assuring because maybe whatever was wrong was something he couldn't see. He wouldn't have a clue, as another extremely cute little nurse had just slipped some more excellent drugs into his IV. "Just tell me what you're dancing around."

"They think you're done firefighting."

No. He wasn't done, he couldn't be. *But what if he was?* Maybe he couldn't feel anything because they'd had to cut off his arm—Flailing out with his left hand he slapped at his right shoulder. White hot pain stabbed at him, and he sagged back, gasping. Nope. Arm still there, just numb from the neck block he'd required on top of the anesthesia. "I'll heal." He grimaced and breathed through the pain. "I'll heal and get back to work."

The sympathy in Joe's gaze was far scarier than a thirty-foot fall through hell had been. "You'll need time," he said. "Lots of it and preferably away from here and the media."

Ah, yes, the media. Turned out little Billy *had* broken his arm. Joe and the other inspector on the case suspected that it'd been broken while Billy had been lighting his own house on fire, but the kid claimed Jake had been rough with him, breaking the limb while grabbing and shaking Billy on the roof.

To add insult to injury, Billy's mother was threatening to file a suit against the city, the fire department, and Jake himself, a situation made worse when Jake had groggily picked up the phone an hour after his surgery, telling some reporter that the kid must be on crack as well as being a pyromaniac if he thought Jake would do that.

The press had had a field day with that comment, and Billy's mother had decided to add a civil suit against Jake for defaming her boy in the press, all of which had warranted Jake more publicity than he'd ever wanted.

Joe was surveying the room, and all the flowers Jake had received. "Fan club?"

"Better than the stack of ugly faxes waiting for me at the nurses' station." His words slurred a little, thanks to the drugs. "There's a whole bunch of people who actually believe I hurt that kid, and want to kick my ass."

"And there's a whole bunch of women who just want to kiss it." He flicked a note attached to a basket of roses: *Roses are red, violets are blue, call me when you're better, and our last rendezvous we'll redo.* "Call her," he suggested. "Let her be a slave to your every whim and need for a while."

It was a running joke at the station that Jake could date a different woman every night for a year and not have to repeat unless he chose to. But none of them would be interested in him at the moment, not a one. Sad to admit, but for all the years that he'd been there for others, most of them complete strangers, he had few true connections. So here he was now, needing a little help to disappear, maybe a little TLC to go with that help, and he couldn't think of anyone to call.

Not a single soul.

Three weeks later Jake stared up at the weights he was trying to pull down to his chest at the orders of his physical therapist, feeling one hundred and two instead of thirty-two. Both mentally and physically exhausted, he'd begun to despair of his shoulder, and how he hadn't bounced back as he'd thought. They'd warned him after the surgery that a reconstructed shoulder wouldn't be a walk in the park, but he hadn't believed it.

He couldn't believe a number of things, including how hard it was dodging the curious reporters at his house on the Del Mar bluffs, or how antsy he felt not working, not doing anything but getting tired of daytime TV.

"Take a cruise," Joe suggested from his perch on the next bench over. He came to Jake's physical therapy as often as he could, offering support and dirty jokes as needed.

But a cruise wasn't feasible. Firefighters weren't exactly rolling in dough, and Jake sank every last penny he had into a down payment on his house last year, and was now the proud owner of a mortgage up to his eyeballs.

"Family reunion?" Joe suggested.

"Nah." Jake's mother was currently enjoying conning her sixth or seventh husband out of his retirement, and wouldn't welcome him. Jake's father—husband number two—had died two years ago. Richard Rawlins had left Jake his guest ranch, the Blue Flame, a place out in the middle of Nowhere, Arizona, where people worked like a dog, camped out on rocky ground, and paid for the pleasure. As a city guy who didn't feel the draw of the great Wild West, Jake had pretty much left it to run itself.

It was thirty acres surrounded by three thousand more of open land in the Dragoon Mountains National Forest, reputedly one of the most beautiful areas in Arizona, which might have been exciting for the value factor, if it had value. But the truth was, the place barely broke even most months, and there'd been several where it hadn't even done that. "Maybe I could go to the Blue Flame."

Joe laughed, then got serious when Jake didn't crack a smile. "But you hate camping."

"Yeah." He also hated that his father, a man who hadn't bothered with Jake in life, had in death tried to tie him to a place that meant nothing except a reminder of a relationship he'd never had. "So how about I just go back to work instead?"

"You know what the doctor said."

He'd said it wasn't looking good for Jake to get his shoulder back to fit condition, at least not fit enough for the heavy demands firefighting would put on it. Jake didn't want to think about that. His cell phone rang so he didn't have to, and since he had his hands on the weights, Joe answered it for him.

His friend listened for a moment, then lifted a brow. "No, I don't think Firefighter Rawlins is interested in doing a spread for *Playgirl*—How much?" His gaze flew to meet Jake's while he let out a whistle, but slowly shook his head. "Sorry. That's . . . shocking, but no." He disconnected, then shot Jake a speculative look. "I had no idea they paid so much."

Jake didn't respond because it was taking all his energy to lift weights. Actually, he wasn't lifting so much as budging.

Budging while his muscles trembled like a newborn baby and sweat broke out on his brow. And then suddenly a microphone was shoved in his face by a man wearing a *Tribune* badge.

"Jake Rawlins, what will you do if your victim wins his case? Will you be forced to quit?"

Shocked, Jake blinked up at him. Forced to quit the job that was everything to him? For saving a kid's life?

"Have you admitted guilt?" the reporter asked.

Fury filled him so fast his head spun, but Joe's hand settled on his chest, holding him down. "Ignore him," Joe warned quietly, then stood and hauled the reporter up to his toes. "We're busy here."

The reporter, feet swinging above the ground, paled. "Y-yes, I see that."

"Then why are you still here?"

When the reporter had high-tailed it out the door, Jake lay back, one thing suddenly crystal clear. He did need out. He'd go to the only place he could think of, and the last place anyone would look for him. The last place he wanted to be.

The Blue Flame.

1

Blue Flame Guest Ranch, Arizona

The rocky wooded canyons stretched to the sharp azure sky, unmarred by so much as a single cloud. Spring had been generous so far, and manzanita, mesquite, and Arizona oak grew in bountiful supply. In the center of all this glory a little piglet pumped its short legs, squealing as it ran from a second little piglet, right across the newly seeded area of the front lawn. A third little piglet chased its tail in circles in the flower bed in front of the big house. Piglet number four sat on its own, happily eating the garden hose.

Piglets five, six, seven, eight, nine, and ten were creating mayhem in the hen pen. Hens screamed and squawked, racing around as if their heads had been cut off, with the pigs in merry pursuit.

Callie Anne Hayes opened the front door of the big house, stepped onto the wrap-around porch, and beheld all this in disbelief.

One day away from a highly anticipated spring season of the Blue Flame Guest Ranch, a season she'd carefully orchestrated to be flawless . . . just one day. Clearly, things had been going too smoothly. Hen feathers flew through the air. Dust and dirt rose in a cloud, and above it all came the incredible sound of pigs in heaven and hens in hell.

Amazingly enough, Shep slept on at the bottom of the stairs, oblivious. Callie nudged the old shepherd's hindquarters, but he just kept snoring.

Callie sighed, and eyeing pigs chasing hens chasing pigs, lifted the walkie-talkie at her hip. "The piglets are on the loose and destroying everything in sight. The latch must have broken. Help pronto, please."

She got nothing back. "Tucker? Stone? Eddie? Marge? A little help?"

Still, no one answered, but at least she knew why. This was her crew's last day off. Tomorrow they had a large group of Japanese businessmen coming in, and directly on their heels, a group of Tucson librarians, and then some professional football cheerleaders on break from the various teams they cheered for. After that, a reunion for a group of nine sisters, and then some frat boys. In fact, for the foreseeable future, the Blue Flame was nicely booked.

Knowing that, everyone had made their last day their own, and if she knew her crew, they'd all escaped at the crack of dawn that morning so she couldn't find something to keep them busy.

Which left her on little piggy detail. She headed down the stairs. The two little guys on the grass first, she decided. They had to be caught before they destroyed the new, tender shoots. She chased them around a large Arizona oak, where the two piglets ran smack into each other, and then sat stunned. Scooping one under each arm, she marched them back to their pen. Brushing herself off, she went to shut the gate, figuring she'd duct tape it for now if she had to, but the latch wasn't broken at all.

Whoever had fed them their slop this morning must have gotten lazy. "Damn it, Tucker." He was one of her youngest employees but the twenty-year-old was usually much more vigilant than this.

Bracing herself, she turned around to go about the next capture, assisted now by Goose, an oversized, bossy female Pilgrim goose they kept around as a sort of mascot who ran the grassy area and front walk like a drill sergeant. Together they corralled the pigs while Shep slept on, and thirty minutes later there was only one stubborn little piglet left to nab. He was currently running from her as fast as his short little legs would carry him, his curlycue tail swinging around madly as he squealed loud enough to wake the dead.

She chased him around the large front yard, gritting her teeth as he led her back over the baby grass, followed by a honking Goose, who hated it when anyone happened onto "her" grass. Around the trees again, and then toward the water pump and hose at the side of the house, which one of the little pigs had already destroyed. Callie pictured a new account in her expenses this month labeled *Ridiculous Costs* and cringed.

To complicate matters, someone had left the hose on, and by the looks of things, water had been leaking all night, turning the entire area to mud.

The little piglet stopped to enjoy the sloppy mess, joyfully rubbing its snout in it. When it saw Callie coming, it prepared to run.

And to think she'd thought today had had perfection written all over it, the beginning of spring, a new time for the ranch, where she'd hopefully prove that the Blue Flame was worth every second of stress it caused the current owner—that is if Jake Rawlins ever even gave this place a second of his thoughts, period. She'd bet her last dollar he didn't, which really ate at her because she'd give her left arm to own the Blue Flame.

But that was a worry for another day. Not today. Today was to be her calm before the storm, and if it hadn't been for the out-of-control pigs, she wouldn't have been able to take her eyes off her surroundings. God, she loved this place, where people could come to relax on a ranch setting, or join in and work it alongside her ranch crew.

The Blue Flame had been the first real home she'd ever had, and it held her heart, her soul, her very inner spirit. She scanned the three hundred and sixty degree vista around her. At an altitude of five thousand feet, the hundred square miles of national forest around her had been unchanged for centuries, probably longer. The Dragoon and Chiricahua Mountains, the Sulphur Springs Valley, the stories of Cochise, of his Chiricahua Apache braves, the legends of Geronimo, the feast of the Buffalo Soldiers . . . so much history right here.

In fact, the big house behind her had its own history. Once upon a time it'd been a country farmhouse for an early settler and his Indian wife, but now it was where their guests stayed in quaint rooms and shared meals together. The place reflected the air of the Old West, meaning rugged, which was more by necessity than design. It was actually in desperate need of renovation, but they hid that behind all the warm, friendly service they offered.

The house sat on a slight hill, overlooking the rest of the ranch. The large wooden deck housed their hot tub, all cleaned and ready for use. Each bedroom was neat and clean as well, and decorated with individual furnishings, all in poor farmhouse chic. The heart of the house was the living room, where ranch hands and guests alike all gathered. There was a large brick hearth there for long winter evenings, and the place looked hopefully inviting despite the fact they hadn't replaced the scarred hardwood flooring last year because profits hadn't allowed for it.

But this year would be different. As ranch manager, Callie had spent long nights working on their website. She'd scrimped in every way possible to spend more money on advertising, and as a result they were getting more bookings every week.

A surge of excitement went through her, as it did every time she thought about the Blue Flame slowly turning itself around from the dump it'd been two years ago; and she knew she'd had a big hand in that.

She moved up on the wayward piglet. "Stay right there," Callie said softly, coming up on him, hands out. "Just stay right there . . ." She dove for him, at the exact moment the cell phone at her hip rang.

With a squeal, the pig ran off, and Callie landed in the mud, arms empty. Lifting her head, she wiped her face off on her sleeve and reached back for the phone. "Hello?"

"Hello, Callie. I'd like to book a room."

Sprawled on her stomach, filthy now, Callie went absolutely still. That voice. She hadn't heard it in a good long while, but she hadn't forgotten it.

It belonged to Jake Rawlins, the one man who had the ability to destroy her perfect life, to have her at his mercy with five short words—"*I'm selling the Blue Flame.*" He was the only man who could drive her crazy, and the last man to have seen her naked.

She'd rather chase fifty more piglets than talk to him. "You need a room? Why?"

"Why?" He gave off a soft laugh that both grated and thrilled. "Because I thought I'd come stay for a while. Get some pampering."

Pampering. No one knew better than she that Jake had an overabundance of charm and charisma, and thought nothing of using said charm and charisma to get a woman in his bed. . . . Only a man like Jake would think of coming to a dude ranch to be pampered.

God, she hated to think back to that night of Richard's funeral service. Grief-stricken at the loss of her boss, her mentor, the man who'd once saved her life, she'd contacted his son. She had picked Jake up at the airport, driven him to the church, taken him back to the Blue Flame.

His first time there.

She'd mistaken his low, husky voice for anguish, his quiet, confident movements for ease in his surroundings, and over a bottle of aged whiskey, had thought she'd found a soul mate to grieve with.

She'd really like to blame what had happened next on her sorrow and the whiskey, or on Jake and his amazing voice, his talented mouth, and even more talented fingers. But the truth was, she'd *wanted* to be held that night, to be taken out of herself, to forget.

She'd done exactly that, until she'd realized that what grief she felt, she felt alone, as the only thing Jake had in him for his father was resentment and anger.

Unfortunately she'd been naked and in his arms by then. Kicking him out of her bed had given her great satisfaction . . . until she was alone again.

She and Jake hadn't talked much since, except to discuss the monthly financials she sent. At least he hadn't uttered those five dreaded words yet. She tried to keep her extremely negative thoughts to herself rather than remind him that he'd like nothing more than to sell this place.

He'd been back to the ranch just twice since Richard's death. Each time had been with a different bimbo—er, woman—at his side and a disinterested smile on his lips as he watched their guests get excited over milking cows and feeding pigs.

Neither time had he indulged in any of the activities available, at least nothing that involved the great outdoors. No, his recreation of choice had been staying in bed with his guest and ringing for room service—which they didn't have.

At least he'd called ahead each time as he was doing now, warning her. She supposed she should be grateful for that consideration. "I'm sorry," she said into her phone. Mud dripped off her nose. "We're booked."

"I didn't tell you when I'm arriving."

"It doesn't matter. We're solid for the month. A group of businessmen is checking in, and we have three more groups booked back to back after they leave."

"I'm sure we can find a spare room," he said easily.

We. That meaning her and the mouse in her pocket, she supposed. "For when?"

"Tonight."

She gripped the cell phone. Mud squished through her fingers. "So soon?"

"Yep." Was that a laugh in his voice? "Why don't you go ahead and finish terrorizing that poor pig first. I'll wait."

Pulling the phone away from her ear, she stared at it,

heart hammering in her ears. Another drop of mud dripped from her nose to the receiver.

"I'd offer to help," he said. "But I'm not interested in a mud bath as a part of my pampering."

Lifting her head, she searched her immediate vicinity. Big house at her right, series of small one-room cabins on her left, where the staff lived. One large barn and stables straight ahead, a smaller hay barn beside it, and behind them the open corrals and fields of the ranch. Beyond that, the Dragoon Mountains, where she'd led countless expeditions to abandoned mining camps and old Apache lookout points along mountain precipices and ridges that rolled along as far as the eye could see.

Twisting around, she looked behind her. The new grass, the driveway . . . and the black truck that hadn't been there before her pig hunt. Leaning against the driver's side stood a man she recognized all too well, despite only seeing him three times in her life.

He looked the same; he always did, which was to say knee-knockingly good. He was just over six feet, with dark hair on the wrong side of his last haircut, thick and unruly to the top of his collar. There was a few days' growth on his lean jaw, and mirrored sunglasses on eyes she knew to be a steely, unsettling shade of gray like his father's had been. He wore a dark blue T-shirt with some emblem she couldn't read over his left pec, probably his firefighter's patch, and nicely fitted Levi's faded in all the stress points. He had running shoes on his feet, not boots, and inwardly she sneered at the thought of him walking in those toward her, in the mud.

Seeming quite unconcerned, his long legs were casually crossed, his broad shoulders relaxed for a man who'd just shown up where he wasn't wanted and knew it.

Or maybe he didn't know it.

In any case, he held his cell phone to his ear, and when he saw her looking at him, he smiled with that mouth that had once nearly made her orgasm from just a kiss, and waved the phone at her.

Gritting her teeth, she pushed herself upright. He looked good and wicked to the bone, which unfortunately she'd learned was a terrible weakness on her part. She had no idea how it was possible to both hate and lust after someone at the same time, but with Jake, she'd always managed it.

Mud dripped off her red tank top, the one she'd put on that morning with a smile and anticipation of the spring ahead. Her fresh, dark blue jeans were now brown. She shoved the phone back onto her belt and put her filthy hands on her equally filthy hips.

To add insult to injury, the last little piglet ran right up to his pen and stood still, waiting to be let in. "I'm feeling hungry for bacon," she hissed at it, then straightened and looked at Jake.

He slid his cell phone into his pocket and shoved his sunglasses to the top of his head, eyeing her with those eyes that made her want to squirm.

She held her breath and waited to hear him say, *"I'm selling the Blue Flame."*

Instead, he smiled a smile of pure sin.

And slowly, slowly, she let out her held breath, trying to remain unmoved. Maybe he really was just here for a visit, just like those other two times since Richard's funeral. Maybe just like then, he'd stay holed up in his room with whatever woman he had with him, appearing only to eat, looking rumpled and sated and far too sexy for his own good.

And then he'd go away, far far away, until she had enough money saved that she could get herself a big, fat loan and try to buy Blue Flame herself.

That was her dream, and no one could take that from her.

Except him.

Nothing but pure stubborn pride kept her from throwing herself at his feet and begging him to wait to sell until she had enough money to buy. Instead, casual as she could, she opened the pig pen, let the errant piglet in, then carefully latched it. Then she walked over to him and thrust out her hand.

He stared at it, then smiled. "Formal, given what we've done, don't you think?"

"I was trying to be polite."

"Okay . . ." Instead of giving her his right hand, he leaned in and kissed her cheek.

She jerked back. "What was that for?"

"A *polite* hello. For two people who've—"

"Don't. Don't you dare say it."

He grinned, and she turned away from the sight because it scraped at her tummy uncomfortably. Like ulcer-inducing uncomfortably. "So you need a room for two?"

"Two?"

She looked back. "Don't you have a woman with you?"

Jake lifted a brow.

"Last time you had a blonde with you," she reminded him. "And the time before that, a different blonde."

"I didn't have a blonde with me the first time I came up here."

No, no he hadn't. He'd had her. A redhead.

His smile spread as he pushed away from the truck and came toward her. "Sweet of you to concern yourself with my social life, but sorry. I'm solo. Unless you're offering— No? Well, then, count me as one."

"So you're here to what? I know it's not to camp, you hate to camp. I know it's not to milk a cow, or to go on a roundup, or hike along ancient Indian trails."

He had his right hand hooked in his front pocket, and lifted his left shoulder. "Like I said, I'm up for some pampering."

"The Blue Flame specializes in camping expeditions, hiking, and ranching activities. Not pampering. You know that."

"You have a hot tub. Food. A massage therapist on call—Macy, if I recall. That'll add up to enough pampering for now." His gaze traveled slowly down her mud-covered body, and then back up again, making every square inch tingle with an awareness that pissed her off. "You're looking a little tense, Callie."

"Oddly enough, I'm feeling a little tense."

"Why?"

"Why?" She let out a disbelieving laugh. "Come on, Jake. You're not that thick."

Uninsulted, his lips curved. "Do you greet all the guests so friendly-like?"

Only the ones who made her world feel like a roller coaster. Damn, she wished she could look at him without remembering what had happened between them on one dark, drunken, foolish night. "I'm sorry." She sounded stiff to her own ear, and lifted her hands to indicate the mud she wore. "Let me take you inside. I'll change, see what accommodations we can find for you, even though I can tell you we really are booked."

"Great."

Great. She told herself she wasn't going to worry. She wasn't going to waste energy thinking about him or what he could do to her life—such as ruin it.

They stepped onto the grass, and with a loud, aggressive honk, Goose waddled toward them, head down, picking up speed as she went.

Jake stopped short.

Goose charged him anyway.

"Goose!"

At Callie's sharp voice, the goose let out one more honk, but slowed. Glared at Jake.

He shook his head. "You haven't eaten that thing yet?"

"She'd be too tough to eat."

His laugh said that he agreed, but he eyed the goose with a healthy mistrust as they walked by her.

Callie tried not to think about why his laugh had somehow softened her, or why his being afraid of a silly goose made her want to hold his hand. Clearly, she had hormonal issues today. Nothing a good hard day of work couldn't cure.

They headed toward the big house, Jake moving with a natural grace that reminded her that she dripped mud with every stiff step she took. She'd never felt more unfeminine or unattractive in her life.

There. Hormonal issue resolved.

"Where is everyone?" he asked.

A safe enough question, and one that didn't surprise her. "Eddie and Stone are most likely in town enjoying their day off." Stone was probably drinking too much, too, she thought with a flicker of worry that she kept to herself.

"Tucson?"

"Tucson's too far for a day run. Three Rocks."

"Three Rocks isn't a town. I blinked on the way in here and nearly missed it."

"Not every place is as big as San Diego."

He lifted a brow in agreement. "Okay, so the Motley Crew is out on the 'town.'"

Callie smiled at the nickname for Stone and Eddie McDermitt. The brothers might have been hell on the myriad of other ranches they'd been fired from because monotony bored them, but the Blue Flame catered to their guests' whims, which always varied, so there was no monotony. She'd known when she'd hired the brothers that she wouldn't be sorry. They had a good work ethic, were fast on their feet, and delighted their guests with their "real cowboy" charm.

In fact, she couldn't have managed without them. That they had some personal problems was another story. "You know Kathy left us last week. I just hired a new cook. Amy Wheeler. I faxed you her employment form? She's probably in town today, too. Marge left yesterday to take a break from cleaning and preparing bedrooms, but if I know her, she's at her mother's house doing more of the same, and Lou's looking for work as he just got laid off from his full-time job in town."

"Lou?"

"You remember Marge's husband? He works for us on an as-needed basis doing all our mechanical stuff?"

"Right. But I guess when I said others, I meant Tucker."

Now that did surprise her. "His day is his own today as well."

Jake nodded, and she couldn't tell if he was relieved or disappointed.

"So why are *you* here today?" he asked. "Don't you ever take time off from this place?" He looked around as if he couldn't understand why one would choose to spend their free time out here. That insulted her, and since she couldn't come up with something nice to say, she took a lesson from Thumper's mother and said nothing at all.

They stepped onto the porch that might have needed some refinishing, but did he have to look at it like it wouldn't hold their weight? She kicked off her muddy boots, not wanting to ruin the clean floors inside. Opening the door, she gestured him in ahead, but he stopped in the doorway with her and put his hand on her arm.

She looked down at his fingers on her skin, then up into his face. He was crowding her, darn it. Please, God, don't let him say he was selling. Not yet. She wasn't ready yet—

"I saddled you with him," he said quietly. "Is it working out?"

It took a moment for her brain to shift gears. "You mean Tucker?"

He nodded, and she let out a low laugh. "You 'saddled' me with him nearly two years ago. You're just now asking?" She shook her head. "Tucker is amazing with the horses. This place is better for having him here. You should know that. You *would* know that if you'd looked around at all on your last two visits."

Jake's steely gaze searched hers. "I'm just making sure. He's stubborn as hell, and hard-headed to boot."

"And brooding and moody, too. All traits that run in the family, I'm taking it."

"He's only my half brother."

She knew this, of course. She knew far too much about this man that stood too close. "Look, make yourself at home, okay?" He would anyway. He had every right to do so more often than he did. She needed to remember that, and be grateful this was probably no longer a visit than his others had been. "I'll be back in a few." She turned to go back out, but they were still in the doorway together, too close in her opinion, and she accidentally bumped into him, making him hiss out a breath. "Sorry," she said, a little surprised at his reaction.

His expression shuttered. "No problem."

She looked him over, trying to figure out what she was missing, but he gave off no clue. "When I get back, I'll try to figure out where to put you for a few nights—"

"More than a few."

"So . . . three or four?"

"Yeah, three or four. *Months.*"

And he turned and walked into the living room.

2

Callie ran to her cabin, mind whirling. Three or four months. Was he crazy? Jake Rawlins was a city man, through and through, and a firefighter who loved his work. She knew those two things about him at least.

Clearly, he'd been messing with her, just to drive her crazy. She stepped inside her cabin, and let herself be soothed by the interior. She'd painted the walls in the color of sand, with adobe-colored trim, and had hung a few tapestries she'd picked up from the occasional art shows on the Indian reservations around the area. Everything was clean and in its place. "*Anal*," Richard had called her fondly, and she had to agree. She washed up and changed quickly, and then stepped back outside into what had begun as such a glorious day. She inhaled the fresh, crisp air that held a hint of the warmth to come, and looked at the row of cabins. Tucker had the one next to hers. Then followed Stone's, Eddie's, Marge and her husband Lou's, and lastly, the newly hired Amy's. There wasn't an extra cabin for Jake.

Instead of crossing the poor grass, which had taken a beating that day, she took the path up to the big house, wondering what to do. There were twelve guest rooms on the second floor, all booked by the Japanese businessmen coming tomorrow, each excited about their first time out in the wilderness.

Which left Jake out in the cold.

Or sharing with Tucker—

That would have to do. Callie could handle him there for several nights, but several months . . . the thought boggled her mind. She wondered how Tucker would feel about it.

She stopped to check on the horses. They had twenty in all, though four belonged to her and the crew, and one was Richard's old horse, leaving fifteen for their guests. Most of those fifteen would be riding out with their guests tomorrow on a mock roundup that wasn't really a mock roundup at all. They really did need to gather up their small but valuable herd of cattle and get them back to the main arena area for their inoculations before shipping a portion of them off to market. What the businessmen couldn't handle, Eddie, Stone, and Tucker sure as hell could, with Lou's help if they needed it, so Callie wasn't worried.

Not about that anyway.

She checked on the poor hens next, fully aware she was stalling. But the pigs had riled the hens up, and many were still clucking and fussing and pulling at their own feathers. "Poor babies." She scattered out some feed as a treat. "That was worse than letting in a handful of roosters, wasn't it?"

She glanced at the big house, painfully aware of the rooster in *her* hen house. With a grim sigh, she passed by the pigs, all now perfectly content to be in their place, and looking quite innocent. "Don't think you're off the hook," she whispered to the littlest one, then headed up the porch steps, wondering what Jake was up to, what he'd really come for. Her heart pounded uncomfortably in her chest as she let herself in. She looked around at the wide comfortable arc of couches in her living room, empty of one big, bad, sexy-but-irritating San Diego firefighter. He wasn't in the small weight room, either, or in the game room playing pool.

She tried the kitchen next. Large and roomy, it smelled like ... she took a big breath ... *blueberry muffins*? Having skipped breakfast, her mouth watered. Amy had been a desperate hire—on both their parts, she suspected—but the incredible scent gave Callie hope. She searched until she found the big, fat muffins in a basket on the counter, and then nabbed one. It melted in her mouth, and she stopped to let out a moan. Oh yeah, Amy was going to work out just fine.

She left the kitchen and put her hand on the wood banister. Upstairs were the bedrooms and bathrooms, all clustered around a central hall, but at the sound of bubbles behind her, she turned. Reversing her steps, she went back into the dining room, and headed directly to the sliding glass door there, which was ajar.

Just outside it, on the back wooden deck, she found her rooster.

Jake sat in the large hot tub, head back, body sprawled out, covered by the frothing, bubbling water. Was he lying there trying to figure out how to tell her he'd already sold the place? Just the thought made her want to throw up. She couldn't handle the suspense. Stepping outside, boots clunking on the wood, she hunkered down at his side.

He cracked a slate gray eye.

"Did you sell?" she asked. "Just tell me."

"What?"

Reaching out, she hit the large red button that

turned off the bubbles. Silence descended. She kept her eyes on his and off his body. "Come on, Jake. You're not here to relax. You hate this place. You always have. Are you here to sell or what?"

"No one's going to buy it until I fix it up."

Right. Good. Okay. Part of her wanted to ask him to wait on her, until she'd saved just a little bit more, until she could get a loan to buy it herself, but she took a deep breath and fought with her own ego because she couldn't bring herself to ask him for anything, especially help in buying the ranch. She'd do it on her own, without anyone's help, especially his. "Are you here to do that then? Get the place fixed up?"

"If I can do it for cheap."

"You're having money trouble?"

He sighed. "I have a heavy mortgage on my house and . . . some other unexpected expenses. This place drains me dry lately—"

"It's going to do better now."

"You mean for this month, but after that, you don't know for sure."

No, she didn't. She stared at him, gauging him for honesty, and he stared right back. Guileless but not innocent. She doubted he'd ever been innocent, but she decided he was telling the truth. He hadn't done anything toward actually selling. Yet. He needed to, though. More than she'd thought, which made her relief short-lived. "So you're hanging here in the hot tub figuring out how to get this place renovated for cheap?"

"You did say I should make myself at home," he reminded her, and ran his wet fingers through his hair. Now it stood straight up, which should have made him look ridiculous but didn't. "Don't tell me that was one of those female things, where you say what you don't mean, because at the moment I'm too exhausted to play that game."

"I'm taking it by that sexist statement you've dated some real winners."

He laughed.

She didn't. Up close, she believed his exhaustion claim. He had fine laugh lines fanning out from his eyes, the kind that gave a man character but only aged a woman. There were dark smudges beneath his eyes. His mouth, now that it wasn't smiling, seemed grim, tired. And he hadn't moved an inch of his body, not so much as twinged a muscle, as if he just didn't have the energy.

And still, he took her breath.

She'd changed into fresh jeans and another tank top, and had hastily splashed her face clean in her bathroom, but she hadn't taken the time for a shower. Just looking at him in that clean frothy water, when she'd been bathing in pigs and mud, made her feel . . . grimy.

It didn't help that he was truly one of the most attractive men she'd ever met, with all the dark, unruly hair clinging to the back of his neck, those see-all eyes, that smile that could kill a woman at ten paces. She'd once kissed that smile, and had never quite managed to forget it. Actually, she'd kissed a lot of that long, hard body, now quite visible through the hot, steaming, still water. Damn it.

He smiled again. "You're looking at me."

"I'm thinking you don't seem all that exhausted."

A speculative look came into his eyes. "Depends on what you have in mind."

Her tummy quivered. Bad body. *Down* body. "What I have in mind is putting you to work."

"Now that's no fun."

"Everyone pulls their weight around here."

He sighed, gave her the puppy dog look, but she didn't back down. She had a feeling he was used to getting his way from any female in his path, but not with her.

"Fine," he finally said, sounding resigned. "If you really need help, I suppose you could count me in. If it'd get us some more guests with money in their pockets."

"It's all easy enough. You can feed the pigs, brush the horses, rake the hen pen . . ."

"Yeah." He looked decidedly unenthusiastic. "I guess."

"You look like you'd rather leap into a burning building."

"Yeah. Just not off of one." With another sigh, he straightened, and then stood so that water sluiced off him.

He had one of those chests that could make a woman drool. Solid. Ripped without being overly muscular, and just enough chest hair to be incredibly masculine. Then her gaze caught on his shoulders, specifically his right, and not just because water was running off it so nicely, but because of the scar running from the top of it, slashing downward, vanishing into his armpit. It was a quarter of an inch wide, and still pink and shiny. New.

Before she could ask about it, the sliding door opened behind them, and out stepped Tucker Mooney.

"I thought you were in town," Callie said, surprised.

"Just got back." Tall and lean, bodywise he was a younger carbon copy of Jake. But Tucker was blond, not dark like Jake. Apparently Tucker had gotten their mother's coloring, along with his father's, whoever he'd been.

At age twenty, he had an attitude to match his age—unless he was working with the horses, that is, in which case Callie had found him to be a beautiful, patient old soul. No horses here, however, and at the sight of his older half brother standing with one foot in and one foot out of the hot tub, his jaw tightened.

Callie knew why *she* had a problem with Jake. He held the strings of her future in his big hand, and God knew how she hated that. Truth was, she'd have distrusted and disliked anyone who had that power over her. It was nothing personal—well, mostly not.

But for Tucker, his dislike of Jake was definitely personal, and that had never made much sense to her. Twelve years Jake's junior, Tucker needed a place to go at age seventeen when their mother had been looking to take off for an extended Greek vacation with her latest husband. She'd been relieved when Jake had stepped in and coaxed Tucker into working at the ranch. It hadn't been an easy coax, either. Tucker had been in trouble with the law at the time, and had a serious authority issue. Chances are Jake had saved Tucker's life by dragging him here, and yet Tucker acted like Jake had never done a thing for him.

"Vacation time?" Tucker asked Jake edgily.

"Sort of." Jake stepped all the way out of the tub and looked around him. "Forgot a towel."

He hadn't forgotten a swimsuit, Callie noticed. The wet material of his dark blue trunks were slung low on his lean hips, hanging nearly to his knees, nicely showcasing a body she wanted covered. Immediately. She grabbed a towel out of the bin at the foot of the deck and tossed it to him.

Offering her a smile of thanks, he tried to wrap it around his waist using only his left hand. Callie realized he hadn't used his right arm for anything, not his phone, not to wave, nothing. She looked at his scar and found herself wanting to help him.

Which was as smart as trying to hand-feed a leopard.

"So how's it going, Tuck?" Jake asked, still awkwardly fighting with his towel.

Tucker let out a sound that was either a muttered "fine" or a different f-word entirely, and completely ignored Jake's obvious injury.

Jake's towel slipped. He swore, then began all over again.

What had he done to himself? Callie felt another tug in her chest, and realized it was sympathy.

Tucker, however, didn't look sympathetic at all. "You bring another chick with you?"

"What is it with the two of you?" Jake divided a disgusted look between them. "A guy can't just show up on his own?"

"You never have before."

Jake paused at that. "No, I guess I haven't," he finally said.

No excuses, no explanations, no apologies. That was such a guy thing, Callie barely resisted the urge to roll her eyes, but she let it go. She figured Tucker had his hackles up because he was young and full of stupid pride. He loved this job, and hated that his brother had given it to him.

And yet Jake must have fond feelings for Tucker, or at least responsible feelings, to have done so. She knew they hadn't seen each other in a long time. Why didn't they just do what brothers do and hug and move on?

"I talked to Mom a while back," Tucker said. "She said she's been trying to call you. You don't know how to return a phone call?"

"Oh, I know how to return a phone call. When I get one." Lazy as can be, Jake sprawled his long body out in one of the lounge chairs. Only Callie seemed to see how carefully he really moved, clearly not using his right arm or shoulder.

Tucker stepped closer, his hands fisted. "You saying she lied?"

"I'm saying she's doing what she does best. Stretching the truth."

Callie stepped between them, mostly because she recognized that look dawning in Tucker's eyes. Trouble. She didn't want it here. "Let's stick to the bigger issue, boys. We're booked in the big house," she said to Tucker. "We need a place for Jake to stay."

Tucker stared at her.

She stared back.

"Fine. Damn it." Muttering to himself, he headed back inside.

"Tuck, wait," Callie said. "I forgot to ask you. Who fed the pigs this morning?"

"Me."

"You left the latch open."

"No, I didn't."

"Well, someone did. They were running loose and enjoying themselves when I got outside. Took me an hour to catch them all."

He turned to look at her. He eyed her hair, which she knew probably still held some mud, readily visible in the long, strawberry red strands, but at least he was wise enough not to mention it. "Couldn't be," he said. "I always wait for the latch to click because they like to push at the gate as I walk away. I'm going to go have a look." With one last annoyed glance shot in Jake's direction, he stalked off.

The slider shut hard.

In the silence, Jake lay on the lounge, suddenly beyond exhausted. "Well, that was a touching family reunion."

"Yeah." Callie stepped to his side. She was frowning, a little pucker appearing between her wide green eyes. She had a spec of mud there, too, which had made Jake want to laugh earlier.

Now he didn't have enough energy to laugh. Flying into Tucson, then driving eighty-five miles into this godforsaken middle of nowhere had taxed him. It used to be he could run five miles a day and wear sixty-five pounds of gear for hours upon hours in relentless, dangerous conditions, but ever since the roof incident and subsequent surgery, he'd been a worthless piece of shit. His physical therapy had been brutal but he was on his own now, with a list of exercises he had to do every day to work his shoulder. He'd been doing that for a month and could still hardly do a damn thing on his own.

God, how he hated to admit that.

And now to be here, on his father's land . . . Jake tried not to think about Richard often. The man had been just one of a slew of short-lived marriages in his mother's life, and the only one Mary Ann Mooney hadn't managed to con. Because Jake had lived with his mother, a woman who hated the Arizona desert more than she hated being single—and that was saying something—she'd moved with Jake to LA after his birth. Richard had called Jake once a year on his birthday until his twelfth, when Jake had told his father he didn't want to be a cowboy, but a firefighter. After that, the annual calls stopped, as if Richard had decided he hadn't had a kid after all.

And yet he'd left his entire legacy to Jake. The idea of it only added to his exhaustion.

Idly he wondered if he could just sleep right there in the lounge so he wouldn't have to muster the energy to get up. Callie, of average height and average weight—and perfectly sized curves, he had reason to know—probably had more strength in her little pinkie than he had in his entire body, and if that didn't rankle . . .

She still looked hot in the whole cowgirl setup, he couldn't help but notice. Long fiery red hair braided down her back, brilliant green eyes that flashed her every emotion, heart out on her sleeve for the world to see.

They'd once spent an unforgettable evening with a bottle of whiskey in her cabin, sharing confidences and shots, talking about much more than either of them would have if they'd been sober. He'd had some timing that night, when it came to talking about his father. He still regretted not waiting until after they'd done the deed to tell her he thought Richard Rawlins had been a selfish, thoughtless asshole and an even worse father. But no. Callie had addled his brain with her big, expressive eyes, her warmth and compassion, the sexy little sounds she made when he touched and kissed her—

But then they'd stopped for another shot, and had started talking. Big mistake, talking to a woman while naked. She'd kicked him out of bed and her life in one fell swoop.

Now she might look at him, she might even want to touch, but she was far too stubborn to ever admit she'd acted hastily. He figured some of that stubbornness

came naturally to her. With all that red hair, she probably couldn't help it.

"What happened to you, Jake?" She gestured to his
shoulder.

"A tumble through a roof."

She gaped and moved closer. "You fell through a
roof?"

Three stories. Into flames. "No big deal."

She pointed to his scar, her finger nearly touching
him. In her eyes and voice was a new softness that
made him wonder if they shared another bottle of
whiskey now, if she'd—

"It looks like a big deal."

Uncomfortable with what he was afraid was pity, he
shrugged, a movement that caused not a little shaft of
pain. "Worried? 'Cause we could get comfy and . . . talk
about it."

"Do you want to talk about it?"

Hell, no, he didn't want to talk about it. "I'd rather
you kiss it better."

"Don't be a jerk." A little hesitant, she kneeled at his
side. "Are you going to be okay?"

"Sure."

"Really?" She lifted her gaze from his scar to his
face. Studied him. "Because it looks bad."

Apparently he was far more tired than he'd thought,
because he would have sworn she was actually concerned. That touched him, when he hadn't planned on
being touched at all. Not knowing what to do with that,
he laughed. "You want to play nurse, Callie? Because
I'm game."

She let out what could only be called a growl and
surged to her feet. "For your father, I would have."

A strange feeling filled his chest, and he was afraid

it was jealousy. His father had treasured her as an employee, while pretending he didn't have a son because that son had dared to have different hopes and dreams than his.

"I'd also play nurse for any of your animals," she said. "Anytime."

But not for him. Yeah, he got that loud and clear. He just didn't know why he'd hoped for something else. Or why, for that matter, he'd never been able to forget her. Jesus, he was crazy to be here, on his father's land, near his brother, with the daily reminder that no one, *no one* who shared his blood gave a shit about him.

"Do you really intend to stay for three or four months?"

"Maybe." What he didn't intend to do was tell that he had nowhere else to go and no one else who cared. That he needed help with even opening a damn can of soup, never mind reaching up into a cabinet for a bowl to dump it into.

Or that he could really get behind selling this place for the money to pay down his mortgage, get the best attorney he could to fight this whole Billy thing, and maybe even take that cruise Troy had suggested.

"I don't get it." She sounded bewildered and unsettled. "Why would you want to stay so long?"

He stretched out his legs even further in preparation for the nice nap he intended to take.

"Don't you have to get back to work?"

He wished.

She was close again, her knees brushing the lounge. Her gaze ran over his body. If he hadn't been so dead . . .

"Jake? No work?"

"Not for a while." When he was on the job, he will-

ingly risked life and limb. And when he wasn't on the
job, he still risked life and limb, just not his heart.
Never his heart. So it really needed to stop thudding
uncomfortably at the way she was looking at him. Had
he thought her annoyed? Maybe mildly curious on top
of that? And then, finally, concerned?

Where, then, had that heat in her gaze suddenly
come from?

"Why would you stay," she repeated softly, once
again hunkering down so they were eye to eye, "when
you don't like being here? Is it because you *can't*
work?"

He wasn't ready to admit that, but she was searching for the answer in his words, his face, and he didn't
know what exactly she thought she'd find in either. She
knew this place wasn't his thing. They were out in the
boondocks, with no nightlife, no city sophistication,
nothing to do except ride horses and feed the pigs, and
possibly try to enjoy the long, endless nights, which is
why he'd brought a woman with him on his last two
visits.

But he doubted his body could handle that kind of
enjoyment now, humiliating as *that* was to admit. Not
that she was offering. "I told you, it's time to work on
this place, give it some value."

"It has value."

"Not resale it doesn't."

"So you *are* selling."

He closed his eyes because he didn't have the energy
to do anything else. He understood she had to be concerned about her own livelihood, and that of her crew,
but he wasn't a heartless bastard. At least not entirely.
He needed to get out from beneath the ranch and the financial obligation, but he also would do his best to

make sure the people here were cared for. "I'll make sure you and Tucker get to keep your jobs. Don't worry, that will be an important contingency about selling. You won't be affected, other than getting someone new to report to, someone better suited than me, I'm sure."

She didn't say anything, and he no longer could even think about opening his eyes. His shoulder was aching again, reminding him he hadn't taken a painkiller that day. Knowing he'd be driving, and also that he'd need a clear mind, he'd kicked the pain pills cold turkey.

Now he wished he'd at least brought them.

"Does it hurt?"

With his eyes closed, Callie's voice sounded sweet, warm . . . caring . . .

She ran a finger over his scar, from the shoulder tip down to the sensitive skin of his armpit.

Jake's flesh flinched.

She jerked her hand back. "I'm sorry."

"No." He wanted to grab her hand back and place it over the healing incisions. "It's okay, the area just isn't used to touch." He rubbed his own hand over it, and grimaced. "The nerve endings keep misfiring or something as they regenerate, shooting random points of fire. It's driving me crazy."

Lightly, she took over, running her finger down the scar. "You need to reintroduce it to stimulation," she whispered. She hesitated, as if daring him to make a sexual innuendo, but he didn't want her to move away so he didn't say a word.

And with that same light, almost unbearable touch, she glided her finger from the top of his shoulder, downward, to the crux of his arm. "Like this . . ."

Then back again.

"Callie."

Her gaze dropped to his mouth. "Or like this . . ." She leaned in for a kiss—

And he jerked awake, sitting straight up so fast he winced and grabbed his shoulder.

He was alone in the chair by the hot tub, and given the new slant of the sun, had been for quite a while. Someone had covered him in a light blanket.

Callie.

She'd not touched him. She'd not leaned in close for a kiss, and he had to laugh at himself for even dreaming it.

Amy Wheeler thought she might never get used to how quickly night fell out in the high Arizona desert. One minute the sun shone brilliantly, and then the next dusk fell hard, followed by sudden and total darkness.

She stepped inside the cabin she'd been given when she'd hired on at the Blue Flame, and locked herself in. She turned on every light, which in the one-room cabin consisted of the kitchen and bathroom lights, and a floor lamp by the futon. Then she pulled a small bag out of her backpack, the purchase she'd just made in Three Rocks at the hardware store with her last few bucks.

A deadbolt.

No stranger to tools, she spent the next few moments installing it with a drill and screwdriver she kept in her pack. When she had the lock on and in place, she backed to the small couch in the center of the room and sat.

And let out her first breath in what felt like forever.

She took a long look around her. The cabin's small kitchen and living space opened to each other, and the bathroom was smaller than a postage stamp. She liked that. She liked that a lot. She could take in the whole place with one sweep of her eyes. There was an old oak table and two chairs by the even older refrigerator. There was a fireplace with the logs neatly stacked to one side and a rug in front of it. Then there was the futon on which she sat right now, covered with a quilt. The self-standing armoire in the corner was for her things, not that she unpacked. She never unpacked.

Everything was small, neat and tidy. She liked that, too.

There were a lot of things she liked today, which was a pleasant surprise, given her life and all she'd experienced in her short eighteen years. She had a job, one she actually enjoyed. She worked for a woman she thought she could respect if not actually trust. Amy didn't do trust. And she had a place to lay her head at night, where she could let herself fall into a real sleep— her first real sleep in too long.

Things hadn't been this good since . . . well, ever. With all her tentative heart, she just hoped they'd stay that way.

3

The dry ground crunched beneath Jake's feet as he walked through the black night from the big house to the row of cabins across the yard.

His father's first and only love, his legacy. And here Jake was hating it. The night was chilly enough that his breath crystallized as he breathed, and he hunched his good shoulder, trying to stay warm in just his T-shirt. He hadn't expected the altitude to affect him, either, but it did, shortening his already too short breath. As he walked, he glanced around, wondering what kind of wild animals roamed the desert at night.

The place had a rather eerie glow to it with the pale blue light from the moon dancing over the rocky hills around him, casting shadows, flickering on the landscape like blue flames, and he wondered if that's where his father had gotten the name for the place. He tried to take it all in but he couldn't; it all seemed too big.

What if he'd come sooner, when Richard had still been alive? What if he'd tried harder to understand the father he'd never known, would he then feel something for this land? Something more than the disconcerting nothing he felt now?

The utter silence around him was abruptly broken

by the lonely bellowing of a range bull, the wind sighing through the hills. And then, thundering hooves. Jake tensed and searched the darkness. There, about a hundred yards to the north of the barn, came a galloping horse. Its rider had a stream of long deep garnet hair blowing behind her, and she rode as if one with her horse.

Callie.

Since the last time he'd seen her had been in his dream, he had a little trouble separating the sweet warm soft woman who'd kissed him with the tough impenetrable woman racing across the rough desert floor. He supposed this was her idea of relaxation time, which seemed crazy to him. Bouncing on a horse in the night across the hard, unforgiving ground seemed as much fun as a physical therapy session.

And still he watched, mesmerized in spite of himself. She rode as if she'd been born to it, leaning over her horse a little, her body fluid with the horse's every movement. The moment seemed so intimate, he felt as if he were trespassing, and he nearly stepped back, but then she let out a heart-stopping scream.

The hair raised on the back of his neck. Was her horse racing out of control and she couldn't stop it? If so she could fall and break her neck. That was all he could think as he started running, gritting his teeth against the jarring his shoulder took with each step. He got to the corral as her horse came thundering in.

"Hang on," he yelled, and leapt up onto the fencing, not sure if he could catch a rein or Callie herself, or what the hell he thought he was going to do, only knowing he had to do something. "Callie, hang on!"

But then, about fifteen feet from his precious perch on the corral fence, the horse suddenly pulled up, slowed to a trot, then a walk, and then right before him, stopped entirely.

"Jake?" Callie blinked down at him. "What are you doing?"

"Uh . . ."

The horse snorted its displeasure at the fun being over, and pranced around restlessly until Callie's softly uttered, "Whoa" calmed her. Perfectly in control now, the horse stilled. Callie looked at Jake. "Why are you up there like that?"

"You screamed."

"No, I didn't."

"I heard you."

She lifted a shoulder. "It felt so good to be out, I might have let out a little 'woo-hoo' or something."

"Yeah." His breathing was still choppy from his run, proving that a good fall and surgery played hell on a man's conditioning. And his balance on the fence wasn't so good, either. He didn't dare jump down; his shoulder was leaping in pain with every heartbeat. Carefully he climbed down, gritting his teeth so hard he thought he just might grind them down to nothing, but hell if he'd show her he wanted to drop to the ground and whimper like a baby. "Just a little woo-hoo."

"What did you think I—" She stared at him as her horse snorted again, stomping a long leg and hoof uncomfortably close to Jake's foot. "Did you think I needed help? On a horse?"

The insulted tone was there in her voice, but with the adrenaline—not to mention pain—pumping through his blood, he didn't much care. "You shouldn't scream like that. I thought you were in trouble."

"You thought wrong. Jake, you're not at work. You're not the hero out here."

Right. He wasn't the hero anywhere.

She bent over the horse's neck, embracing the huge animal. Then, with one last pat, she hopped down. "And even if I had been in trouble, I can handle myself." She grabbed the reins and led the horse toward the barn, sending him one last long, hard look over her shoulder.

Great, she could handle herself. "Good to know," he muttered and rubbed his shoulder. He was an idiot. He wished he was in San Diego; at the station playing cards waiting for the fire bell; at his small house with a good hot pizza and cable TV; at a bar sharing drinks with a woman . . . anywhere but here.

For the second time that night, he headed toward the cabins. He pulled a key out of his pocket, the one Callie had given him with an unusual look on her face; as if she'd wanted to both laugh and wince in sympathy.

In this case, he'd take the sympathy. He came to a stop in front of the second cabin. His brother's.

Half brother, he reminded himself, because blood didn't seem to mean much to Tucker these days.

It hadn't always been that way. Once upon a time, Tucker had thought the sun rose and set on Jake's shoulders. That had been nice, real nice, but Jake shook off the memories and reached for the handle just as the door opened. Light spilled out into the night.

Tucker stood in the doorway with a scowl on his face. "You going to stand there muttering to yourself all night, or are you coming in?"

"This was a bad idea."

"No shit." Tucker stood back and gestured him in.

"But there's no other choice until morning, unless you want to sleep in your rent-a-cowboy truck."

Jake glanced at the Toyota in the driveway, the one he'd rented at the airport. He had no idea why Tucker might object to it. "What other choice will present itself in the morning?"

"You can leave."

Jake smiled grimly and stepped inside. "You used to come running when I came home. You'd throw your chubby little arms around my legs and laugh while I tried to walk with you on me." Nothing had ever made him feel more important, not before, or since.

"Yeah, well, I was just a stupid kid then."

Jake refrained from asking him what had changed, and looked around. To say the place was small would be an understatement. There was a kitchen nook and living space, which held a fireplace with a couch in front of it. Behind the couch was a cot. He looked at it and groaned.

"There's always the truck," Tucker reminded him.

"You know, you might show a little more gratitude to the guy who got you out of your one-way ticket to juvy-hall, moved you out of the town where at least half the population wanted to kill you, and handed you a job."

Tucker just stared at him from sullen eyes.

"Or not," Jake muttered, and weary beyond exhaustion, sat on the couch.

"Try again, Sherlock."

Jake got up, walked around the couch, and kicked the cot. "Do I at least get a pillow—" It hit him in the face. "Gee, thanks."

"Don't thank me. You paid for it."

"Is that what's up your ass? You're mad at me because you owe me money?"

"I don't owe you anything."

"You know what, Tucker?" Exhausted, he sank to the cot. He toed off his shoes and lay back carefully. "Remind me to pound the shit out of you tomorrow." He just prayed he had the energy. He closed his eyes and, fully dressed, fell into a deep slumber.

Later that night, Callie lay in her bed watching the moon's shadow play across her ceiling. She could still picture Jake balancing himself on that fence, trying to save her from a runaway horse.

The idea was laughable, and yet . . .

What kind of guy did such a thing for a woman he hardly knew? A firefighter, she had to admit. A man well used to putting others' safety ahead of his own.

She might almost like him for that, if their earlier conversation wasn't haunting her.

"It's time to work on this place, give it some value."

"It has value."

"Not resale, it doesn't."

The words had stuck with her ever since he'd fallen asleep after uttering them by the hot tub. The first time she'd stepped foot here, she'd been seventeen years old, with twenty bucks in her pocket and no more possessions than could fit into her ratty old backpack . . .

The memory never failed to make her smile, though she hadn't been smiling then. She'd been secretly shaking in her boots. Richard Rawlins had stood in front of her, looking so big and formidable, hands on his hips as he stared down at the bedraggled young homeless girl asking for a job.

"Whatcha got in the way of skills, girl?" he'd demanded in a craggy voice that suggested he'd been yelling at bedraggled young homeless girls just like her for years.

But she was good at not letting anyone see her squirm. Real good. Some might say that she was too proud as well, but she didn't think so. She was just independent, fiercely so, but having never been able to depend on anyone but herself, she had good reason. "I can clean up after the animals," she'd told him. Her mother had been a small-time singer, chasing fame in bars across the south for most of Callie's youth. This had meant nocturnal sporadic mothering, and she used the word mothering quite loosely, because really, if there'd been any mothering done at all, it had been done by Callie herself.

In any case, she'd been left mostly alone during her days. During the summer months, she'd spend her time wandering around whatever town they were staying at, often finding herself near whatever horse stables she could locate.

By age six, she wanted to be a horse when she grew up. A wild stallion, with no fencing and no drunk mother. No adults, period.

Unfortunately, by the time she'd turned eight, she'd realized that dream was impossible. So she'd forged another—she wanted freedom. She'd discovered people were willing to pay her to clean up after their horses, and if she did a good job, they'd pay even more. Freedom granted.

By the time she met Richard Rawlins, she was a loner, a somewhat cynical teen who knew only that she instantly liked the feel of the Blue Flame. The yards had been clean, the barns and house the same if slightly shabby, the animals happy enough in their corrals.

BLUE FLAME 51

Plus, unlike most of the ranches she'd spent time on, this one was for people to come and play at living in the Wild Wild West. New people in and out all the time, exciting people from all over the country, and new adventures every day. The thought appealed to her more than anything else she'd seen.

"So . . ." Richard had watched her with an inscrutable gaze. "You clean up after animals . . ." He hadn't been known for being patient or even particularly kind, but then again, having not experienced much of either in her life, Callie hadn't expected anything. She just wanted a place to sleep at night and a job she could live with.

"We'll start with you clearing the stalls then," Richard said, nodding. "But I'm thinking you'll want to aim higher next time I ask you what you can do, so keep your ears open, girl."

She had, and still did. That had been twelve years ago, and she'd been here ever since, working her way up through the ranks, watching other employees butt heads with Richard and his stubborn, unbending ways, marveling that they didn't understand that all he wanted was to be left alone and for them to do their job. Employees had come and gone, and she'd laid low, wondering why anyone would ever leave.

She hadn't, except for the occasional vacation.

Oh, and then there'd been the one time she'd quit to do something really stupid—like get married.

But that had lasted only long enough for her to realize her foolishness, and Richard Rawlins had been more than willing to hire her back. Once again, she'd settled in at the Blue Flame, wiser, smarting from her mistakes, but time—and the place—had eventually soothed the pain away.

Then two years ago Richard had gone off for a long ride. No one had thought anything of it, not then, and not when he didn't show up for four days. He'd often taken his own adventure for that long a period, or longer.

But this time he'd suffered a fatal heart attack, twenty miles away from his ranch, in the wilderness of the Chiricahua National Forest, all alone.

Callie had been devastated, but as she quickly learned, she'd been the only one to feel that way. Some of the employees had moved on, some—like Lou and Marge—had stayed. Stone and Eddie had come to work for her, and then Tucker, and Jake had been content to let her run the ranch. She'd made the most of that time, slowly changing things, improving where she could.

She'd also been saving, getting financial advice from Michael Dawson, a man she had several ties to. One, he was her best friend. Two, he was her ex-husband's partner in a mortgage company, where she was hopefully close—maybe two years close—to getting her finances in good enough shape for a loan.

But as she'd felt all her life, not quite close enough.

Dawn was still a good hour off when Shep let out a bark and Callie jerked awake. Had that been a car driving down the gravel road out of here, or had she been dreaming? In any case, she got out of bed and went to the window. Squinting through the gray light, she could only see as far as the first barn.

With a sigh, she moved to her front door and opened it. Now she could see the hay barn and the hen house as well, but nothing out of the ordinary.

The big house was dark, as were all the other cabins,

but she trusted Shep implicitly. Mourning the thirty minutes before her alarm would have gone off—she dressed and stepped outside. Still nothing.

Except the soft whinny of her horse Sierra, and it held the sound of . . . pain? At that her heart dropped to her stomach and she started running. Sierra was *her* horse, *her* baby, the love of her life, and she couldn't get there fast enough. When she reached the barn, breathless from nerves and worry, she hauled the door open and hit the lights. Normally she'd have been met with quizzical glances from the horses they kept there in the two rows of stalls.

Instead they peered at her anxiously, and Sierra whinnied again.

"Sierra?" Callie rushed over to her. "Why is your saddle on?" Callie had definitely taken it off after her ride last night, it would have been cruel to keep it on overnight—

And crueler still to leave the stirrups tucked beneath the saddle, digging into Sierra's flanks. The horse was rubbing up against the wall of her stall in a desperate attempt to get comfortable, something that only succeeded in making the stirrups dig into her all the harder. A line of blood ran down both her sides, dripping into the straw beneath her, and Callie's heart nearly stopped at the sight. "Oh no. Oh, baby, hold on." She slipped into the stall, but Sierra was long beyond spooked. Eyes rolling back in her head, ears flat, she reared up, catching Callie between twelve hundred pounds of frightened animal and the unforgiving door of the stall.

Stars burst in Callie's vision as her head hit the wall hard. A knifelike pain exploded in her ribs. Dizzy, she pushed on Sierra with all her might. "It's okay, Sierra, it's okay. You just have to scoot over—" The horse shifted just enough that Callie could draw in a lungful of air, and she shoved the saddle off.

It hit the ground with a thump. Staggering a little from the blow to her head, Callie stared at the sight of the horse's flanks, rubbed raw and bleeding. "Oh, Sierra." Throat thick, she stroked the horse's face. "Oh, baby. It's okay now, I'm here. It's okay."

Sierra tossed her head, the whites of her eyes still rolling as she blew out breath after loud, fearful breath.

"I know. I know." For a long, long moment Callie just stood there, her arms wrapped around Sierra's neck. "Who did this to you?" Only when both of their heartbeats had settled a little did she leave the stall to get some medical supplies, coming back to Sierra just as the barn door opened.

Once again Sierra reared in alarm, knocking Callie back against the stall door. She raised her arms to protect her face and head from the animal's flailing hooves and braced herself for serious injury, but a pair of hands grabbed her, yanking her out of the stall.

Jake sank to the ground with her in his lap. "Jesus, Callie. Are you all right?"

"I'm not sure."

"What hurts?"

He ran a hand over her, gently probing until she put her hands over his. "No, it's okay. I'm okay." She was still gasping for breath, each inhale burning her already bruised ribs. "What are you doing here?"

"I was out pretending I still run in the mornings, and I heard another scream. And this time it sure as hell wasn't a happy little woo-hoo warrior call, so don't even try to tell me I'm being stupid again."

She was becoming increasingly aware that she sat

cradled in his lap with his hands on her. "I never said you were stupid."

"No, it was just implied. So why is that horse trying to kill you?" Jake shot a grim look into the stall, where Sierra had gone still, head down, puffing out panicked little breaths that made Callie want to break down and cry.

"She's not trying to kill me." She held her spinning head, then tried to get up but Jake kept her against him. "Some idiot put her saddle on—wrongly I might add. I need to calm her down. Let me up."

He helped her and stayed close, even as he eyed Sierra and the other horses with a healthy distrust. Stone's, Eddie's, and Tucker's horses had stalls in here, as well as Moe, Richard's old horse. With Richard gone, Moe had gotten a little ornery, so they kept him out of the corral unless he was being exercised or ridden on a trek by an expert guest.

Sierra still shook and trembled, and Callie's heart broke. Just like the people that worked the Blue Flame, many of the animals had come to them through circumstances that proved life could be unfair and cruel. Before being rescued by Richard, then purchased by Callie three years back, Sierra had been abused on another ranch.

She looked it now, and that pissed Callie off so that by the time they were done cleaning her up and calming her down, Callie was shaking, too. "I just can't believe it," she said, her throat thick with tears.

Jake touched her face. "Callie, I think you should just sit a minute."

"I'm a little dizzy, that's all." Dizzy enough to let him take her hand in a big, warm one as they moved down the row of stalls toward the barn door. Moe stuck his head out of his stall and tried to take a bite out of Jake's shoulder.

"What the—" Jake jumped sideways and stared at the horse. "Is he hurt, too?"

"No." Callie patted Moe, but the big horse kept a baleful eye on Jake, enough to keep Jake a good few feet back. "He just doesn't play well with other horses so we keep him inside."

"He doesn't play well with other people, either."

"He usually does." As she said this, Moe tried to take another bite of Jake.

"He's crazy," Jake said, jumping back again. "Why do you keep him?"

"He was your father's horse."

Jake went still, looking at the animal for a long moment.

Moe looked right back.

Then Jake turned and walked right out of the barn.

Callie followed. Only a half hour had passed, but dawn had just arrived, and she blinked into it. Her head pounded, and she felt just a little sick with it.

Jake stood right outside, his expression unreadable. "You okay?"

She nodded and took a step toward the big house, where her crew would probably be looking for hand-outs now that Amy was leaving out things like amazing blueberry muffins. "I'm going to find out what the hell happened."

"Not yet."

She didn't have the time for this, plus she hurt so badly she nearly whimpered when she moved. "Jake—"

"Humor me." He took her to her cabin. Once inside, he flipped on the lights, then turned to her. Sinking his

hands in her hair, he gently probed her head and the
bump on the back of it.

She hissed out a breath.

"Yeah, nasty lump. Trust me, I know how that feels.
Follow my finger."

He had her track it back and forth. Then, tilting her
head up, he stared into her eyes for so long, she
squirmed.

"Close your eyes," he demanded, and when she did,
he said, "Now open them." He kept staring into her
eyes, then finally nodded. "Not concussed. Your head
is too hard, thankfully." He put his hands on his hips.
"Now strip."

4

Callie managed a raw laugh. It'd been a hell of a long morning, and standing there feeling so vulnerable and shaky in front of the one man she didn't want to see her weak in any way was difficult. Not to mention what her hormones had done when he'd quietly ordered her to "strip." "I know I let you think I was easy the night of Richard's service, but—"

"You're favoring your ribs, I want to see them."

She hugged herself and felt her eyes water from the pain of that little gesture. "I want to go find out what happened, then I want to check on Sierra again. I'm fine, and even if I'm not, I can get Marge."

"Let me see, Callie."

"You have a real save-the-girl thing going, and I'm sure most women find that sexy, but—"

He lifted his hands to her short-sleeved blouse, and started unbuttoning her. His head was bent to his task, their jaws only an inch apart. He hadn't shaved but smelled like soap, and like the man she'd once held too close.

He spread her blouse wide, exposing her hot pink and black satin bra, at which he executed a comical double take.

"I . . ." She closed her eyes, felt her face heat. "I have a thing for lingerie."

"I remember."

His voice seemed a little hoarse, a little thick, and she searched his gaze but all she found was concern as he ran the tip of a work-roughened finger over the already black-and-blue ribs on her left side. "Not good."

"Nothing's broken." She held her aching head. "But who would do such a thing to her?"

"Let's find out."

She shivered at the edgy, underlying danger in his voice. "*I'll* find out."

"Maybe you're forgetting whose place this is."

"Trust me, I have never forgotten whose place this is." She shrugged her shirt back on, buttoned it. Then moved to her front door and opened it, hinting for him to leave.

"Callie—"

"I'll meet you at the big house."

He came close, put a hand over hers on the handle. "You're ready to get rid of me. I get that. We rub each other the wrong way. I get that, too. Just . . . don't go to sleep, okay?"

"Of course not." She straightened her spine. "I know what time it is, and what has to be done—"

"I don't mean—Jesus, you're hard-headed. I meant because of your head. I don't think you have a concussion, but sleeping isn't a good idea."

"Oh. Right. Jake—"

But he was already walking away.

She stripped in private this time, showered gingerly, and dressed carefully, already feeling as if she'd been hit by a Mack truck. She couldn't find any aspirin, so she went to Marge and Lou's cabin.

Marge had two boys, both grown and on the rodeo circuit, but she'd always pined for girls, and loved to mother Callie. She was of average height and build, her long brown hair streaked with gray always in a ponytail. She wore jeans and T-shirts that hid the fact she was built enough to lift a calf and budge the most stubborn of horses. When she heard what had happened, she smothered Callie in affection, clucking worriedly as she doled out aspirin. By the time Callie escaped the older woman's clutches, another half hour had gone by. She had until noon before their guests arrived, but mornings on a ranch were never idle, not even a dude ranch.

And she still had to figure out what the hell had happened to Sierra last night. She checked on the horse, and found Eddie with her. The twenty-five-year-old led all their hiking and camping expeditions, and assisted with the animals when needed. He had the build of someone who'd spent his entire life working hard outside, and the good fortune to be as pretty as a cover model, which only added to his playful, charismatic persona. Hands down, he received the most fan mail from their guests. It amused the rest of them, who teased him mercilessly about it, not that he cared. He liked his reputation, and in fact, spent a lot of money to keep it. Fancy truck, fancy horse and gear, expensive exotic dates with a variety of women . . .

The laid-back guy rarely got too riled over anything, but he whirled on her now, eyes flashing with a fury she'd never seen from him. "What the hell is this?" He gestured to Sierra's bloody flanks. "Jake said someone did this on purpose."

"Looks that way." She entered Sierra's stall and, ignoring her aching ribs, hugged the horse tight. Sierra set her big head on Callie's shoulder and huffed a soft, welcoming breath in her ear. Her throat closed as she held on.

"No one here is that stupid or cruel," Eddie said. "No one."

"I don't want to think so, either."

Eddie ran an aggravated hand through his hair, then touched her arm. "Jake also said you got knocked around some. You okay?"

Reluctantly, she pulled away from Sierra. Her head throbbed. "Nothing a good soak in the hot tub won't fix." She kissed the horse's forehead, then left her to Eddie's care. She made her way to the big house and let herself in the front door. Normally the first thing she did was make a huge pot of coffee. The scent would draw in her crew one by one as they went about their own chores. Several times over the past week since Kathy had left, she'd even attempted breakfast. Everyone ate, but they finally begged her to stick with coffee. She'd happily complied.

But today as she walked down the wide hallway toward the kitchen, the scent of coffee already filled the air. Coffee and something . . . cinnamony. Mouth watering, she pushed open the double swinging doors.

Amy stood in front of the stove stirring something, but when the double doors swung shut behind Callie, clanking together, the young woman jumped as if she'd been shot.

Callie's easy smile faded. Had that been guilt flashing across Amy's face? She moved closer. "Morning."

"Morning," Amy mumbled, turning back to the stove.

"You okay?"

"Sure." Barely eighteen, Amy had shown up on the ranch in much the same way Callie herself had.

Poor and homeless.

And, Callie guessed, apparently afraid of her own shadow. Callie looked at the petite, dark-headed, skinny girl with the most wounded eyes she'd ever seen and tried to picture her as someone who could hurt a horse. She couldn't. "Something smells heavenly."

"Yeah. Cinnamon rolls." Amy wiped her hands on a towel she had slung over her shoulder. Her jeans were threadbare and had holes in the knees that had nothing to do with being fashionable. She wore a T-shirt that invited the general public to GO TO HELL.

Callie looked at it and grimaced. They hadn't discussed suitable attire for the ranch when they had guests; she hadn't thought to. "How long have you been up?"

"A while."

"Have you been in the barn?"

"What?" Amy looked at her in surprise. "No, why?"

"Someone went in there late last night, or early this morning, and put on Sierra's saddle."

"Why?"

"I don't know, but it really spooked her. She rubbed her sides raw—"

The oven buzzer went off. Amy pulled out a large glass dish, her face red from the heat, her thin arms bulging with surprising strength as she lifted the dish. Blowing a loose strand of dark hair out of her face, she set the dish on the stove top and stared at it as if looking for flaws. "It's an egg and sausage and potato casserole, but we didn't have potatoes, all we had was frozen Tater Tots . . ."

The scent alone drew Callie close. "I love Tater Tots. Listen, about Sierra. I've got to figure out what happened—"

"I never went in there, I swear."

Callie looked into Amy's uneasy face, and managed a reassuring smile. "Okay."

"I was in here until late last night, getting used to where you keep everything, and making lists and stuff, and then I went straight to my cabin. Is Sierra going to be okay?"

"Yes."

Nodding, Amy took out a serving spoon, set it in the casserole. In spite of herself and her aches and bruises, Callie's stomach leapt with anticipation. She'd tested Amy's cooking abilities the other day when she'd first hired her and had been excited at the stew she'd whipped up on the spot with what they'd had in the pantry. "You know you didn't have to cook until tonight."

"I know." Amy bit her lower lip. "But I noticed yesterday everyone just grabbed junk for breakfast, and I thought you guys might want something better—"

The kitchen doors opened. "God-almighty," Tucker exclaimed. "I've died and gone to a ranch where someone knows how to cook." He followed his wriggling nose to the steaming casserole dish. "Man, that's going to make up for a really bad morning."

Amy, who barely came up to his shoulder, started to back away but he snagged her wrist in his hand.

That was all he did before Amy grabbed his arm with her free hand, whipped around, and with a grunt, tossed him right over her shoulder.

Callie gasped.

Tucker landed with an *oomph* on his back on the

kitchen floor, blinking somewhat confusedly up at the ceiling.

"Ohmigod," Amy said, and clasped her hands over her mouth.

Callie leaned over Tucker lying there, all gawky and long-limbed, and offered him a hand. "I think it's safe to say, hands off the cook at all times."

"Yeah." Tucker carefully got to his feet, then glanced over at Amy, who'd backed herself against the oven, hands still over her mouth. Above her hands, her eyes were wide as saucers. She looked sick.

Any flash of amusement fled Callie's chest. When she glanced over at Tucker, she could tell he felt the same.

"I'm sorry," he said quietly. "I smelled the food and lost my head. I was just going to say that you're my new best friend."

"You grabbed me." The words were muffled behind Amy's fingers.

"Yeah. I was going to hug and kiss you, actually. Good food does that to me." He tried a grin that tugged at Callie's heart because she realized she didn't see him smile all that often.

Amy nodded, looking like she wished a hole would swallow her up. "I'm sorry."

"We can put a bell around his neck," Callie offered, trying to lighten the tension for Amy's sake. She hated the pink glow of humiliation on the girl's cheeks. "I've been tempted before now to do so, believe me."

"A bell would be good." Amy turned her back and studied the casserole dish steaming right in front of her. "Did I hurt you, Tucker?"

He rubbed his jaw and eyed the petite Amy. Clearly he couldn't figure out how to proceed. If he said she hadn't hurt him, she might doubt herself next time when it came to self-defense. But if he admitted to being hurt, that would stab at his stupid male pride, and maybe make Amy feel even worse.

Plus, the "sorry" had been uttered through Amy's teeth, and sounded so insincere it might have been funny, if anything about this had been funny.

"Don't worry, Amy." Callie looked at Tucker. "I don't think you could hurt this lug." To show it, she knocked her knuckles against his head. "See? Hard as a brick."

"Which I heard yours is as well." Tucker muttered at her beneath his breath.

Amy's shoulders remained rigid.

"I'm sure if you feed him quick," Callie said. "He'll forget all about it."

Tucker nodded. "The key is the quick part."

Amy let out a sound that so perfectly conveyed her disgust with the entire male race, Callie laughed.

Happy just to get fed, Tucker reached for a plate and a fork, which he handed over to Callie. Then he grabbed a platter for himself, blinking innocently when Amy finally turned to him with a spatula. She gave his huge makeshift plate the once over.

He smiled hopefully.

Without a word she gave him a heaping serving.

"Thanks." But he waited until she looked up into his face to move aside. "Thanks," he said again softly, smiling.

Amy didn't smile back.

Apparently undisturbed, Tucker waited for Callie to get a plateful, then gestured her outside. "I need to talk to you." He held open the back door for her.

"Jake told you what happened," she said when they got on the small porch step.

"Yeah. You okay?"

Sure, if she discounted a mother of a headache. "Better than poor Sierra. Who did it, Tucker? Who would have done such a thing?"

"I haven't a clue, but it wasn't that girl in there. No way." Tucker shoveled in food at an alarming rate. "It could have just been a stupid mistake."

"Yeah," she said, unconvinced.

"We've got two others things as well."

"Good or bad?"

He chewed and considered. "Bad and badder."

"Terrific. Let's hear it then."

"The easier one first. We're short-handed today." This was said around a huge mouthful. When he swallowed, he stopped talking to moan in pleasure. "Oh my God, this is better than sex."

Callie lifted a brow, refraining from pointing out that he was barely twenty, how much could he really know about sex? But though she felt ages older than he at times, truth was, he probably knew more than her about the matter. "Short-handed?"

"Stone's hungover."

That Stone'd had too much to drink the night before was nothing new. He was Eddie's younger brother and hadn't outgrown his party years yet. But it had never affected his work before. The unsettled feeling in the pit of her belly grew. "How is that an easy problem?"

"Trust me, compared to the other thing, it is."

"Oh, God, Tucker, what else? You and Jake had problems last night?"

"This has nothing to do with him. Who can we call to fill in for Stone, someone who can help us handle a big group? I asked Lou, but he's got something he has to do in town."

"How about Michael? I can see if he wants to play hooky from work today. Remember how much he loved filling in for us when we needed another guide a couple months back?"

"He told me last night he had a busy day."

"He partied with you and the guys?"

"Not as hard, but yeah. Waxed poetic all over you, too."

"Tucker, we're just friends."

"*You're* just friends."

Callie sighed. She loved Michael like a brother. He was always there for her, they had fun together, and actually, he'd introduced her to her ex-husband—a fact she didn't hold against him.

Michael was her sounding board, her rock, and if a small part of her suspected he felt more for her than mere friendship, she didn't have to face it as he'd never mentioned it, especially not after what had happened between her and Matt. "How about Jake? He can help."

Tucker snickered. "Yeah, right."

"Tucker . . . you've never said, and you don't have to, but—"

"But what's the bad blood between Jake and me?" Tucker stared morosely out at the yard. The chuck wagon they sometimes used on camping expeditions lay near a tree. There were a series of benches lining their vegetable garden, which had begin to thrive with the early spring. "It's all too old to even give it the time of day," he finally said.

"So you can work with him, if it comes to that?"

"Hell, I'm living with him, aren't I?"

"I'm sorry about that."

"Not as sorry as I am, believe me. But as for the work ... He won't want to. It's not his thing. He says he hates camping, hates the desert. Needless to say he hates it here."

"Then why is he here?"

"Why don't you ask him directly?" Jake asked from behind them. "And how do you know what my thing is? Neither of you have bothered to ask me."

With her fork halfway to her mouth, Callie glanced at Tucker, who'd also stopped eating.

Jake let out an annoyed sound as he moved between them down the steps. "Christ, there's some serious chips on some serious shoulders around here. How's the head and ribs?" he asked Callie.

This wasn't a polite question, it was a demand, by the man who'd seen her in her bra only an hour before. She reminded herself he'd seen her in far less. "They're fine."

"You find out what brainless idiot was messing around in the barn?"

"No."

"Me either." He still looked so serious, and somehow more intense than she'd ever seen before. Also the firefighter side of him, she guessed. In any case, it was startlingly, unexpectedly attractive, and she swallowed her last bite of breakfast with extreme difficulty. Then smiled weakly. "How about you? How's your shoulder?"

"Fine."

"Yes, but ..." She trailed off at the closed look on his face. Men and their stupid pride. She supposed she was one to talk, when she herself had more than was good for her. "You're not fully healed. I figured if the injury took you out of firefighting, it would take you out of ranching, too."

He rolled his neck, then stretched his shoulders. And winced, gingerly putting his left hand to his right shoulder. "It might."

Tucker let out an obnoxiously loud sigh, as if he didn't believe Jake could really be hurting.

Jake glanced at him. "What's your problem?"

"How do you know I have one?"

"Maybe because it sounds like your head gets a flat every time I so much as look at you."

Callie had no siblings, though she'd always dreamed of a big, older brother to beat the crap out of anyone who bugged her. But in her dreams, she and this fantasy brother always got along, no bickering.

She had a feeling Jake and Tucker didn't dream about the same kind of relationship.

"What is it?" Jake pressed Tucker. "What's eating at you?"

Tucker stood up. "I already told Callie. There aren't enough hours in the day to discuss it." He stacked his plate on top of Callie's empty one, then brushed past Jake.

"Hey, wait," Callie called. "What's problem number two? The bad one?"

Already ten feet away, Tucker swore, then turned back. "Unless you moved them, someone's stolen all of the serum we were going to use tomorrow to inoculate the herd."

"What?" Callie set the plates down beside her and stood up, managing not to grimace at the ache in her ribs. "They're not in the barn refrigerator?"

"Nope."

"But they can't just have vanished . . ." Her words trailed off at Tucker's grim nod.

"Maybe it was the same person who messed with Sierra," Jake said, frowning. "Has anything like this happened before?"

"No," Callie said. "Never." They'd need to call the police and make a report. Damn it. "Bring Stone some coffee and tell him to suck it up. I don't care how hung over he is, we're going to need him."

"Yeah." Tucker stalked off.

Callie started to calculate how many hundreds of dollars they could be out if Tucker was right and the serum was gone, when Jake stirred, reminding her she wasn't alone.

"You should cancel the incoming guests," he said.

"No. They're paying big bucks."

"You're not ready for guests, not with this shit going on."

"We're ready."

"Look, if a bunch of businessmen want to play at being cowboy bad enough to come all the way out here to Nowhere, USA, then they'll be willing to wait a week. We can use the time to start fixing stuff up. Cheap stuff though." He scratched his jaw. "Really cheap. Like painting. The barns look like crap."

"We're booked next week, too."

"So they'll wait—"

"No, they won't, Jake. If you want to make money—"

"You know I do."

"Then the show goes on. This is our job, our life, and it means everything. *Everything*," she said, knowing she was standing on her own personal soapbox, but the emotions of the day were showing and she couldn't help it. "I don't know if you can understand that, but—"

"Hey. Hey, slow down, I was just—"

"I know." She shook her head. "I just thought that given how this place was left to you by your father, it'd mean something to you."

"We've been over that," he said tightly.

"Right. You didn't like Richard. You don't care about this place."

"I care about how much it's worth. Which is nothing if we don't have guests in here. I care about keeping all of your jobs available to you, even after I'm no longer here. I care about a hell of a lot, Callie, so don't tell me what I feel."

"Fine." Angry, frustrated, hurt—and not really understanding why—she moved down the stairs. She was so full of conflicting emotions it took her a moment to realize the decibel level of barking.

She followed the barking around the back of the house to the basement entrance. It wasn't Shep barking, though he stood there.

Or sat anyway, because Shep was twelve and he never stood when he could sit, and never sat when he could lie down. Tongue hanging out, he happily panted at the mud-colored brown dog next to him, which Callie had never seen before.

She was a good-sized dog, too, despite being so malnourished. Still, it wasn't her size that stopped Callie from going into the basement, but the bared teeth and menacing growl she let out between ear-splitting barks, now aimed right at Callie herself.

5

Jake stood on the porch for a long moment after Callie walked away from him, staring blindly out into the yard. He heard a dog going crazy but it didn't penetrate his other more pressing thought—that Callie wanted this place to mean something to him, wanted him to understand how much it meant to her, to all of them working here.

"But how can I?" he said to the morning air, to his father's ghost, to no one. Maybe if Richard hadn't been so ornery and stubborn, maybe if he'd been willing to meet Jake halfway, maybe, maybe, maybe.

It was far too late for maybes with the man dead and buried.

But why had Richard left him this godforsaken ranch in the first place? It was nothing more than a money pit for him. Maybe it'd been a cruel reminder that Jake had never been the son he wanted. Maybe it'd been a joke. Or, maybe it'd simply been a way to reach the son he'd never tried all that hard to reach in life. And how pathetic was it that Jake wished for the latter.

He didn't belong here in the land of Oz, where these people all had each other and looked at him like he was an alien. That had been made painfully clear to him when he'd questioned everyone about Sierra. They'd all stuck together with genuine care and affection, Eddie covering for his brother's hangover, Stone covering for Tucker's temper, and Tucker covering for Eddie being alone in the barn.

And each of them had vouched for Amy as well, a young woman they knew even less than they did Jake. He didn't have to wonder if any of them would have done the same for him. They wouldn't have.

And damn if he didn't feel lonely as hell.

He also felt stupid for letting it all get to him. He should have left this morning. He still could, and he pulled out his cell phone to call Joe to tell him he was coming back as soon as he could get on a plane.

But Joe had left him two text messages: "*Playgirl called again, offered a firefighter calendar. Mr. July . . . can I have your autograph?*"

And then the second: "*Just heard from the chief . . . brace yourself for a nasty lawsuit.*"

He also had a message from his attorney. Just an ominous: *Call me today.*

Rubbing his aching shoulder, Jake sighed, a whole new can of nerves opening inside him. He would have to get up to date on the proceedings, and also pay for the nuisance. With what, he had no idea.

In any case, going home didn't seem like a viable option, not yet.

The wild barking finally penetrated his thoughts, and shrugging off his own problems, followed the noise around the back of the house. Callie stood in front of the basement entrance, facing off with a mangy old mutt who looked as if she hadn't eaten in a week.

"Hey, there," she murmured to the dog, reaching out her hand.

Teeth bared, the mutt growled, and Callie hastily pulled back.

Jake moved in and put himself in front of her. "You want to lose a few fingers to go with those bumps and bruises? Back up."

"You never give up with the hero thing, do you?"

He could have argued that point. He sure as hell didn't feel like a hero out here in the middle of nowhere, being needed by exactly no one. "Just move." Hunkering down to the dog's eye level, he smiled. "Whatcha doing, pretty lady?"

Callie let out a rough laugh. "That voice might work on the females of *my* race, but a dog isn't going to"— she broke off with a frown when the dog relaxed her stance enough to sit—"fall for it."

"So whatcha doing all the way out here in the middle of nowhere? You lost? Poor thing, you look hungry." He held up his hand for her to sniff.

"What do you think she's all up in arms about?" Callie tried to step beyond the dog to see past the open basement door, but the dog growled again.

Jake put his left hand out in front of Callie to hold her back from getting bitten, and ignored her irritated huff of breath. "You sure look like you've had a rough time of it." At the sound of his voice, the dog stopped growling again. "Maybe if we fed you, you'd be happier. What do you think?"

The dog let out a long whine.

The sound was oddly heart-breaking. Jake tried to decide what could be disturbing her, but couldn't see into the dark basement. "So what are you guarding?"

"We don't use that space for much," Callie said. "She could have cornered anything in there."

Jake continued to hold out his hand to the dog, and

took it as a good sign when she didn't resume her growling. He let her sniff him again, then stroked her down her thin, scruffy back.

Her tail let out one weak wag. Permission granted, Jake moved around her and to the door, but when Callie tried to follow him, the dog once again bared her teeth.

"Wait here," Jake said.

"But—"

Ignoring her, he pulled the door the rest of the way open, and poked his head inside. There was a landing there, and then a set of stairs that went down about five feet, then turned ninety degrees and went down another five feet. It wasn't the stairs that drew his attention, but the second landing.

In the far dusty corner he found what the poor dog was trying so desperately to protect, and even as he looked, she pressed her cold nose under his arm to see as well, making him see double when she jarred his shoulder.

"Jake?"

Hearing Callie's voice behind them, the dog growled low in her throat.

"Hang on," he called back. "She's got—"

"Puppies," Callie guessed, sounding resigned.

As his eyes adjusted to the dark and he started counting the softly mewling puppies, the momma again nudged his arm with her wet nose, sending shots of fire down his bicep all the way to his fingers. "Yeah, I see your babies." With his left hand, he patted her as they looked them over. "Five?"

The dog walked down the steps to the landing and whined softly, plaintively. Jake moved in, then peered down the crack between the landing and the wall. He heard the rustling in the dark. Reaching down there was a whole new kind of pain, and he gritted his teeth as he paused to take a deep breath. "One's slipped down between the landing and the wall. I'll get it." It cost him. By the time he set the puppy in the midst of its siblings and next to the mother who finally allowed herself to relax now that her last baby was back, Jake was a sweaty, shaky mess. His shoulder was leaping with each heartbeat, pulsing with pain, and he felt light-headed. The weakness was humiliating.

"Jake?"

"I think you can come in now. She's calmer." He stayed where he was, on his knees in front of the dog and her puppies, waiting for his world to stop spinning.

Callie had run somewhere for a flashlight. When she scooted in behind him, with Shep pushing in as well, she also dropped to her knees to take a look. "Oh, Shep." She sighed and put an arm around him. "They're adorable though, aren't they?"

Jake would have laughed if he could. Adorable isn't what he'd call the mangy-looking things, but then any amusement backed up in his throat because Callie, so close he could feel her soft breath on his ear, put her hand on his shoulder. "You're shaking." Her fingers lightly danced over the incision beneath his shirt, much like the motion he'd dreamed her doing, only this wasn't a dream. "Torn rotator cuff?"

"Among other things."

"Such as?"

He wanted to be big and strong. He wanted to not feel any weaknesses, but a man could only be so tough with a woman looking at him like she was. "Actually, it was a complete shoulder reconstruction."

"Oh, Jake."

Her expression made him want to touch her, cup her face, stroke his fingers over her jaw and sink into her hair. A shock, because it wasn't just the usual surge of lust. Here was an opportunity he hadn't even known he wanted—to talk to her, to have her know him, to convince her he wasn't a jerk, because suddenly it mattered what she thought of him. Suddenly he wanted her to be as warm and sweet to him as she was to everyone else.

Too bad he couldn't move without whimpering.

"Probably climbing around after dogs and puppies is a bad idea," she said, her hand still on him.

"Probably, but you shouldn't be doing this, either."

"I'm fine."

"Headache?"

"Only a little." She glanced at the puppies now being fed by their mother, who still watched her and Jake carefully. "Looks like we got ourselves a new dog."

So accepting. So willing to gather whoever and whatever to the Blue Flame.

Had his father been like that? It surprised him to feel sad that he didn't know. "And six puppies."

She sighed. "And six puppies. You were good with her; she didn't want anything to do with me."

"Animals like me."

"Women do, too."

He slanted her a glance. "Most, but not all, I'm learning."

She mused over that for a long moment. Dropped her hand from him. "Sometimes I don't know what to say to you."

"Then don't say anything." With a great effort, he

leaned in so their mouths were a mere fraction of an inch apart. He put his left hand to the curve of her jaw. "Let's try this instead." And even knowing he was crazy for wanting this, he put his mouth on hers.

Her hand slid up between them, until her palm settled against his chest. To push him away? Pull him closer? She did neither but let her lips cling to his for a long moment before pulling back.

"What was that?" she whispered.

"Just one little kiss." He tunneled his fingers up into the wild silk of her hair, glad it was loose, and leaned in again, needing one more taste.

She held him back. "You said *one* kiss."

Right, but he'd also said little. It'd been neither. He wanted more but he couldn't move his other arm worth a damn. With his good hand, he slid his fingers down the length of her hair to the small of her back, nudging her forward into his body.

Her hand fisted in his shirt, gripping him tight, getting a few chest hairs in the mix. He didn't care if she pulled them all out one by one as long as she stayed with her body up against his for another moment.

"Jake . . ." She rocked against him, just a tiny little movement of her hips, which was all the encouragement he needed to lower his head and kiss her again.

She moaned softly, then hooked an arm around his neck, and just like that, it was that long ago night all over again; so hot, so sweet and wet, sending an unquenchable hunger skittering down his spine to pool in his groin. He forgot the puppies, his shoulder, his father, everything but the taste and feel of the surprisingly sensual woman in his arms. Her breasts pressed into his chest, and he cupped the sweet curve of her ass in his hand. A sense of déjà vu filled him at that. They'd done this before, and as it had then, the pleasure of her blew him away. Like then, he wanted a hell of a lot more than a kiss, a hell of a lot more than he could get from her while kneeling on the dirty ground surrounded by puppies and dust.

And still she didn't pull away. Neither did he. Needing more, his hand slid beneath the hem of her shirt, seeking warm, sleek, soft skin. She was slim but not fragile, never fragile. He'd seen her toss a heavy saddle, lift a pig, and face down a panicky horse. He knew exactly how strong she was. And he knew something else. He wanted her, so damn much.

It made no sense. Nothing about this made sense. He didn't have a place in his heart for the Blue Flame or the woman who ran it, and yet the longer he kissed her, the more he wanted. He kissed her long and deep. He kissed her until he was dizzy with it, until she was making little sounds in the back of her throat that told him she was as far gone as he was. He was fantasizing about how much further he could take them both when she pulled back. Not out of his arms, just away enough that their lips disconnected with a sucking sound that didn't help any. God, her mouth.

Her eyes fluttered open. "Was that just a kiss, too?"

It took him a long moment to get his brain in gear. Slowly he pulled his hand back, lingering for a few seconds to stroke her warm skin one more time.

"I need to get to the barn." She rose to her feet. Wobbled. She put a hand to her head as if that would help her think. "Tucker'll be waiting. I'll figure out what to do with these puppies later."

"Callie." He rose, too, and felt just as wobbly. When she would have moved away, he put a hand on her wrist. "You're not going to be able to blame that on the whiskey."

Her lips were still wet, and he thought of a thousand things he'd like her to do with those wet lips.

"I never blamed it on the whiskey," she said.

"What did you blame it on?"

"Having a misguided sense of what's right for me."

"So you're not denying there's something almost chemically addictive between us."

"Like I said, I have a misguided sense of what's right for me." She stepped away, subject apparently closed. "Tucker might enjoy your company today."

"So apparently we're done talking about us."

"Yes."

He actually managed to laugh. Now he remembered why he didn't want a woman in his life. They were unreliable, unpredictable, and insane. He should thank her for reminding him. "How do you figure Tucker might enjoy my company?"

"I know he puts up a tough front, but I think it's been hard for him having no family."

"He doesn't consider me his family anymore."

"Why not?"

From the day Jake and his mother had parted ways, Tucker had stopped loving Jake. It hadn't helped that his mother had done her best to keep them separated, and with her traveling, she'd succeeded. A habit that had stuck, even when Tucker had gotten older.

Until he'd been in trouble with the law and had needed Jake. "You'd have to ask him."

"But you consider him *your* family, right?"

"I got him this job, didn't I?"

She let out a sound of annoyance, and he frowned. "What does that mean?"

"It means you're as stubborn as he is."

His mind was still addled by the blood loss to his groin. "Look, I'm glad he took this job. I'm glad he's helpful to you, and having a good time while he's at it. It's kept him off the streets and out of more trouble. I don't know what else I can do. That's not stubbornness, that's just the way it is."

"You could take more interest."

"I'm here, aren't I?"

"To sell."

The indignation left him. "I know you guys consider this place home. I'm not going to let anyone get kicked out in the street. I told you, if I sell, I'll make sure they'll keep you both on, and I meant it."

"If you sell? Or when?"

There'd better be a when. "I've called a few Realtors to come out this week. After we paint."

"We?"

"We. You've seen the books. You know I can't afford to get a painter out here."

That was definitely disappointment on her face now, but he only got a quick glimpse before she started walking toward the barn.

Well, what the hell else could he say? He was good for his word. He'd do his damnedest to make sure her life didn't change, or his brother's. With one last look at the puppies, he headed back toward the house. His shoulder throbbed, his head was beginning to match. He decided to spend the day doing what he'd gotten good at since he'd fallen through a burning roof and had broken his fall with his shoulder—nothing.

Callie would have dwelled on that kiss—*kisses*—all day if she could have, but she had plenty of things to do to keep her distracted. Feed her new dog for one. The poor thing inhaled her food as if she hadn't eaten in days.

The serum for the inoculations was indeed missing, a problem made all the more strange because of what had happened to Sierra. Odder still, it didn't appear as if anyone had broken in, and nothing else was missing, even though the tack room hadn't been locked and was filled with expensive gear.

Callie would swear she was losing her mind except she'd seen the shipment of serum arrive herself. They searched everywhere: the barn, their storage shed, even around the yard. She had no choice but to accept the fact it was gone.

Before their guests arrived, the sheriff came out and took a report. And through it all, Callie was aware of a humming in her blood that she knew she had Jake to thank for. She'd let him put his hands on her, and at odd moments throughout the day, her face and body went hot at just the thought.

Idiot. When would she remember that he turned her into a blathering, drooling idiot? The next time he had her naked? And would that be before or after he sold the Blue Flame? A hundred times today she'd nearly told him she wanted to buy the ranch and a hundred times she'd held back. The guy had to sell, sooner than later, so what could telling him possibly get her besides pity? Nothing.

She was standing on the porch when Marge came out, hand extended, aspirin in her palm. "Hey, honey, take these."

Callie didn't question how or why Marge was keeping track of when she needed aspirin. Marge took pride in doing such things. Callie dutifully took the pills for her aching head and ribs. "Thanks."

"You okay?

"Always."

Marge patted her shoulder, then went back inside. Callie took a deep breath and put the morning into perspective. The small-town gossip train would go into effect now. She knew this. In no time, whichever Realtors Jake had called would hear about the missing serum and what had happened to Sierra. Terrible as it sounded, it would put a question mark on the property—a definite disadvantage to selling.

Torn between hope and regret, she was still standing on the front porch when the airport vans arrived with their next guests. Things went fast after that. Checking in the group of Japanese businessmen, seeing them all happy with their accommodations and Amy's big pot of chili that night for dinner, getting everyone into the spirit of the Wild West was fun but hard work.

Their guests didn't speak much English, which was a challenge. So was the four-year-old son one of them had brought on the spur of the moment. Keito had run his short little legs all afternoon. The horses and hens had been an unbearable excitement for him, and the puppies had sent him into ecstasy.

At sunset, Eddie lit a bonfire for the guests to sit around, and Amy brought out the makings for s'mores, which was met with such enthusiasm, Callie actually caught the girl *almost* smiling before she walked off toward her cabin. Callie had hoped Amy would stay outside, but her duties would begin early every morning now, and they didn't include having to socialize with the guests. But still, Callie wished she'd want to. The others always did; it was a huge part of the Blue Flame's charm.

Stone, obviously feeling better than he had earlier, pulled out his guitar. With the stars out and the chill of the spring night being beaten back by the warm, crackling fire, he and Eddie taught everyone silly campfire songs. The guests all fell for their easy appeal. Marge came out of her cabin and sat next to Tucker, humming along with the songs. Lou came out a few minutes later. Fifty-something, he was a tall, beefy man with a wild shock of gray hair and chocolate eyes that usually twinkled. Tonight, he hunched his broad shoulders and jammed his hands into his pockets as he came close. "Callie." He nodded his Stetson at her.

"Hey, Lou." She knew how worried he and Marge were about money ever since he'd been laid off from Roger's Garage in Three Rocks two weeks ago. That he looked so unhappy tugged at her. "Any luck finding a new job?"

"No, thanks to Roger."

"What do you mean?"

"He's telling people I stole from him. Tools and money." He looked at his feet. "There weren't many other jobs out there to begin with, but now . . ." Helplessly, he shrugged.

"Why would Roger do that to you?"

"I don't steal. You know I don't."

"Of course I know that."

"I think his punk nephew Tony did it, so he could have my job." He kicked the dirt. "Not that Roger'll ever believe me over him. Tony's a slimy weasel but he's a smart slimy weasel."

"Oh, Lou. I'm sorry."

"It's all right. I know the truth, Marge knows the

truth. We'll be all right." But he sighed heavily, then walked over to his wife and sat next to her. She hugged him hard and kept singing.

Everyone else had smiles on their faces, too, especially their guests as they sang in heavily accented English, and after a few minutes, some of Callie's tension eased. They had problems, they all had problems, but in spite of it, she loved having guests to entertain and her makeshift family all together.

After a few songs, she caught sight of a silhouette at the edge of the fire's glow. A slim, petite shadow with her shoulders hunched against the night's chill, too far from the warmth of the fire.

Amy had stayed outside after all.

Callie figured she was used to being the outsider, and was just about to wave at the girl, to urge her back into the circle, when Tucker beat her to it, motioning Amy over, squishing into Marge and Lou to make room for her.

Amy shook her head.

Tucker tried again, adding a sweet, charismatic smile that made Callie blink because for a moment he looked so much like his older brother Jake she couldn't believe it. A woman would have to have ice in her veins not to respond to that smile, but Amy remained where she was.

Callie understood perfectly. With the exception of kissing Jake today, she herself had resisted all wily masculine smiles for a good long time, and with good reason. She'd followed her heart down the wrong path before, and didn't intend to do it again.

But Amy was too young to have learned such a thing.

"The day redeemed itself nicely," said an unbearably familiar masculine voice.

Jake. Wearing soft, worn jeans and a dark shirt, he came up next to her. He had a plate in his hands, filled with the largest s'more she'd ever seen—melting marshmallow on melting chocolate, squishing out of the sides of the graham cracker, designed to make one's mouth water on sight.

So did the smile he wore.

All on a dark, starry night in front of a bonfire, which was almost too much to resist. She kept her gaze on the crowd around the fire. "The day did redeem itself."

He offered up his dessert but she shook her head.

"Sure?" His eyes were sparkling with good humor, mischief . . . and much more. "How can you resist?" He lifted the plate to his nose, sniffing appreciatively. "Warm, soft chocolate, toasted marshmallows all gooey in the center, sandwiched between—"

Her stomach growled, and given how his grin widened, he'd heard it. "Fine, damn it, hand it over." Leaning in, she took a big bite, barely managing not to moan as the chocolate and marshmallow liquefied in her mouth.

"Isn't that just about the best thing you've tasted all day?" he murmured.

No, *he'd* been the best thing she'd tasted all day. She set the s'more down on his plate.

"You have . . ." He reached out with a finger toward her face.

She slapped his finger away. "I'm not going to fall for that."

"Okaaaaay, if you want to walk around with . . ."

"What?"

"Nothing, just a little chocolate—"

She swiped at her mouth with the back of her hand. But he just laughed softly, and with a shake of his head, lifted his hand again. His finger hovered right near the corner of her mouth. "May I?" he asked softly.

Her tummy fluttered. She ignored it. "Just do it."

"Tsk-tsk." The pad of his thumb glided over her lower lip. "So impatient."

Definitely, but she was far more concerned with why her nipples had suddenly gone so happy. "I'm too tired for this."

"For what?"

"For . . . you." Tired, and off-kilter, too, from him watching her with that smile that suggested a sensual earthiness, and from the knowledge he could drive her crazy with one touch. "I'm outta here." But the words weren't out of her mouth before she caught sight of Keito running wild around the campfire. Since his father didn't seem inclined to stop him, she moved forward and stepped into Keito's wild path, catching him. "Hey, little guy."

Laughing, he wriggled free. "I am running," he said in the English none of his group had mastered. "See me run . . ."

And off he went again.

She caught him on his next round, wincing at the pain in her bruised ribs as she hoisted him up. "Running around the fire is dangerous, Keito. You could get hurt."

"No hurt. More run."

From her back pocket, her cell phone rang. Setting Keito down, she held on to his hand as she reached for her phone. Michael. "Hi," she said. "I've got to call you back—"

"You don't have everyone off to bed yet?"

"Are you kidding? It's their first night here. They're still all around the campfire, singing songs and eating s'mores." She smiled at Keito, who smiled back.

"Run," the little boy said, tugging on her hand.

"You've got a crew," Michael reminded her. "A good one. Say good-night and come meet me for a drink. I'm buying."

This was not an unusual request. Michael routinely coaxed her off the ranch and into Three Rocks for some fun. He said she worked too hard, she never gave herself any time off, whatever he could come up with to get his way. Often, she went, and never regretted it. He was easy to be with, and made her laugh. But she was so tired tonight. "I'm exhausted."

"Because you give that place too much of yourself. Come give it to me instead. Come on, I'll spoil you rotten. Dinner, dessert . . ." He paused, knowing she never could resist the promise of dessert. "And whatever else floats your boat. Just name it."

"Bed."

He laughed, his voice a little husky now. "Done."

"I meant *my* bed. Alone," she said, laughing, because he was just teasing. He'd never made a real move on her, not once.

"Come on, Cal. That place is sucking the soul right out of you." Suddenly he was no longer kidding. "You never give yourself a life."

She'd been planning on telling him what had happened earlier with Sierra and the missing serum, but doing so would only prolong the conversation she suddenly didn't want to have with him, not now. "This place *is* my life," she said gently. "And today has been a long day."

"Yadda, yadda." But there was a fond smile in his voice again. "Fine. I'm going to try again for tomorrow night."

"We're doing a roundup."

"The weekend then," he said firmly.

"The weekend," she promised, and slipped the phone back into her pocket.

Keito was gone. Whipping around she searched the fire. No little boy. And no one seemed to realize he was gone. They were all laughing and toasting themselves, probably planning their adventures for the next week.

Tucker looked up and caught her obvious panic. "What?" he mouthed across the fire.

"Keito," she mouthed back, and Tucker craned his neck, looking around him. Then pointed behind Callie.

She turned around and came face to face with Jake. She tried to go around him but he blocked her way. "I'm sorry," she said. "I've got to—" She tried to go around him again, but he didn't move.

With her teeth gritted, she looked at him. "Can I help you?"

"Wow, that's impressive," he said. "That tone you use. Cool, icy, yet utterly professional. As if I was a guest here."

"You are."

"Really?" He leaned in. "You kiss all your guests the way you kissed me today?"

"Look, I've got to—"

"Find Keito?" He turned around and showed her the small four-year-old cuddled on his back, off center a little, clinging to Jake's left side. "Got him."

Keito lifted his head from where he'd had it tucked against Jake's broad back and giggled.

Callie let out a breath and pulled him off Jake. The moment she put Keito down, he took off running again, but Eddie stood up from his perch near the fire and nabbed him, nodding to Callie. He'd take care of him.

Grateful, she let out a breath and combed her fingers

through her hair as she turned back to Jake. "Thanks," she said, and knew by his grin she could have sounded more genuine.

"Bet that cost you," he said.

"I can't help it, you have this habit of trying to sweep in to save the day."

"Trying? Correct me if I'm wrong, but you'd be squished like a grape if I hadn't hauled you out of that horse pen this morning."

"Stall," she corrected. "Horse stall."

"And me finding Keito just now saved you some trouble."

"Fine, you've saved me twice. Thank you. Thank you."

"The dog."

"What?"

He was still smiling, looking quite sure of himself, and quite kissable, damn him. "I also saved you from the dog," he reminded her.

She blew out a breath. "Thank you *three* times then."

"You're very welcome."

"You really miss work, don't you?"

His face closed. "This isn't about me."

"You know what? *Bed*." She was *way* overdue for bed.

"An invitation?"

"In your dreams."

"How about a hot tub trip instead?" he purred, a warm smile accompanying it, one that had a rather melting affect on her bones. "Both our sore bodies need it, want it."

No. What her body needed and wanted were two very different things.

She needed rest.

She wanted him.

6

Under the glow of the three-quarter moon and more stars than he'd ever seen in San Diego, Jake knew Callie was going to shake her head even before she did.

"No hot tub," she said.

That didn't surprise him, but what did was the pang of regret. He'd watched Callie and the others kick into gear after the guests had arrived, effortlessly offering hospitality and service as a unit. A tight unit.

As for himself, he'd attempted to help. Attempted being the key word. Tucker had given him a list of stuff to do, which had included saddling up a few horses. Jake managed to feed and water the pigs—ruining his running shoes with muck that didn't bear too close inspection. He'd not been able to get a saddle on a horse. Hell, he couldn't have lifted his own arm above his head much less a saddle. The only reason he'd been able to hold Keito for that brief moment had been because the kid was light, and had happily crawled up Jake himself, holding mostly to his good side.

In any case, Jake had not been successful moving the few cows from one pasture to another for Tucker, but he had a feeling his brother hadn't expected him to. He'd just watched as if Jake was the biggest disappointment on earth.

Jake had made the mistake of letting that get to him, enough so that he'd actually tried to get on a horse. Eddie had helped him. Sitting hadn't been a problem. Even walking hadn't been a problem. But when he'd dropped the reins, startling the big animal into a trot, it had jarred his shoulder enough that he'd nearly slid off into one miserable, whimpering heap on the ground.

Humiliating. But then again, he suspected Tucker had enjoyed that, too. Everything about being here seemed so foreign. There was just so much damn open space, all surrounded by rocky ridges, lined with overgrown brush, and miles and miles of wide horizon. No Thai food. No twenty-screen movie theater complex. No traffic unless he counted the occasional lost cow blocking the driveway.

It'd only been two days, and he was going to lose his mind, never mind what three months would do. Coming here to recoup had been the stupidest idea he'd ever had, and he was exceptionally bad off if baiting this beautiful, prickly woman in front of him had become the only entertainment available. "You afraid of a little hot tub adventure?"

"I'm not afraid of anything."

"Except opening up to me."

"Is this a story about the pot and the kettle, Jake?"

He sighed, and ran a finger over the black smudge of exhaustion beneath her eyes. "I watched you work your pretty ass off today. It's late, and you're probably aching. All I'm saying is that you deserve a little break."

"Not with you."

He toed the dirt at his feet. It rose up and choked him. Shit, there was a lot of dirt out here. Beyond the fire, where everyone was still gathered, having a great time, the dark night settled over him like a smothering cloak.

"So who's Michael?"

"A close friend."

"Ah."

"What does that mean, "*ah*"?"

"Women never use 'close friend' as a description for a guy they want."

"And does it matter to you one way or another?"

"Definitely," he said. He stood close enough to see the pulse flutter at the base of her neck. "Since you and I, whatever we are, includes a hell of a lot of wanting."

"That whole kissing episode today was a mistake, Jake."

"Maybe we should repeat it, just to make sure." He laughed at the expression of annoyance on her face. "Okay, fine. You're a workaholic who doesn't need much wild fun. I get it."

"I've done wild."

"Uh-huh."

"I have." She lifted her chin defiantly. "I was once introduced to a perfect stranger in a bar, eloped with him that same night, and then left him a month later. Wild enough?"

He took her left hand in his, rubbing the pad of his thumb over her ringless ring finger.

She yanked her hand back. "It turns out, he wasn't husband material."

His eyes cut to hers, wondering at all she wasn't saying. "Had a rough time of it, did you?"

"You could say that."

"Well how about this . . . you try fun and wild again, this time without tying yourself down."

"A particular talent of yours?"

"You know it." He smiled coaxingly, because he was dying out here, and desperately, shockingly lonely. "Look, I don't know why we're arguing. We want the same thing, really."

"Really? And what's that?"

"What anyone wants." He lifted his hand and tucked a stray strand of fiery hair behind her ear, just for the excuse of touching her. "Happiness. Contentment."

"Well, I have them. I have it all." She stared at him for another moment, as if wanting to make sure he believed it, before walking away.

He let out a long breath. Alone again. "Must be nice to think you have it all."

The next day started early for Callie. Besides the unsettling fact that no one knew where the serum had gone or who'd messed with Sierra, it turned out that their guests had misunderstood their forms. They were not experienced riders, but beginners. In fact, most of them had never ridden horses before. That wasn't a big problem, but it did mean an adjustment of the plans.

She stood in her office in the big house, looking out at the corral, trying to plan out the day in her head, when Jake appeared in the doorway holding two mugs of coffee.

"Wow," she said. "I'm impressed."

"Because I can pour coffee?"

"Because you're wearing boots."

"Yeah. Had to borrow some from Lou." He handed her one of the mugs, blew into his own, and took a sip. "What do you say, Callie, to making a deal." He looked right into her eyes. "We start over."

"Start over?"

"Getting to know each other. Since I always seem to be on the wrong foot with you."

Shame might have filled her that she'd made him feel that way but a few remembered words stopped it.

"When I sell this place . . ."

"Starting over isn't going to change anything," she said.

"We could at least try." He started to thrust out his right hand, winced and hissed out a breath, then set down his coffee and offered her his left. "The name is Jake."

"Jake—"

"What's yours?"

She rolled her eyes. "Callie."

"Lovely name." He shook her hand, then ran his thumb over her knuckles. "How can I help you today, Callie? I'm here, at your service."

"You don't like anything about ranching."

"Ah, but see you just met me. You don't yet know that."

"Right. So you want to move some more cows around, see how the pigs are doing, gather eggs, that sort of thing."

"Well . . ."

"Yeah, thought so. If I need you, I'll let you know."

He waited until she brushed past him and got to the door before he said her name. She hesitated, then turned back, gasping in surprise because he'd come up right behind her and now her front bumped his.

Slowly he reached for her face, tilting it up. Smiled. And her heart took off on a race she didn't want to be in. "Jake—"

"Shh." He lowered his mouth to hers in one soft, melting kiss.

When he was done, it took her a moment to open her eyes. She found him focused in on her, just her.

"See how nice and simple that was without any baggage?" he asked.

"Nothing about that was simple." She had to force her limbs to work, and turned away. "But . . . it was nice," she admitted to the door.

She didn't see his grin, but she felt it, all the way to her toes.

The sun was warm, steaming off the dew. Callie and the others spent the morning in the center horse corral leading the guests around on horseback, teaching them to ride.

Between the language barrier and their innate fear, it took the entire ranch crew. Callie even recruited Marge, Lou, and Amy to come out and lead around a guest or two. Marge had been riding horses all her fifty-some years, and loved getting back outside for a day, having fun telling stories of her wild youth, even though most of the guests didn't have a clue as to what she was saying. Lou was quieter than usual, his smile rare, and Callie silently hoped a meteor fell on Roger's garage.

Amy didn't say much either, but Callie caught her smiling at little Keito a couple of times as he sat in front of his father on a horse, giggling for all he was worth.

But even with all of them outside helping, they were still short-handed for this unexpected chore of teaching every single one of their guests to ride. "Call a few friends from town?" Callie begged Tucker at one point.

"Everyone's on a three day camping trip to the Cochise Stronghold." He took off his hat and scratched his head. "How about Michael?"

"He's got some big thing today. I'll go see if Jake—"

"We can do it without him."

"You know he's here for a while."

He shoved his hat further up on his head and scratched his forehead in frustration. "I'm living with him, aren't I?"

"I think you should talk to him, try to work out what's bugging you."

"What's bugging me is his presence. And why are you defending him?"

She had no idea. "We owe our jobs to him."

"So you think he went and bought paint today out of the kindness of his heart?"

"The place needs some paint."

"And when we're done, he'll sell that much easier."

"He said we'll keep our jobs, he'll make sure of it."

Tucker let out a sound of disgust. "The guy can't milk a cow to save his life. And he went green when he fed the pigs."

"He's never done those things before."

"And he won't again, is my guess. We did get him up on a horse though, which was amusing."

"Not Moe," she said quickly, well aware that Moe had taken an instant dislike to Jake, one that seemed eerily personal.

"I'm not looking to kill him. He rode Molly."

"That's good, right?"

"Please. Molly would let a toddler ride her."

"Still, he tried."

"You're the most logical, smartest woman I know," he said, baffled. "Don't go soft now, just because there's a pretty face to flirt with."

She laughed and hoped she didn't blush with guilt. "Have you looked in a mirror? Your face is just as pretty."

"Callie." Suddenly he looked very young. "Listen, he walks away. That's what he does. Know that right now."

She remembered how angry and brooding Tucker had been when he'd first come here, a seventeen-going-on-thirty-five-year-old man, looking for a purpose. Her heart had broken for him then.

And it broke now. This land had given him his purpose. She wanted to be angry at Jake for not doing more, but truthfully, she suspected he would have done anything for Tucker, if only he'd known what.

She wished she could fix this for them, but she couldn't. She could only try to get them back together, help them learn about each other, and hopefully, eventually trust each other, too. God, she hoped Jake was worthy of Tucker's trust. As for herself, plenty of people had walked away from her, or proven unworthy of her heart. Her father, her mother. Matt. It no longer mattered to her. "I'm not looking for another husband here, Tuck, just a spare hand."

"Whatever."

Without another option looming, she went looking for Jake. She found him lounging in the hot tub, head back, body sprawled out, snoozing. She nudged his arm with the tip of her boot.

He opened his eyes and smiled. "I knew you'd come to your senses and join me."

"Did you mean it?"

"Are you kidding?" He scooted that long, lean, hard-as-rock body over and made room. Patted the water.

She shook her head. "I meant about helping."

"Are you asking?"

She let out a breath. "Yeah."

He just looked at her, and she let out another huff. "Could you help us out today, please?"

"Does it involve the pigs?"

"Nope."

"Does it involve Goose?"

"Nope."

"How about rounding up anything with four legs?"

She lifted a brow. "No."

His smile was slow and sexy as hell. "Well, then, I'd love to." Good as his word, he stood up, water running down his heart-attack-inducing body. She quickly turned her back, and his soft laugh scraped at her belly.

"You've already seen it all," he reminded her. "In fact, you've even touched or kissed most of it."

"I'll meet you in the corral," she said quickly, and walked away, grinding her jaw when he laughed. She didn't need the reminder of what she'd done to and with that body. If she didn't know exactly what she'd missed out on that night, she'd guessed a million times since.

But the truth of the matter was that *he* hadn't wasted time wondering, he'd simply replaced her with another woman, countless times over. *Remember that*, she told herself.

When he met her outside a few minutes later, he was dressed the part of a horse handler in jeans, a white T-shirt with a blue plaid flannel unbuttoned over the top of it, complete with boots. No hat though, and no gloves, bringing home that this was not just another Eddie or Stone, or even Tucker. This man didn't belong here, didn't really want to be here. "It's simple," she said, and handed him a spare set of gloves, along with the reins of Misty, another particularly kind, sweet mare. On her back sat one of their guests, a forty-something man named Lee who spoke little to no English.

Callie smiled up at him, then she said to Jake, "Just

walk them around the corral until Lee gets used to the feel of the horse beneath him. Misty'll be good."

As if looking to agree, Misty lowered her head and bumped it into Jake's chest.

He took a staggering step backward. "Jesus."

"She's waiting for you to take a carrot out of your pocket."

He sent her a baleful look. "That's not a carrot in my pocket."

"Ha, ha." She pulled a carrot out of hers and stepped close, slipping it into his front pocket. She hadn't meant anything by it other than to put him more at ease, and to give him something to bond with Misty over, but when the horse started nudging him for the carrot, his eyes widened.

"Holy shit—" He hastily pulled the carrot out and practically threw it at Misty. "Now stop frisking me."

Misty knocked his chest again, and snorted her thanks.

Callie laughed. "Maybe *I* should save *you* this time."

Jake turned his head, interested. "Really? What did you have in mind?"

"Nothing. Never mind," she said hastily at the heat flaring in his eyes. "But if you want to back out of this—"

"No." He shot Misty another long look. "I can do it."

And he did. He walked that corral for hours, without another incident or complaint, making her rethink some things—such as his willingness to adapt, to change and accept. It appeared he had plenty of that, for whatever he came up against, leaving her to wonder exactly whose willingness to adapt and change and accept was really at stake here.

7

It took a day longer than planned, but eventually all of their guests did get the hang of being on a horse by themselves. Jake continued to help, and though he used only his left arm, he seemed to manage well enough for a guy who had no more horse sense than their guests, twice catching Keito from falling off his father's lap. In fact, their guests thought Jake was the best cowboy they'd ever seen.

Tucker decided it was beginner's luck.

Two days later, the guests helped round up the cattle as planned, driving them into the main corral—with Eddie's, Stone's, Tucker's, and Callie's help.

Jake didn't ride.

Tucker had no idea if that was because he'd had enough of being involved, or if Callie hadn't invited him, or if he'd just not gotten up in time.

He didn't care. Sure, he'd cared once, but then Jake had walked out of his life and hadn't looked back.

And Tucker had woken up to the ways of blood ties. They meant nothing. He'd found his real family right here at the Blue Flame, and it had nothing to do with genes.

After the roundup, they inoculated the cattle with

the new serum Eddie had driven into town for. The guests loved it all. In fact, Tucker didn't think they'd ever had a more enthusiastic group than this one, who even with no experience and hardly any grasp of the English language seemed to be having the time of their lives.

It was infectious. Typically Tucker just . . . existed, glad to be away from what had been a vagabond life, glad for the steady job, glad to be around people he cared about and who cared in return. But once in a while, like today, something bubbled up from within that he nearly didn't recognize—happiness.

It felt good, very good.

That night, Amy served the guests homemade stew and cornbread. The scent of it teased his nose as he came inside the big house. In fact, he stood there in the hallway, taking the time for a big sniff, listening with pleasure as the dining room on his left rang with laughter and conversation he couldn't understand.

Amy burst out of the double doors, carrying a tray of empty plates, her cheeks glowing.

"Hey there." Smiling at just the sight of her, he reached for her tray.

She pulled back. "I've got it."

Remembering how fast she was, and just how strong, he held up his hands in surrender. "Fine, you've got it— Are you blushing?"

"No."

More laughter rang out from the dining room. He eyed her some more. "They loved your food, didn't they?"

"I thought they'd hate western food, but . . ."

God, she was something to look at. Long, dark hair, and even darker eyes, which were looking anywhere but at him. She wore black jeans and a white T-shirt layered beneath a black long sleeved one, with an apron around her slim waist that read: TODAY'S MENU—TAKE IT OR LEAVE IT. "I have to go." She indicated with a jerk of her chin that he should move out of her way.

Because he wasn't stupid, he backed up to give her plenty of room, then followed her into the kitchen.

"You're probably hungry. I'll serve you." She didn't look at him as she moved directly to the sink and dumped her tray.

Typically, the staff either ate with their guests in the dining room or by themselves in the kitchen afterward. Tonight, with the language barrier, he'd assumed everyone would be waiting in the kitchen, but there was no one there but the two of them.

Amy turned to the cabinets and reached for a plate for him.

"Where is everyone?" He took the plate from her hands.

She snatched it back. "Callie just left to have a late dinner with Michael. Eddie and Stone went out, too. They said you didn't want to go."

No, he hadn't felt like making the usual rounds tonight. But he was restless. Truth was, he'd been restless for some time now.

She took the plate to the stove and lifted a lid off a pot, from which came such a mouth-watering smell he brainlessly moved toward it. "I swear to you," he said, leaning in. "I've never smelled anything so good in my life."

She pointed at him with the wooden server. "I don't want to have to hurt you again, but I don't appreciate personal comments."

Tucker fought with a grin. "I was talking about your stew."

At the priceless look on her face, he lost his battle and let his grin loose. "And though you smell heavenly yourself, I promise, I would never have dared told you so."

Silently, she ladled some stew into his bowl. He reached for it, and as he had before, waited until she looked at him to take it. "Thank you. But I don't expect you to serve me."

"It's my job."

"It's your job to serve the guests. The rest of us are just grateful for your leftovers. You cook like an angel, Amy."

"No offense, but I've seen you eat chili right out of a can, so I'm not going to consider you a great judge."

He laughed, but started eating where he stood, stopping to let out a heartfelt moan at the first taste. "Okay, maybe you could have served me anything and I wouldn't have complained, but honestly, there's just something about your food."

And about her, he thought.

Clearly deciding to forget about him, she began working at the counter, dropping some ingredients into a large bowl, sometimes stopping to stir, but rarely measuring anything. Eggs, flour, sugar . . .

Still eating, he watched her, and when she got to the chocolate, he was drawn closer. He came up beside her, not behind her. He'd learned that much. He'd like to know why she hated to be touched, or who'd put that trapped doe expression on her face that she sometimes got, but he knew she sure as hell wasn't going to tell him a thing.

She slanted him an irritated glance. "What?"

"What are you making?"

"If I said 'nothing for you,' would you go away?"

"Nope."

She sighed. "Cookies. For the picnic you're taking the guests on tomorrow."

"Cookies." His stomach rumbled hopefully. "Maybe I should stick around and taste them, just to make sure you've got it right."

"I don't think so."

Her face had gone sullen, and he went still. He'd been flirting playfully, harmlessly, but she wasn't. In fact, she'd clearly been happier when she'd forgotten he was watching her. Surprised, he took another long look, but realized the truth. This was not Amy trying to flirt back, or being coy. She really wanted to be left alone. That was hard for him to imagine, as he hated to be alone. But he figured she had good reason to prefer her own company to anyone else's.

With a big spoon, she began dropping little balls of dough onto a cookie sheet, her movements stilted now, and he didn't miss how she kept him in her peripheral vision, where she would know where he stood at all times.

Suddenly he was no longer hungry, or interested in playing with her. "You're safe here, you know," he said quietly.

Going still for one telling second, she went back to dropping cookies on the greased cookie sheet.

"The Blue Flame." He managed a smile past the odd lump in his throat. "We're sort of a collection of misfits and outcasts and former wanderlusts."

Picking up the full cookie tray, Amy let her shoulder jab him in the chest, just hard enough to set him back a step, as she passed him on her way to the oven. "Excuse me."

Her charming little way of reminding him not to get too close, he supposed, rubbing his chest. When she'd settled the cookie sheet in the oven, she straightened and wiped her hands on her apron. Then she looked him right in the eyes. "I'm not a misfit or an outcast or a former wanderlust. I'm just trying to do my job and stay out of everyone's way, yours included."

"My mistake, then."

"Yeah." She turned to the sink and began to rinse dishes. Dismissing him.

With a sigh for the brick wall he'd hit, he took one last envious look at the cookies beginning to rise in the oven, and did as she wanted, left her alone.

Late that night Callie sat on her bed reading a magazine instead of sleeping because images kept popping into her head. Jake pulling her from beneath Sierra's flailing hooves before she could get stomped on. Jake coaxing that poor, starving dog into letting him save her puppy. Jake finding Keito and keeping him safe.

Jake kissing her, touching her, as if she'd been more important at that moment than air.

She couldn't get the thought of him falling off a roof out of her mind, and all that he must have suffered. He had to be hurting, and missing his life. Missing his job. She was so lost in the wondering about that, when the soft knock came at her door, she nearly fell off the bed.

She looked down at herself. The sunshine-yellow spaghetti-strapped satin tank top and matching panties she'd just gotten on sale from the Internet absolutely weren't suitable for company. She grabbed a robe. "Who is it?"

"Me."

She had no trouble recognizing the low, deep voice, and even if she hadn't, the way her body tightened in response would have told her it was Jake. Her body always knew him, craved him, even when her mind tried to resist.

He knocked again, just once, and she rested her forehead on the door, her heart beating like a wild drum.

"Callie?"

She put a hand to her chest as if she could hold her heart safe. In the light of day she could have resisted him, but there was no light here, no warmth, no sun, and suddenly she needed him. "I'm not dressed."

"I don't care. I just want to see you."

He sounded like maybe he was hurting, and one thing she'd never been able to do was ignore someone in pain. She debated with herself for another second, then opened the door.

He didn't say a word, just looked at her with that intriguing, irresistible mixture of affection, the need to strangle her, and a longing that nearly brought her to her knees.

So he felt it, too, she marveled, all the pent-up emotions that drove her so crazy. "Are you all right?"

"Yes." He paused. "No." He let out a breath. "Actually, I'm not sure." He started to step in but she mustered up some pride and blocked him. He just looked at her with those eyes of his and everything within her quivered in reaction to the hunger there.

"Is your shoulder hurting?" she asked.

"If I said yes, is that the password?"

"Jake—"

"Because it's killing me. But that's nothing new."

Her heart melted. There'd be no resisting him, not tonight anyway, and she moved aside.

He shut the door behind him, then leaned back against it and pulled her to him. "Callie." Just that, just her name whispered in a raw, tortured voice as he skimmed a hand down her hair, over her shoulder.

"What is it?"

"I don't know."

He sounded nearly destroyed. "Oh, Jake," she murmured, and unable to resist soothing him, she slid her arms around his neck. "Is it being here? Tucker? Not fighting fires? What?"

"All of the above."

She tightened her grip on him. "I'm sorry."

He buried his face into the crook of her neck and held on tight. "I feel a little dead inside. But not when I'm with you, never with you. Make me feel alive tonight, Callie, the way only you can."

Her breath caught. Any resistance she'd managed to hold on to flew out the window. "I do that for you?"

"Oh, yeah." The silky robe slid off one shoulder, not enough to expose her but enough to change his breathing. The pad of his finger danced lightly over her collar bone, and then he tipped up her face and kissed her, his mouth tasting so good, his body firm and warm against hers. He cupped her breast, his thumb gliding over her nipple, which was already tight and aching for his attention.

He looked a little dazed at the heat they seemed to generate. "Stop me now if you're going to," he murmured hoarsely. "And I'll go."

Her body throbbed with sensual hunger. Stopping wasn't on her mind.

"Callie? I'm not much for subtleties, so you're going to have to give me a sign here."

She didn't understand how much she wanted this. Him. But she slipped out of the robe, nudging off her straps while she was at it, then took his hand from her face and set it against her breast.

He let out a shaky breath. "That's a damn good sign." He tugged the satin down to her waist and let out a purely male growl before bending his head and opening his mouth on her. He used his lips, his tongue, his teeth, until she was burning up from the inside out. Other thoughts tried to invade. This was crazy; she couldn't possibly want him this way; she would regret this come the light of day; but she shoved them all out of her head the way she nearly had that long ago night, and held on as if he were her lifeline.

He touched the bruises flowering on her ribs and made a low sound of regret. "Looks like I'm not the only one hurting." He took her hand and led her to her bed. She sank to the futon mattress and he followed her down, facing her in the low light.

"You're overdressed," she murmured.

"I feel overdressed." He began to lift his arms when she tugged on his shirt, then hissed out a pained breath.

"Let me," she said, and helped him out of his clothes, taking the utmost care with his poor abused body, putting her lips to his scar. She couldn't take her eyes off him, because despite various other scars he sported from head to toe, he was still the most beautiful man she'd ever seen. She was just worrying about how she couldn't possibly compare when he pressed her back. He whispered her name and then kissed her, long and deep, sliding one warm palm inside her panties, tracing her wet flesh with his fingers, drawing another rough sound from both their throats. His mouth made its way from her jaw to her ear, and there he told her what he wanted to do to her, using words that should have shocked her but only made her wetter.

His mouth forged a path with hot, open kisses over her collarbone, down to a breast, skimming the silk off her as he went. He kissed her belly, her thigh. And then in between. She was so primed and ready that she nearly came on the first stroke of his tongue, and on the second she did.

He had a condom. After he put it on, he looked at her from between her splayed legs, jaw tight, body trembly. "Callie . . ."

She realized it was pain, not pleasure on his face, and she sat up. "What? Your shoulder?"

"Yeah. I can't—"

He couldn't brace himself over her, and when she thought about it, she marveled that they'd gotten this far. But they had, and her body was still throbbing with pleasure. She had to give him the same. "Oh, Jake . . . here—" She pulled him down to his back.

He looked up at her from beneath heavy-lidded eyes so filled with heat and desire he took her breath. Poor wounded warrior. He sucked in a breath when she threw a leg over him, and not from pain this time. Her hands went to his jaw, wanting to ease the tension there. "How can I make it better?" she whispered.

"Trust me, you're well on your way."

She ran her hands down his chest, over his belly, which besides being ridged with muscle, quivered at her touch. She didn't expect that sign of nerves, or her reaction to it, which was a slow melting of her insides. There was a connection here that she hadn't counted on. Then he deepened it by whispering her name softly, longingly, and she stared down at him, her already wired senses completely overcome.

"If you're changing your mind again," he said in a ragged voice. "Just kill me now."

"No." Her fingers wrapped around his impressive erection, and holding his gaze, she lifted up and guided him home. But he didn't get very far, and frustrated, she slumped over him. "It's been a long time."

"Shh." He lifted a hand to where she was trying to help him inside her. Moving her fingers away, his thumb brushed across her center in a light, teasing circle that had her gasping at the delicious touch.

He sent her up a dizzyingly wicked smile. Had she thought he wouldn't fit? His touch opened something deep within her, and she sank down on him, discovering he fit just right.

His fingers dug into her hip, urging her to move, and when she did, he arched up into her, their twin moans mingling in the air. With him filling her to bursting, and his thumb sliding over her, pleasure rocked her world. As they moved together in perfect rhythm, something very deep and soul-grabbing flickered between them, and she felt herself start to spiral. As she took the plunge, he went with her, pulling her down closer to him, burrowing his face in her hair as he groaned.

Afterward, they lay there entangled, breathing as though they'd run five miles uphill. Afraid she might be hurting him, she tried to slide off but his arms tightened around her.

So she stayed, her muscles still spasming periodically in pure overloaded bliss, absorbing the lazy stroke of his hand up and down her spine. Eventually he got up and went into her bathroom, and when he came out, he sat next to her in all his naked, unself-conscious glory.

"Feeling alive now?" she asked.

"Yeah." He smiled and ran a finger over her shoulder. "I'm feeling far more than half a man, too."

"Is that how you see yourself?"

"Without firefighting, yeah."

"Oh, Jake."

He stood up. "I don't want your pity."

"I'm not offering you any. Just a little sympathy."

"I don't want that, either. But I'd take round two."

A moment ago she'd felt like cuddling him. Now she wanted to chuck a pillow at his head. "We should talk about it, Jake."

"About what?"

"About how you're hurting. Missing your job. Your father. Tucker—"

"I don't want to talk." He moved around the cabin, picking up the clothing they'd so haphazardly tossed in all directions only a little while before, pulling on his jeans before he glanced at her. "I should go."

She had no idea why she'd expected something different. "Right."

He sighed again. "Callie—" He looked at her for a long moment, hair tousled, clothes disheveled, looking so damn sexy she could hardly stand it. "Nothing."

Disappointment was a vice on her heart, cooling her still-heated skin. "Bye, Jake."

"Bye." Her front door shut behind him.

Body still humming, Callie lay back. "That was it," she told herself. "No more." So why her body quivered and hungered for more, even as she turned over and forced herself to sleep, was a complete and irritating mystery.

8

What seemed like only ten minutes after he'd crawled onto his cot, Jake awoke with a start. This was due to Tucker climbing off the couch and kicking him on the back of the head with his foot as he did—not, Jake was certain, entirely by accident.

"Sorry," Tucker muttered, sounding anything but.

Jake had been dreaming about being back in Callie's bed, which had been a great place to be. So great that when he'd been there last night, he hadn't wanted to leave, which in turn had given him a panic attack, and he'd nearly killed himself to get out. "What the hell time is it?"

"Five thirty. Time to rise and shine, city boy."

Jake had to laugh at that. "You used to be a city boy yourself. You used to whine like a baby when I'd wake you for kindergarten."

"Yeah, well, that was a damn long time ago." Wearing only his boxers, Tucker grabbed his jeans off the floor and headed toward the bathroom.

"I'd have to peel you off me to get you on the bus," Jake called out.

Tucker tripped but caught himself. The bathroom door slammed behind him.

Jake lay back and studied the ceiling. Dawn never seemed this early when he was in the firehouse. And it was butt-cold out here for spring. The windows were fogged.

He didn't want to get up. He'd have liked to just lie there and think about the amazing sex he'd had last night, but as with everything out in the boondocks, even that had ended badly.

His own fault. He'd been a shit for leaving like that, when all she'd wanted to do was talk, and he deserved whatever she dished out today. He wondered what form his torture would take. Feeding more pigs? Moving more cows?

And who willingly did those things every day?

Maybe these people were all crazy. Yeah, that would explain a lot.

The shower turned on.

All hell, they weren't crazy. No one crazy would get up at dawn like Tucker and work so hard or be so dedicated. And Jake had to admit, stretching, wincing at the ache in his shoulder, that his baby brother was both. He wore responsibility surprisingly well.

An extremely welcome change.

After a few more minutes, the bathroom door opened and a fully dressed Tucker headed toward the front door.

"Tuck?"

One hand on the door, Tucker hesitated. "Yeah?"

"When are you going to forgive me for leaving you?"

"I was only five, you were nothing to me."

A lie. They both knew that. They'd been everything to each other. "You know I had to go," Jake said softly. "Mom—"

"I don't care."

"She was jealous of us. She had all the control then, and she used it—"

The front door slammed shut. Before Jake could lie back, it was whipped open again. "You going to help with chores or what?" Tucker demanded.

"I'll help."

"I know you don't want to get your hands dirty, so maybe you could just show up in the tack room and help organize the gear for our day trip."

"I don't give a shit if my hands get dirty. I just wasn't used to trying to direct a damn cow—"

The door slammed again and Jake was left alone. He got up slowly, shoulder stiff, feeling twice his age. A hot shower didn't help.

He stepped outside and glanced at Callie's cabin. He could still be in there right now, holding her gorgeous body and getting lucky again. But no, he'd had to run out like a bat out of hell rather than talk. He hated talking, especially about what she'd wanted to talk about—himself and his feelings.

He made his way to the barn. Moe gave him the evil eye as he entered. "Okay, listen," he said, stopping at his stall, extending a hand to pet him. "How about a peace treaty?"

Moe bared his teeth.

Jake yanked his hand back. "Or not," he muttered and went to the tack room. A few days ago he and Eddie had moved the puppies and their mother there, onto a soft bed of hay. They'd named the brown dog Tiger, for her fierce protective tendencies, and she seemed proud of it. Now the dog raised her head and sniffed at him, and then let him pet the puppies, which sent them all into wiggle, mewling mode.

At least somebody here liked him.

Living alone and working twenty-four hour shifts didn't suit a dog's life, so he didn't have one. But he stroked the belly of a warm, chocolate brown puppy and felt a yearning inside him.

Knowing he couldn't take one home, he sighed and went looking for some sign of what Tucker needed done. He had no idea, and no one was around, so he left, walking up to the big house in the early-morning sun. He didn't hear a sound. No planes, no cars, no honking trucks, nothing. Just the occasional snort of a horse, the clucking of a hen or two.

The sky yawned wide in front of him, as vast as the land around him. Towering rocky canyons surrounded them, outlined by thick oaks and sycamores. Nowhere to go, no fires to put out, no purpose. Even more depressing was the little niggling voice inside saying, *What if this is all you have? What if you can never go back to firefighting?*

Outside, Lou kneeled before a toolbox in front of Callie's Jeep and Eddie's truck. They'd upped his hours at the ranch because he and Marge needed the income, but the truth was, the man kept all their equipment running smoothly and was damn handy. Just yesterday he'd made a hero out of himself when he fixed both the fussy hot tub and the microwave in the big kitchen.

Lou nodded to Jake but didn't say a word. Eddie stood in the corral working with one of the horses. He nodded to Jake, too, but also kept to himself.

Everyone had a purpose, a reason for being there. Everyone but him.

Jake shoved his hands in his pockets and headed inside. Still no sign of Tucker. In the kitchen, he pilfered one of Amy's excellent banana nut muffins off the stove. He could hear the guests conversing in Japanese in the dining room so he wandered into the weight room and over to a weight bench. Lying down, he reached up for the bar. There was only thirty pounds on it, and his left hand gripped just fine but his right . . . he couldn't even get it to the bar. He had to physically maneuver it with his left hand. Ridiculous. He'd been doing his exercises, including a brutal set of thirty push-ups a day, and he still couldn't reach for anything. Lifting the weight was out of the question, he knew that, and yet out of apparent stupidity, he tried anyway.

And nearly strangled himself when his right arm collapsed and the bar landed across his windpipe. He fought with it for a moment, but couldn't move, couldn't breathe. *Good one, Ace,* he thought as his vision swam. Nice way to go—

"Ohmigod." He caught a whir of fiery hair, which hit him in the face, and then the weights were lifted.

Callie glared down at him, looking more furious than he'd ever seen her. "You have a death wish?" She put a hand to his chest, holding him down when he would have risen. "Don't you know your own damn limitations?"

Grabbing her hand in his, he pushed it aside and sat up, trying not to gasp for breath or look like he hurt like hell. "I would have been fine." This was spoken in a thin, hoarse voice that didn't fool either of them.

Callie shoved her hair out of her face, and let out a breath. "I was in my office, and heard the clang of the weights. I thought it was a guest, and nearly didn't come check." She shook her head. "You could have killed yourself, you idiot."

Idiot? Did he call *her* an idiot when she got hurt? "I'm not paying to stay here to be insulted."

"You're not paying to stay here at all," she pointed out. "I mean it, Jake, that was the stupidest thing—" She broke off when he sank back to the bench, lifting his left hand to rub his shoulder. "Did you hurt yourself?"

Yes, he hurt like hell, and was damn tired of it, too. "I'm fine. Thanks for the lecture. You can get back to work."

"Let me see."

"What? No."

"Take off your shirt."

A laugh choked out of him. "Didn't we do this in reverse a week ago?"

"Here—" Impatient, she unbuttoned his shirt herself, her tongue caught between her teeth with concentration.

Jake stared at that tongue while her fingers brushed his bare skin, sweeping the material off his chest and shoulders. "I decided sleeping with you again would be extremely detrimental to my mental health. So I'm begging you, put that tongue away."

Ignoring him, she touched his scar, from armpit to the tip of his shoulder. "You didn't split anything."

"No." Apparently his lower body didn't get the memo about not sleeping with her, because it was reacting to her touch. "The incision's closed."

"But it hurts?"

"Only when I breathe."

Her fingers kneaded lightly, in a motion that was both torture and pleasure. "You're not massaging it enough. The scar tissue is stiff." She dug in with her fingers, stopping when he sucked in a pained breath. "Too hard?"

"Nah." Sweat broke out on his brow.

Shaking her head, she let out an irked mutter and continued to massage his shoulder and scar, manipulating it much the same way his physical therapist had. "You hanging in?" she asked a few minutes later.

He decided not to answer that because he wasn't sure. Eventually she stopped and pushed him back to the bench when he would have risen. "Stay," she said, and whirled away, only to come back a moment later and set an ice pack on him, making him yelp at the cold. "Ten minutes, you big baby."

"Damn, such a bedside manner. Are you this kind to all the men in your life?"

"You could ask my ex. I once held his own shotgun on him."

He shuddered. "And here I thought you were so sweet. Why did you get married so young?"

"Besides being stupid?" She lifted a shoulder. "It's a long story."

"I'm not going anywhere."

She touched his ice pack. "It's a little pathetic, actually."

"Well, I'm feeling a little pathetic myself. Tell me."

"It's just the same old poor neglected kid story. You know, where no one looks at the girl twice, so when a guy finally does . . ." She shrugged again, looking embarrassed. "I fell for Matt hard. Hook, line, and sinker."

"You got your heart broken."

"I lived." She smiled grimly. "I'm tougher than I look."

"Yeah, you are," he said. "And softer, too."

She looked at the weights that had nearly strangled

him. "I still can't believe what an asinine move that was."

"Gee, don't hold back."

"I never will." She looked at his shoulder. "Your father fell off the barn roof once. He'd been up there fixing a leak, insisting he knew what he was doing—he didn't, by the way, but he was so stubborn. I guess I know where you get that."

"I'm not like him."

"How would you know?" she asked softly. "I mean, in all the years I was here before he died. I never saw you here. How come?"

"Did he talk to you about that?"

"Never."

"Well, there's your answer."

"You mean he never asked you to come?"

Pride dictated he change the subject, but he decided to tell her the truth instead. "Not since I was twelve and told him I wanted to be a big city firefighter."

She looked at him for a long moment. "His loss then, for believing a twelve-year-old could possibly already know what he wanted in life."

"I did know what I wanted. I wanted him to work a little harder at wanting me." The minute the words slipped out of his mouth, he wished he could take them back. They were too open, too raw, and far too revealing.

"His loss," she repeated gently, and adjusted his ice pack again. "I remember being twelve. I'd see other kids getting rides to school. They'd have a sack lunch, or money. A hug if they wanted. It all seemed so normal." Her wistful tone and soft breath brushed over his skin. "I used to wish for that."

Him, too. Knowing he'd missed out, he'd tried to

give a sense of normality to Tucker, though he'd failed miserably.

"When I landed here, I felt as if I'd come home for the first time in my life." Her fingers danced over his skin lightly. He wasn't even sure she realized she was doing it; he just didn't want her to stop. "Richard was everything to me," she said. "He taught me so much, accepted so much."

Was she waiting for him to say he'd made a mistake in not coming here sooner? Because he wasn't going to. That street had gone two ways, and as she'd said, he'd only been a kid. Richard could have reached out, too, and the age-old resentment balled up in his gut. "Yeah, he was a real saint."

"Oh, Jake." Her smile was so sad. "He was so much more than I'd ever had before, yes, but I wasn't blind. He loved this place over and beyond all else."

"Including his own flesh and blood."

"Including his own flesh and blood," she agreed. "It was just who he was. Stubborn as a bull, hard-headed to boot, and God forbid anyone not agree with him. He knew what he wanted at all times and didn't understand why everyone else didn't want the same thing. He could be"—her smile was wry—"curmudgeonly. Difficult."

"An ass."

"Well, that's a matter of opinion," she said loyally. "But the truth is, most of his employees worked hard for him because he paid well and fair, but he wasn't loved by any stretch of the imagination."

Off-kilter and off balance, he looked at her. "At his funeral service, you were furious with me for not grieving. Why tell me all this now? What's changed in me?"

"Maybe it's not you who changed."

"And maybe it's both of us," he said quietly. "Maybe I'm rethinking things, too."

"Your life has changed."

"Drastically."

"And it makes you sad."

"Extremely."

"I'd say I'm sorry but I don't want you to think I'm pitying you." She smiled softly. "But have you thought that maybe changing your life's path could turn out to be a good thing? That you can find something just as rewarding as firefighting?"

"I'm not that evolved."

Her radio chirped and she rose. "Lie still and cool your shoulder down."

After she'd gone, he tried to stay still, which he managed for five minutes. Restless, he tossed aside the ice pack and stood, carefully rolling his shoulder, telling himself he didn't hurt any worse than usual. A lie. Fire burned all the way from his throat to his fingertips. Buttoning his shirt, he walked down the hall of the house, which was quiet. Too quiet.

Now that he'd nearly killed himself in the weight room, he'd exhausted all options of self-entertainment. He wished for something to occupy him, to take his mind off everything. At home that want would be sex. Sex on the lunch table. Sex for dessert. Sex, sex, sex.

Now he'd be happy to have someone to sit with and talk to.

Christ, he was getting old. He needed to sell and get out of there. Go back to his life.

But his stomach dropped a little because deep, deep down he was afraid of the truth—that the life he wanted to get back to no longer existed.

He stepped out of the house into the warm spring day.

Goose rushed to the edge of the grass, neck out, prepared to attack. Jake actually imagined the obnoxious thing as the spirit of his father, cursing him, waving his fist. "Honk, honk," Goose said, and Jake heard "Loser, loser." He shut his eyes and ears to the image and turned away from the grass, stepping instead onto the driveway.

Goose let him go, but watched carefully.

Callie's red Jeep was still parked on the driveway. The hood was up, and from beneath it came an exceptional pair of jean-clad legs topped with well-worn boots.

She was talking, either to herself or the Jeep or the old dog lying prone at her feet. "You big, worthless piece of shit."

Lifting a brow, Jake moved closer, coming to a stop just next to the hood. Shep didn't waste the energy to lift his head. How he'd ever managed to get another dog pregnant was a big mystery to Jake.

More swearing from Callie.

"Problem?"

Jerking upright, she smacked her head on the hood. With another impressive oath, she rubbed the top of her head and glared at him. "Don't sneak up on me."

"I didn't sneak. What's up with your Jeep?"

"It won't start." She kicked the tire. "And Lou's on a job interview in Boca. Damn it."

"I saw Lou right here only a little while ago. He had his tool box out."

"He was giving the Jeep a tune-up. You'd think he'd have noticed it wouldn't start."

"Maybe I can help."

"Oh no. I'm working on evening out the score between us, not adding to my debt." She vanished beneath the hood again.

"What, you think I'm keeping track?"

"Oh, stop with the insulted, wounded warrior tone. This isn't about you." Her words echoed beneath the hood.

Wounded warrior? "Look, I worked as a mechanic after high school while I was training to become a firefighter. I could probably—"

"I've got this handled, Jake."

She wasn't even looking at him. Damn, he was even lonelier than he thought to be bugged by that. He glanced around him.

Still just wide open space. He was going to lose his ever-loving mind out here. The last two visits hadn't been this way, but they'd been short and quaint and, even better, he'd had a woman with him, tending to his every need.

He didn't know what he'd expected this time, but it sure as hell hadn't been this soul-deep loneliness. He turned back to Callie, buried in her Jeep, and wished she'd look at him, talk to him some more, even if it meant hearing more about his father and his life out here, which made him worse off than he'd even thought. "Callie—"

"Honestly. I've got this."

"Right. Because God forbid you actually need anyone."

She started to jerk upright again, but slowed down just before she hit her head. Looking greatly vexed, she eyed him. "What does that mean?"

"I think I scare you." He had no idea why he was pushing this. Maybe it was the pain. Or sheer perversity and frustration. Pick one. "You've been burned and now you're protecting yourself. I get that, but you still have to put it on the line and live."

"And you're the resident expert on this?"

"I'm not afraid, I'll tell you that." *Just lonely as hell.*

She slapped a screwdriver against her thigh as she studied him. "You know, as fascinating as this conversation is, I have work." She stepped around the lazy dog and hopped up into the driver's seat, slamming the door.

"Please start," she whispered to her beloved Jeep. "Please." Because then she'd be able to drive away and forget the look on Jake's face.

The look that had seemed an awful bit too close to desperation.

She didn't want to think of him as being vulnerable. Hurting. She wanted him to remain as she'd conveniently filed him in her head—arrogant, conceited, and a pain in her ass, not to mention on the verge of selling the Blue Flame, her heart, her home. *That's* how she wanted to think of him.

But she couldn't stop thinking about the night before, and how he'd taken her right out of herself while he'd worshipped her body. And then there'd been his expression in the weight room, when she'd talked about Richard. He'd looked starved for the information, angry at wanting to hear more, and terrified he might feel something other than that anger and resentment for the father he'd never known.

He missed his life, and she knew he was afraid he'd never get it back, that he wouldn't heal, that he couldn't perform. That had softened her, when she hadn't wanted to be softened.

Jake reached under the hood.

"Jake, move."

"Wait." He leaned in further. His shirt came untucked from his faded Levi's.

Not that she noticed. To distract herself, she opened the door. "Shep. You coming or what?"

The old dog groaned, got to his feet.

"I wouldn't bother, old buddy." Jake reappeared and looked at Callie. "Someone pulled your coil wire."

"What are you talking about?"

"It's missing. You think Lou took it?"

"No. Why would he?" She hopped back out of the Jeep and looked under the hood again, unable to believe her eyes. Why hadn't she seen this before? "No wonder I couldn't start the thing."

"Yeah. Callie—" He broke off at the sound of a truck rumbling up the driveway.

Michael's Dodge. He got out of the truck and walked over to them. "Hey, babe," he said, pulling Callie into a friendly embrace. Only a little taller than she, he was blond and blue-eyed, and so perfectly featured he should have been in the movies alongside other current hotties like Orlando Bloom. But financing was his thing and so was Arizona, and she was glad. He felt warm and familiar and safe as he hugged her, and she resisted the urge to put her head on his shoulder.

"Ready for lunch?" he asked, squeezing her gently.

She lifted her head and gave him a baffled smile. "I didn't know you were picking me up. I was coming to meet you, but I have Jeep issues. Michael, this is Jake Rawlins."

"Ah." Michael shook Jake's hand, his eyes assessing. "Figured I'd meet you sooner or later. What's the matter with the Jeep, Callie?" He stuck his head under the hood. "Your coil wire is missing."

"We know that much," she said.

"We just don't know why," Jake said.

The two men looked at each other for a long moment, doing the size-the-other-man-up thing, and Callie barely resisted rolling her eyes. They were both incredibly good-looking men, and also incredibly different. Jake was taller, leaner, and definitely edgier, with an air of mystery Michael could never achieve. But truthfully, any man would have paled a little standing next to the sheer maleness of Jake.

"You shouldn't let just anyone drive the thing," Michael said to her. "I saw Stone in it last week, and Eddie in it yesterday getting gas for you. And you just let Lou tune it up. You do know why he was let go from Roger's."

"Yes, but he's innocent of those charges."

"Roger's an ass," Michael allowed. "Still, anyone could be messing with you. We can get a new coil wire in town after we eat."

"Well, if Lou took it while he was working on the Jeep, he had a good reason. Maybe he's just getting me a new one." Callie turned to Jake. "I'll be back. We're just going to go over some financial—"

"No, we're not. No wasting our lunch date on business talk." Michael waved at Jake before leading her to his truck. "Everyone deserves a break, and that's what this is. A lunch break."

Callie craned her neck as she pulled on her seatbelt. Jake was already walking away. "Why did you do that?" she asked Michael when he got behind the wheel.

"Do what?"

"Let him think this is a date. It's a working lunch,

and you know it. I want to talk about getting a loan, and what I need—"

"He was looking at you funny. Like he wanted to gobble you up." Michael's searing blue eyes suddenly weren't light and friendly, but protective. And worried. "You want to buy Blue Flame from that man? Then you want to be friendly but distant. Nice but cool. *Not* a pushover, and definitely not available."

Callie shook her head, but laughed at his twisted logic. Being distant and cool just might keep her out of Jake's arms. "Maybe you're right."

"I always am, babe. Always am." He shoved the truck into gear and drove into town.

The Japanese businessmen left. That night, when Lou came back from town, Callie asked him about the coil wire.

"It was there when I was working on the Jeep," he said with such confusion that she believed him. He went out to check for himself, and scratched his head. "That's odd."

More than odd, but she'd already picked up another coil wire, so she put it out of her head because her poor brain was too full to dwell.

A group of Tucson librarians came the next day for a ride to an abandoned ghost town, guided by Eddie and Stone. Stone had been sick in the morning but thankfully had recovered enough to take them. Callie had a bad feeling he'd simply been hungover yet again, but since he'd been able to do his job, she didn't interfere.

While they were gone, Lou, Tucker, and Jake painted the barn. Lou worked on the inside, Jake and Tucker on the outside. Callie joined Lou until the fumes got to her, then moved outside in time to hear Jake telling

Tucker about the coil wire. The two men looked at each other for a long moment.

Later Callie went in to get drinks and when she came out, she found them arguing.

"Something's up," Jake was saying. "I can feel it."

"What's up is your horrible painting," Tucker said.

"I'm doing it left-handed. And you're changing the subject."

"I'm not sure it'd matter if you switched hands, bro."

"I'm trying to talk about Callie."

"Stow the save-the-world complex. Save it for fire-fighting."

Jake stopped painting altogether at that and squared off to face Tucker. "You're as bad as she is. Something's going on out here. Don't tell me you're so selfish that you'd put your hatred of me before her safety."

Tucker stopped painting, too, and dropped his brush into the paint. "No. Damn it. I'll keep my eyes out for her."

"Both of us will," Jake said firmly.

"How about I keep my own eyes out for myself?" Callie handed them their drinks. "Because if something's going on, and it would seem that it is, it couldn't be about me."

"How do you figure?" Jake asked. "Your horse, your Jeep."

"The ranch." She rubbed her temples. "It's got to be about the ranch. Look, we'll figure it out." She could see the worry and strain in each of them and managed a smile she didn't quite feel. What she did feel was a lump in her throat for these two tall, stubborn, beautiful men looking at her in mutual concern, not even realizing how alike they really were. "And anyway, we have much more to worry about."

"Like?" Jake asked darkly.

"Like . . ." They both looked so serious. So intense. She wanted to change that. She wanted to see them laugh. Lifting her brush from the red paint tray, she turned to Tucker and dabbed it right in the middle of his chest.

Tucker sputtered.

Jake grinned.

"Oh, you like that?" she asked him silkily, and repeated the favor on his chest.

He looked down at the hand span–wide mark of red paint in shock. "I can't believe you did that."

Tucker moved behind her, gestured to Jake over her shoulder. She knew this because Jake's face split into an evil grin. "Callie?" he said.

"Yeah?"

"You'll want to run now," he said softly.

Before she could, her arms were seized from behind by Tucker, and she was pulled back against his chest.

"Warned ya." Jake reached down for his brush with his left hand and came up with that wicked smile. He stepped close.

Laughing, she tried to tug free from Tucker. "Don't even think about it."

"Oh, I'm thinking about it. How about you, Tucker?"

"I'm thinking about it, too," Tucker said in her ear.

"Don't you dare—"

Jake painted a big X on her chest, taking his time about it, too.

Tucker let go of her, and the two of them looked at her and laughed uproariously.

She tried to remain indignant but the sight of these two men laughing, together, was a sight. Almost unbearably touched, she turned her back, not wanting them to see, but they only laughed harder.

Because she was also wearing the paint from the front of Tucker all down her back.

That night Callie spent some time in her office, working on the ranch's books. Normally she loved this part of her job, being alone, entering numbers, seeing the light at the end of the tunnel, but tonight she felt distracted and it wasn't just the scent of paint still on her skin.

Michael had dropped off the loan application she'd requested. It was a few years early in her life plan, but her life plan had been altered. She'd talked to Michael about it in detail. As a solution, he'd offered her a job at his mortgage company, which she took to mean he didn't think she could qualify for a loan.

The job was in data entry, a starter position, but she could make more money than here at the Blue Flame. He said she could rent one of the houses he owned in Three Rocks real cheap. He'd offered this countless times since Richard's death, and she'd never even considered it. She didn't now, either.

Alone, stressed and worried, she dropped her head in her hands and rubbed her temples. When the phone rang, she looked at the clock, startled to discover it was past nine already. "Blue Flame."

"I'm looking for Tucker Mooney."

The voice was feminine and carrying what Callie would have sworn was a fake English accent. Odd. Tucker had led a colorful early life, she knew this, but since he'd come here, he'd had no contact from anyone

from that old life. That had been part of the deal when
Jake had given him the job two years ago. He hadn't
looked back.

He had a tight-knit group of friends in town, including some young women, one of whom was Macy, the
ranch's on-call massage therapist. Callie knew them all,
and this woman on the phone was one she'd never
met. "I'm sorry, but he's gone into town for the
evening."

"Oh, damn." The European accent took a dive,
straight into an annoyed American one.

"Can I take a message?"

"How about Jakey?"

"Excuse me?"

"Jake Rawlins. My other boy. I know he's there; I
saw his face plastered across every single newspaper in
San Diego, so I called his station. They told me where
to find him."

"Uh . . ."

"Tell him it's his momma. And hurry up, honey, I
don't have all night. This is a long distance call."

9

Jake had done his physical therapy every day. It was time-consuming and not a little painful, but he wanted to get back to work—God, did he want to get back to work—so he'd been diligent.

But he hated the weight room. No doubt that was due to the humiliation of Callie's rescue there, but he'd been doing his exercises in the barn and been happier for it.

Tonight he walked between the stalls lining either side, watched by a curious Sierra. He stopped to pet her and check on her sides, which were healing. While he stood there Moe stuck his head over his stall, and before Jake could figure out what that meant, the horse opened his mouth and clamped his teeth on the back pocket of Jake's jeans, which held his cell phone. "Hey!"

Without letting go, Moe eyed him.

Jake broke free and clamped his hand over the spot. "What the hell is your problem?"

Moe snorted and turned away.

Jake rubbed his butt. "I could send you off to the glue factory. You know that, right?" He stared at an unrepentant Moe, then had to shake his head at himself for even caring that the horse hated him. Still muttering, he began his pull-ups on a hanging wood beam. He got to three before the muscles in his shoulder and bicep started trembling like a baby's.

He forced himself to five, then hung, panting. His physical therapist had demanded ten, building up to three sets of ten. He could no more do that than hop to the moon, and yet once upon a time he'd have been able to do them forever. Now, as he hung there, he tried to consider what life would be like without firefighting, but his heart took a slow roll in his chest.

No. He wasn't going there. Arms quaking wildly, he forced his sixth and seventh pull-up, then dropped to the floor.

Moe stuck his head out again, and snickered.

"Yeah," Jake said, flat on his back, his shoulder on fire. "Get a good look."

The door of the barn opened. Moonlight spilled in, as well as the silhouette of a woman holding a flashlight. "Jake?" She rushed forward. "What happened?"

"Nothing. You just go about your life, maybe even on another date with Michael, and I'll go about mine."

She stared down at him. "What is your problem?"

"No problem." Jake got to his feet even though he wanted to curl into a little whimpering ball.

"I wasn't on a date with Michael. Not a *date* date, anyway. Not that I need to explain myself to you."

"Whatever." Christ, listen to him. He was an ass.

"I thought you were painting," she said.

"Was. It got dark."

"We have a weight room."

"I remember." He looked around at all the horses watching them and let out a mirthless laugh. "This felt more private than the weight room."

"You have a phone call."

"All right." He followed her to the door, suddenly remembering another night—the night of his father's funeral service. He'd found her out here, staring around her with a lost, haunted expression on her face. They'd shared a bottle of whiskey because he'd wanted to see that expression erased, and in the process had ended up sharing far more of himself than he'd ever intended. "Remember the last time we stood in this very spot?" he asked her.

"No."

"You were crying."

"Was not."

"I hugged you, told you it would be okay."

"You were trying to get laid. You got me drunk."

He laughed. "Is that your story?"

She crossed her arms. "It works for me."

"You're the one who got that bottle going," he reminded her. "And you kissed me first."

"A gentleman wouldn't say so."

Looking down at her, with those luminescent eyes and those full naked lips that he wanted open and willing beneath his own again, not to mention her gloriously lush body and what he wanted to do to it, he didn't feel like much of a gentleman. "I'm sorry you had to grieve. I'm sorry you miss him."

She sighed and put her hand on his. "And I'm sorry that he never got to know you. You should have had him in your life."

They started back toward the house. There was such a stillness to the air now that darkness had fallen, and a starkness to the lines and shadows of the hills. *Mars.*

"She said to hurry," Callie said as they walked up the back steps of the big house.

"Who's calling for me on the house phone instead of my cell?"

Callie opened the back door and turned to face him, bumping into him on the threshold of yet another door. "Your momma."

"Why?"

"I have no idea." She pointed to the phone in the kitchen. "You can take it right there, or in my office if you'd like some privacy."

"Office," he muttered, then brushed in past her, shutting the door behind him.

Callie stood for a moment, then shrugged and turned away. Unlike the others here—Tucker, Amy, Stone, Eddie, Marge, and Lou—Jake wasn't one of hers. Not really. And yet he just kept reeling her in with that way he had, making her care.

Not smart. She turned to walk out the door but came to a startled halt at the thundering crash of glass from within her office. Without thinking twice, she whirled back down the hall and hauled open the door.

Jake stood behind her desk, wearing a mask of pain and holding his shoulder.

"What happened? Are you okay?"

"Nothing. I'm fine." He jerked his chin toward the glass shards on the floor against the wall. "Your glass isn't. I threw it," he said to her unspoken question. Clearly in agony, he turned away, but she rounded the desk and put her hands on his arms.

"Sit. *Sit*," she repeated in a firm demand when he tried to pull free. "Throwing the glass was stupid. I bet it hurt pretty good."

"Like a red hot poker through my shoulder," he said through his teeth.

She began to massage the area with her fingers,

lightly at first, feeling the knots of tightened, abused muscles, then a little harder to try to loosen them up and get him some relief. He was holding his breath. "Breathe," she commanded, and kept at it.

The only sound in the room was his labored breathing and the ticking of the clock on her desk. After a long time she felt the knots give a little, and his slight relaxation. "Better?"

He rolled his shoulder carefully. "Yeah."

Taking her hands off him, she moved to the door. "Next time maybe you could stomp your feet, or just scream your head off."

"That's all?" He let out a low laugh. "I figured you'd have a longer lecture than that."

"I'm too busy resisting your sexy charms."

That caused a ghost of a smile to cross his lips. "You think I have sexy charms?"

"You know I do."

"Actually . . ." He pushed to his feet, and made his way close. Too close. The light from her lamp danced in the gray of his eyes. "I don't know any such thing." He lifted his hand, then winced and let it drop again.

"Stop using it, Jake."

"I was just trying to thank you."

"For what?"

"For putting up with whatever my mother said to you. For giving me a moment of laughter with my brother earlier. Or how about for letting me intrude on your life out here. . . . Hell, I don't know, pick one."

"Your mother didn't bother me." She put her hand over his. "But she bothered you."

He turned away. "She's worried I'm going to be a bad influence on Tucker."

She tugged him around, not thrilled with the protective feeling that rose inside her. "As if Tucker would let anyone be a bad influence on him."

"Yeah."

"Isn't she worried about you? About your shoulder?" She ran her fingers over the spot.

His laugh was harsh. "We're not . . . close. She had me when she was just a kid." He mirrored her action, running a finger over her shoulder, too. "She never really forgave me for that."

"Right, because her getting prepared was all your fault."

He looked surprised for a moment, then laughed. "I'm sure it doesn't help that I remind her of my father, a man she hated by the time I came around."

"Again, totally your fault."

His smile slowly slipped away but he didn't take his eyes off her. His hand came up, cupping her face. "The way you barged in here, eyes hot, hair wild . . . what were you going to save me from, Callie?"

"I . . ." She laughed. "I have no idea."

"You're something."

"Something annoying, I'm betting."

"No. Sweet. Hot." He frowned. "Confusing as hell—"

"Jake."

"I don't want to fight with you anymore, Callie."

"You don't?"

He let out a slow shake of his head. "No."

Her breath caught. "What is it you want to do?"

"I think you know."

"Yeah." And damn, but it made her yearn and burn. Her arms helped themselves, getting comfy around his neck. Her fingers sank into his hair.

"Callie," he said hoarsely.

"You shouldn't say my name like that."

"Callie," he said again, and then one more time, even softer.

"Oh, damn." She slammed her eyes closed. "Just kiss me."

His mouth closed over hers so fast her head spun, while the feel of his lips, warm and soft and firm on hers, simply electrified.

"I was going to leave," he murmured, dragging hot, wet, open-mouthed kisses down her throat. "A hundred times in the past week I've wanted to leave."

"Why didn't you?"

His tongue traced the pulse leaping at the hollow of her throat, and her eyes crossed with lust. She grabbed his hand and made him look at her. "Why, Jake?"

"Well, if you think things are complicated between us, you should see how it is at home."

"What do you mean?"

"You don't really want to know."

"Yes. I do."

"That fire, where I fell through the roof . . . I was rescuing a kid. He's suspected of starting the fire."

"Oh my God, a kid?"

"A teen. And now he's suing me and the department and the city and the state and probably God, too."

"You saved his life and he's suing?"

"Yeah. And when I got out of the hospital, the press was having a field day on me, my shoulder was killing me, I was getting broker and broker, and . . ."

"And you needed out."

"I needed out." He sighed. "And now here I stay until I can go back to work."

She looked at his shoulder. "You're not ready."

"Not yet."

In his eyes, she saw what he didn't say, that he

feared he might never be ready again, and her heart broke for him.

"Maybe you should take better care of me," he said softly.

"Back to that pampering thing, are we?"

A slow grin tugged at his mouth as he crowded into her space again, leaning in, lips parted, eyes dark and sexy, but a knock at the door, just behind her back, made them both jump.

Michael poked his head in, bumping the door into them. Callie dropped her arm from Jake, but Jake was much slower to pull free. His shirt was askew from her hands, her hair messed from his, and guilt flashed through her for reasons that made no sense.

"Did I interrupt something?" Michael asked, his welcoming smile gone.

"I'm just surprised to see you." Callie glanced at Jake, who'd turned his back now, jamming his hands in his pockets, looking out the window. "What brings you out here this late?"

"You seemed down on the phone earlier. I brought you dessert." He eyed Jake, then Callie again, and held up a gallon of Rocky Road ice cream. "Thought I'd cheer you up."

It was so awkward, Callie couldn't stand it, but she forced a smile. "Thanks. Ice cream is always appreciated. Jake? Do you want—"

"No. Thanks." He moved to the door. "'Night."

When the door shut behind him, Callie stared at it for a minute trying to get her bearings in a spinning world.

Michael handed her a spoon. "Interesting night, huh?"

"Yeah. Michael—"

"Hey, it's none of my business." He jabbed his spoon into the ice cream with much more force than necessary, then sagged a little bit. "Ah, Cal. Tell me I'm seeing things. Tell me you're not doing this."

"I thought you said it was *my* business."

"I lied. You are my business. I know you hate it when I say this, but honest to God, you're scaring me. This whole thing is scaring me. Things missing and horses hurt. *You* hurt. And now you're . . . I don't know what exactly, with Jake Rawlins. Your mortal enemy."

"*One* horse got hurt. And I don't think I was meant to. And as for Jake . . ." When she trailed off helplessly, not sure what to say, he just stared at her.

"I really don't like you all the way out here in the middle of nowhere with him."

"I'm home, Michael. And I'm not *with* Jake."

"You're not home. Not with him planning on selling this place from right beneath your feet."

She dug into the ice cream and tried not to think about that, or the confusion in her heart. "I'm going to be okay." She always was.

10

The ranch had one full day before its next guests arrived—a group of professional cheerleaders looking for an exciting retreat atmosphere for a team-building experience.

Everyone used the day to catch up on chores. Eddie worked on the inside of the barn. He tried to move the soft, sweet, mewling puppies again, just so he could clean their area, but Tiger wouldn't allow them to be moved. Shep sided with her, and with resignation, Eddie worked around them all, giving the protective, possessive momma wide berth. Only when he accepted the situation did Tiger come close to him, tail wagging, butt wriggling, as she nosed up for some of the attention he'd been giving her every day. "She's aptly named," he told Callie.

Stone painted with Jake, talking nonstop in his usual cheerful manner. Tucker worked with the horses, once again quiet and brooding, making Callie figure he and Jake had already forgotten the paint-Callie incident.

All in all though, things were calm. At least until late in the afternoon, when Marge managed to run her finger beneath the sewing machine needle while repairing curtains in the big house. Callie was good with injured animals, but at the sight of Marge's finger and the blood spurting out of it, she felt faint. Amy was no help, either. She just stood there, mouth covered with her hands, eyes wide.

They were all just beginning to panic when Marge herself leaned out the window of the laundry room and yelled, "*Problem!*"

In two seconds flat, Jake was there with the others behind him. He pushed Marge to a chair, elevating her arm and applying pressure to the wound, calmly giving directions to everyone around him. "Amy, grab some towels. Eddie, get Lou to pull out the truck. Stone, the floor—"

"On it," Stone said and began to clean up.

Callie just sat and held Marge's other hand while Jake dressed the wound with supplies from the first-aid kit Tucker had gotten from the kitchen. She was careful not to look at the wound while reluctantly admiring Jake's cool composure under pressure.

Lou drove Marge into town for a doctor, leaving Callie and Amy hustling to get all the bed linens and towels changed and the house cleaned up. They stood over the dryer, folding the linens as they came out. Hot, tired, and sweaty, Callie rubbed her arm over her forehead. "I appreciate the help in here."

As usual, Amy's face was a study in seriousness. "Did you thank Stone and Eddie? And Tucker?"

"For what?"

Amy kept folding. "For doing their job."

"But this isn't your job."

Amy snapped a sheet in the air, then proceeded to fold it like an army drill sergeant. "It just so happens you needed a cook and I'm good at it. But I can do other stuff, too."

"It's been a while since I've had a thank you thrown back in my face." Callie smiled.

Amy didn't.

Callie sighed, and they continued to work in silence until she couldn't stand it anymore. "You've been here over a week now, right?"

Snap. Amy began to fold another sheet. "Yes."

"Do you like it?"

Amy didn't answer for so long that Callie stopped folding to look at her.

"I like it," Amy finally said.

"And everything is okay?"

Amy looked suspicious. "Why?"

Callie remembered coming to the ranch at about the same age, scared and alone, terrified she'd make a mistake and get kicked out. She'd have done just about anything to avoid that. "Look, I'm not trying to pry but you don't smile very much, and you're so quiet. Marge said she walked by your cabin the other morning when you were coming out and it looked like you hadn't unpacked your bag. I just want to make sure—"

"I'm good." And while she didn't exactly smile, she did look a little less rigid. "Really."

Callie smiled. "Okay, then." She set another folded set of sheets in the basket. "You don't have any reason to know this, but you could talk to me about anything. If you needed to."

"Like what?"

Like who put that haunted look in her eyes. "Anything."

Amy just kept folding.

Ten years ago Callie would have done the same thing, and no one could have convinced her to talk. So they finished folding in silence, and she released Amy from housekeeping duties to start dinner.

Jake showed up while Callie was making the beds. He helped as best as he could with one hand, which is to say he wasn't much help at all.

An hour later, in the last bedroom, he watched her from the other side of the mattress with heavy-lidded eyes as she smoothed out the spread. "We've looked at each other over a lot of beds today." He leaned over the bed, resting his weight on one arm, giving her a secret little smile. "You wanna . . . ?"

"No," she said quickly.

"How do you know what I was going to say?"

"Okay." She folded her arms. "What were you going to say?"

He grinned. "You wanna lock the door and have your merry way with me?"

Her body tingled. Yes. "No. *Double* no."

He leaned in even closer, lightly tugging on the way-ward strand of her hair that was forever escaping its band. "Did you know your pupils dilate when you lie?"

She threw a pillow at him, and he laughed. But he backed off, and when she was done she thought about that.

He walks away.

She thought about that the rest of the evening, through dinner, through visiting Marge in her cabin with her new six stitches, through talking to Stone and Eddie while they fed the animals. By that night she'd have thought she'd fall into bed exhausted, but instead she found herself uncomfortably wide awake and un-able to sleep.

She kicked off her covers, pulled her jeans and T-shirt back on, and headed outside. A few cabins down, Lou sat on his front porch, nursing on a long neck. She sat next to him, tipped her head back, and eyed the stars. "You okay?"

"I went to Roger's for my final paycheck. When I got back here, Roger called. More tools are missing. They think I stole them while I was there."

"What? That's ridiculous."

"Yeah. But customers have been asking for me, wanting only me to work on their car. My guess is that Tony feels threatened. He wants to make sure I can't come back."

"Oh, Lou. What can I do to help?"

"Know a cheap attorney?"

She shook her head, and he shook his. "The truth'll come out," he said with a sigh.

"It will," she said fiercely, and hugged him, aching for both him and Marge.

Lou went back inside his cabin and Callie moved across the yard toward the big house and her office. Goose came running. "I don't have a snack," she said in apology, but patted the goose's head before moving on. Eddie sat on the back porch of the big house, smoking. Seemed it was a restless night for a lot of them. "Hey," she said. "What's up?"

He exhaled smoke and didn't look at her. "Don't ask unless you're up for more bad news."

"You get one of those girls you date pregnant?"

He laughed but shook his head.

"You going to jail?"

Another shake of his head but no laugh, and she sat down next to him. "I hate guessing games, Eddie. Just spit it out."

"I'm worried about Stone."

She absorbed that and tried to hide her alarm. "What's happening?"

"You've seen him. He's drinking like our dad. But he says he doesn't have a problem."

"And you think he does."

"I know it. I've lived through it before. I see the signs."

She rubbed her temples. "Okay. I'll talk to him."

"No." He stood and tossed his cigarette, grounding it out beneath his heel. "It'll just make things worse. It's going to have to go all bad before things change. Trust me, I know."

"You're talking about your dad."

He nodded and looked miserable, which was so unlike the usually upbeat Eddie that she wanted to hug him like she'd hugged Lou, but before she could, he walked off into the night.

With a bigger sigh now, she went to her office and pulled out her own problems, her personal files. She spread out the loan papers she'd been working on, and looked at the numbers that represented what she was worth. Not bad for a single woman. But for a single woman who wanted to buy a guest ranch, the situation couldn't be less promising.

With a disconsolate sigh, she switched to Blue Flame's books to catch up on some accounting. It was tedious, but she welcomed that, as it kept her mind busy.

Thirty minutes later, she frowned and stared into the petty cash box. Something was wrong. Two hundred and fifty dollars wrong. "Damn it." She readded, and yet still came up short. A little overwhelmed by the implications, she sat back, a terrible feeling deep in her belly. Someone had stolen two hundred and fifty dollars in cash, possibly someone she knew well and cared about deeply.

It was two in the morning before she finally slipped back into bed, and though she tossed and turned, she could come up with no answers. There hadn't been any guests around, at least not consistently. Their neighboring ranches weren't that close, nor did they have easy access. Granted, Shep wasn't that effective, but he did have *some* watch guard tendencies.

So who? Not quiet, brooding Amy. Not sweet Eddie. Not Stone, even with his drinking problems. Not Marge or Lou, with his ex-boss and his accusations. Not Tucker, who considered this place home. Despite his crazy youth, she'd trust him with her life. Definitely not Michael who, granted, had been around a lot, partly because he loved being out here with his friends, and mostly because he had the bad fortune to care about her too much. Not a crime in either case.

God. She was so damn tired her eyes were gritty. She needed sleep to think clearly. In a few hours, she thought wearily, turning over, punching her pillow. It would come to her in a few hours.

Once again Jake woke up to Tucker's foot cracking him in the back of the head.

"Oops," Tucker said, glancing back on his way to the bathroom. "Sorry."

"You're so full of shit your eyes are brown."

Tucker stopped short, then burst out laughing. He shut the bathroom door, the sounds of his laughter still ringing in the predawn air.

Jake rolled to his back and eyed the door, surprised. That was the first time since he'd gotten here that his brother hadn't slammed the bathroom door hard enough to rattle both the windows and Jake's bones.

That had to be a good sign, didn't it? And he'd

laughed. He'd laughed a lot in the old days, when Jake had tickled him, or given him piggyback rides, or taken him for an ice cream cone with money they'd stolen from their mother's purse.

Did Tucker remember those times? Jake hadn't, not until he'd come here and seen how these people were a family, in the way he'd never been with anyone other than Tucker.

On that thought he fell back asleep, dreaming about his mother's call the other night, when she'd had the nerve to warn Jake not to drag Tucker into the gutter, as if he'd been the one to do so in the first place. He dreamed about running from Moe and Goose, both of whom leered at him in the dark, their faces turning into his father's. . . . Then he was holding Callie again, sinking into her heat. She looked up at him with her heart in her eyes, smiling, as she slowly faded away into nothing, leaving him all alone.

He woke up, still alone, with the sun fully risen and the sounds of excited voices ringing through the yard.

Their next guests had arrived, which meant he'd need good luck to find someone to help him paint today. He showered and dressed, and picked up his cell phone. There he found Joe's latest text message.

You find yourself a sexy cowgirl yet?

"Yeah, I found one," he muttered to himself. Only he hadn't kept her, had he? Outside there were two large airport vans and a bunch of young, perky women milling around the yard, with enough bags and suitcases to boggle the mind.

Callie stood in the middle of it all with a welcoming smile and a clipboard, checking names. She wore jeans—big surprise—and a bright green tank top with her cowboy hat hanging down her back. Her fiery hair flew around her face in the light morning breeze as she directed her show.

She belonged here.

Tucker came out the front door of the big house. He dove right into the organized chaos and grabbed two armfuls of suitcases, nodding to Callie when she pointed out who they belonged to, and led a group of the women inside.

He belonged here, too.

Jake didn't. He didn't know where the hell he belonged.

"Hello."

He turned to the feminine laughing voice. One of the guests had meandered over to where he stood on his front step, watching the proceedings.

"I'm Vicki," she said. In her mid-twenties, she looked to be a replica of Camping Barbie—tall, blond, and stacked. She wore dark blue ironed jeans with a designer label that had never been meant for camping or ranching. Her blouse was silk, fitted, and also freshly ironed. He had no idea how she was going to feed pigs or milk cows in that blouse. Adjusting her designer cowboy hat on her pretty head, she smiled with her carefully glossed lips. "Are you one of the cowboys who'll be taking us out in the wilderness?"

"Uh . . ."

"I hear there are wolves out there." She let out a full-bodied shiver. "Sounds dangerous?" She grinned. "I love it, especially if there's a bunch of big, strong cowboys around. Do you think we'll hear them howl at night?"

Jake laughed. "The cowboys, or the wolves?"

She laughed, too. "Either. All of us are hoping for adventure. All sorts of adventure."

She was cute, and sidling up to Jake in a way that felt familiar. "All of you?"

"We're professional cheerleaders, looking for a good time." She looked him over from head to toe, and then back again. "What's your name, cowboy?"

"Jake."

"Well, Jake, you're the cutest Arizona cowboy I've ever seen."

"Why do I have the feeling I'm the *first* Arizona cowboy you've seen?"

She grinned broadly.

"Vicki? *Vicki Henderson?*" Callie was consulting her clipboard and looking around.

"Right here." Vicki waved. "Just taking in the sights. The *excellent* sights," she added in a breathy murmur to Jake.

Tucker came back out of the house, took in the way Vicki was practically lapping up Jake, and shot him a long look before he picked up her bags and headed toward the house again.

Vicki took her eyes off Jake and watched Tucker go. "Mmmm, you're *all* fine. Goodie." With an air kiss toward Jake, she followed Tucker.

Callie walked over to Jake, still wielding that clipboard. "We get one every time," she said.

At the front door, Vicki turned to wave at Jake.

He waved back. "One what?"

"Oh, that's right, you've been hit on so many times, you don't even recognize it for what it is anymore." She slapped the clipboard against her thigh. "Well, let me enlighten you. Vicki Henderson is here to pick up a cowboy."

Jake laughed. "*No.*"

"Fine. Make fun." She put a finger in his face. "But

she's picked you now, Jake. Enjoy her." Clearly annoyed, she stalked off, and his grin spread because really, she was quite adorable when she was jealous.

And I pick you, he thought. Before he could tell her so, she stopped and pressed her temples. "Damn it." She came back to him. "I forgot."

Her face was so serious, his smile faded away. "What?"

"I'm sorry. It never should have left my mind even for a second, but you slept in, and I didn't get a chance to talk to you before the guests arrived—"

"Tell me." All kidding and teasing aside, he put his hands on her arms. "Did something else happen to you?"

"Not to me . . ." She closed her eyes, sighed, and then opened them again. "There's two hundred and fifty dollars missing from my office, from petty cash."

Jake and Callie met with the sheriff and made yet another report. As discreetly as they could, they talked to all the employees one by one, working around the new guests. Everyone was horrified; no one knew anything.

And a bad feeling grew deep in Jake's gut.

The cheerleaders were . . . perky. For the rest of the day they were entertained with ranch chores. Eddie and Stone had lots of fun getting the women to feed the pigs, cows, hens, and horses. Both men wore ear-to-ear grins at dinner that night, which they naturally took in the dining room with their guests, all too happy to keep entertaining.

The sheriff came by again after dessert to check on things. When he left, Callie stood in her office and dropped her face in her hands.

Jake put his hand on her shoulder. "This is getting old."

Her face jerked up to meet his. "I'll replace the money myself, from my own account."

Startled at how she'd so misunderstood him, he shook his head. "Who the hell do you think I am that I would ask such a thing of you?"

"My boss."

"I have no idea," he said slowly, "how you can dislike and distrust me so much, and yet let me into your bed to kiss and touch and f—"

She put her hand over his mouth. "Don't go there."

He pulled her hand down. "Too late, I'm already there, sweetheart. There and waiting."

"Don't even try to tell me you've never slept with a woman who didn't like you afterward."

"No," he said honestly.

She laughed, then shook her head. "How do you do that, make me laugh when I don't want to?" Her smile faded. "Oh, Jake. Don't you get it? I don't dislike you at all." And on that shocking admission, she opened the door to leave. Tucker stood there, hand raised to knock.

He divided a glance between them. "What's going on?" He pointed to the cash box. "Did you find the money?"

"No," Callie said. "And I think we should implement new rules—no one goes where they don't belong. Amy, for instance, can be in the kitchen, but she shouldn't be in the barns or my office. Stone and Eddie—"

"Should be only in the barns, not the office. Yeah." Tucker looked grim. "Got it. You think it's one of us."

"Damn it, I don't think that at all. This is for our own

protection, Tucker. A way to make sure no one is wrongfully blamed, okay?"

Tucker sighed. "Okay."

"The guests are all settled for the night, right?"

"Yeah," Tucker said.

"Good. I've got a killer headache. I'm outta here." She glared at Jake when he tried to stop her. "Alone," she said, and walked out of the room.

Tucker looked at Jake after she'd left. "I heard what she said before she opened the door. She likes you."

Jake was still worried about the headache he'd seen lurking behind Callie's green eyes, and the misery there. "Get your facts straight. She said that she didn't *dis*like me."

Tucker dropped into one of the chairs in front of Callie's desk. "She's off limits."

"Really? Says who?"

"Says me."

Jake shot him a look of disbelief.

"She's not like one of those cheerleaders, all right? She gives a shit about people, about everyone. I mean, look how she's protecting all of us, no questions asked. She trusts us, Jake. For no reason other than her heart tells her to. She's been hurt, and still, she trusts."

"What do you mean, hurt?"

"Haven't you ever wondered why we're all so close here? It's because we all have one thing in common. Sucky pasts, Callie included. So don't even think about fucking with her."

"How about," Jake said very quietly, "unless it involves you, you mind your own business, especially when it comes to Callie and me?"

Tucker's voice was just as quiet when he stood and got in Jake's face. "This *is* my business. She cares about me, Jake. She saved my life by letting me have this job, and I'm not going to repay that by letting you screw with her head."

Jake laughed incredulously. "*She* cares about you? How about *me*? How about how much *I* care about you? I dragged your sorry ass here. *I* gave you this job, not Callie. *I* asked her to keep you here."

Tucker stared at him stonily.

"Ah hell." Jake shoved his fingers through his hair and turned in a slow circle, searching for his cool. It was a hard time coming. Things were just so damn complicated. His feelings for Callie, his feelings about not being able to work, and now these problems here at the ranch. It was all changing his perspective, and he was so tired of thinking.

Tucker still didn't say a word and Jake shook his head. "Forget it. Just forget it." And like Callie had only a moment before, he walked out.

"There you go," Tucker said when he was alone. "Walking away again."

11

Head throbbing with stress, worry, and a bunch of assorted other things, Callie started across the yard toward her cabin, the way lit by a blanket of stars. Halfway there, Shep met her, nudging her hand with the top of his head.

At his unconditional love, a lump grew in her throat the size of a regulation football. "Hey, boy. Got your family tucked in for the night?"

He panted alongside her, relaxed and at ease, so she knew everything was okay in the barn at least. The puppies had nearly doubled in size since they'd found them. She'd been checking on them every day, even if Tiger still wouldn't let her touch them.

Letting herself into her cabin, she pulled her shades and started stripping. She needed a hot bath, aspirin, and bed, and not in any special order. Down to her favorite soft silk camisole and panties, she moved toward her CD player. Some music would help her relax, help her think. She had a lot of thinking to do, but unfortunately, her cell phone rang, interrupting her thoughts.

"You sound upset again," Michael said.

Upset? Try tense enough to shatter. "I'm okay."

"Truth, Cal. You're working too hard. Is it worth it?"

"You mean the ranch?"

"I mean Jake. You're heading for hurt."

"I can take care of myself." She rubbed her temples but the ache only increased. "You know that."

"Yeah, I know. I've seen you do it for years." He let out a long breath. "Look, just give it all up and marry me. You can do whatever you want all day long."

She laughed, as he'd meant her to. "So you'd turn me into a housewife now, is that it?"

"Oh yeah."

Laughing again, she plopped to her bed and stared at the ceiling. "You know I can't cook. I can hardly make a bed, and I don't look good in an apron."

"I'll hire a cook, and who needs a made bed? And I bet you look hot in an apron."

Smiling, she shook her head. "Good-night, Michael." She tossed her phone aside, slipped on her headphones, then hit the POWER button. Her ears filled with Sheryl Crow singing about how the "first cut is the deepest."

Callie knew the feeling. The room was warm and her head pounded. She stretched out on her back on the cool wood floor and closed her eyes, wondering how the hell she could fix all that was wrong in her world.

A cold, wet something brushed her tummy and her eyes flew open, landing on two large brown ones. "Shep." She let out a laugh, pushed the dog away, and rolled to her belly. Sheryl continue to wail in her ears, blocking out Callie's world, and she closed her eyes again. Animals loose, Sierra mistreated, her Jeep messed with, serum and money missing . . .

What was happening to her quiet, calm, beautiful world?

Sheryl eased into another song, and Callie sighed, some of the tension finally leaving her body as sheer exhaustion took over.

Jake walked outside, into the night. One of the horses let out a soft whinny, and then another. A pig snorted, and a cow moaned. From somewhere in the hills, not nearly far enough away, a coyote howled.

Had he ever thought this place silent? Without thinking, he stepped onto the grass. A sound came from behind him. He whipped around, and stared into the unblinking eyes of Goose. She honked at him and lowered her head for attack.

"Damn it—"

Menacingly, she honked again, and pawed the ground with her webbed feet.

Jake wasn't a fool. Sometimes a man had to run. So he turned and loped off the grass. *Her* grass.

Goose chased him to the very edge, glaring at him triumphantly, her feet firmly on her domain.

"I'd go on a diet if I were you," he warned, and crossed to the cabins. He looked at Tucker's and remembered his words.

"She saved my life by letting me have this job, and I'm not going to repay that by letting you screw with her head."

He really thought Jake would mess with Callie, purposely hurt her. The knowledge both burned and shamed, because it could quite possibly be true.

There was no denying Jake felt something for her, and up front that something appeared to be no different than what he'd felt for any of the women in his past.

But he knew this time there was another layer to the

attraction between them. He knew it, felt it, dreamed it. He just didn't know what to do about it.

Callie seemed happy enough to shrug it all off, and that would have been Jake's choice, too, but there was more at stake now than just emotions.

Someone was trying to get to her, trying to unnerve her, hurt her where her heart lay. And though she was tough as nails, fiercely independent and strong-willed, it was working. It *was* getting to her. He could see it in her eyes, in the grim lines of her mouth, in the exhausted way she'd held her body.

He'd been wallowing in his own problems for so long it felt good to think of something else, someone else, and as he stood there beneath a night sky, a surge of something filled his chest. It took him a moment to recognize it as the same feeling that had always come over him when he was working on a fire or a rescue.

He had a purpose. He was needed. Since that was rare these days, he began walking again, toward Callie's cabin now. She might not want his help, or want him to check on her, but she was damn well going to get both.

When she didn't answer his knock, he jiggled her door handle. It was unlocked, damn it. Didn't she know how stupid that was? He pushed it open. "Callie."

Light from the small kitchen spilled into the living room. A blue display from a CD player glared in the far corner. Lying on her belly on the floor in front of it, a set of headphones holding back her wild hair, was Callie.

At the sight of her, he sucked in a breath. She wore only a thin, silky camisole and panties, in a pale color that seemed to glow in the dark and didn't do a thing to cover the tight, curvy body he'd been dying to touch again.

Her head was down on her bent arms, her face turned away from him. She hadn't moved an inch. Concern propelled him forward, and he hunkered down at her side, a hand on her back. "Callie—"

She nearly jerked right out of her skin, rolling away from him to her side, then up to her knees. "*Jake?* What the hell are you doing?"

"I just—"

"You don't knock?" She leapt to her feet and put a hand over her heart. Her nipples pressed against the thin silk, and in spite of himself, he couldn't tear his gaze off her, though he did take a moment to bless her lingerie fetish.

"You should have knocked!"

"You didn't answer."

"Maybe I didn't want company!" Whirling around, she revealed a silk wedgie, and a gorgeous ass. It wasn't nice to look, but he'd never been all that nice.

She grabbed her jeans off the floor and shoved a leg in. Nearly falling over, she shoved her other leg in, then glared at him. "Stop looking at me!"

He tipped his head back and studied the ceiling. "You said your head hurt. I was worried that it was related to your fall in the barn—"

"That was a *week* ago. This is just a regular *stress* headache." She snapped her jeans, jerked up her zipper. Sent more daggers his way.

"I just wanted to make sure you were okay."

"Did I say I was falling apart and needed a keeper? No! I've told you, I don't need a hero." She whirled around in a circle, looking for her shirt, her breasts jiggling enticingly in her fury. "And I said *stop looking at me*!" Scooping up her shirt, she held it to her breasts, two high spots of color on her cheeks as she pointed at the door.

But the camisole had slits on the sides, and he'd just seen the vivid black and blue and green bruise on her ribs. That, added to her stress, and the pain in her eyes from her headache, made him hurt for her. He knew, God he knew, how it felt to be overwhelmed, hurting and alone, and he could no more walk away in that moment than stop breathing. He took her hand and pulled her around to the front of her couch. "Sit."

"No—"

He put a hand in the middle of bare chest and pushed. With a squeal, she went down, plopping to the soft cushions. He moved around behind her, and sliding his fingers into her long hair, began to massage her head.

A strangled sort of moan came from her lips.

"I'm sorry." He leaned over her. "What did you say?"

She merely moaned again as he kept massaging her scalp.

"Callie?"

"Shh. I'll go back to yelling at you in a minute." Her eyes were closed, her throat exposed. She still held her shirt up to her breasts. "Just don't even think about stopping."

"I won't."

For long moments there was nothing but silence and the sound of their breathing as he touched her, and when he finished, he merely shifted his attention to the back of her neck, letting out a disparaging sound. "You have a rock quarry in here."

She just let out another little moan that he shouldn't have found so wildly sexy.

"You're letting it all get to you," he murmured.

"No, I'm not."

"Of course you are. You're human, and at some point even you're going to have to admit it." Beneath his fingers, her skin was soft and creamy smooth. He wanted to put his mouth on her, but the knots beneath the surface of all that creamy, soft skin tore at him.

"All I need is to relax enough to get some good sleep," she mumbled.

"I only know one surefire way to relax before going to sleep."

"A drink?"

"An orgasm." Preferably for the both of them.

She snorted her opinion of that so he kept massaging her. When he'd finished her neck, she leaned forward, giving him better access to her shoulders. "Sometimes," she whispered, "I don't know what to do with you."

He had plenty of ideas.

"It's just that you're . . ."

"What?"

"Sexy," she said, surprising him. "And you always smell good. How do you do that?"

"I've got nothing on you." One of the silky straps fell from her shoulder. He helped the other fall, too. "You smell like—"

"Horses."

"Yeah, horses." He'd been going to say heaven. "And pigs, too."

The sound that escaped her was definitely a laugh, and he smiled.

"Sometimes I think to myself, just jump him," she said. "Just do it."

"I'm all for that," he said fervently.

"But then I look at you, really look at you, and I see a pain there. I don't know what it is; missing your job, your life, or something else, but seeing it makes my heart squeeze." She sighed. "I can't lust after you and have it be simple if when I look into your eyes my heart squeezes."

"I can cover my face so you can't see my eyes."

"Stop it. Stop making light of this."

His smile faded, and he came around to kneel in front of her. "I *am* missing my world, you know that. Being out here is forcing me to think about things, make decisions that I don't want to make."

"Like selling the ranch."

"Like selling," he agreed. "Even when doing so to save my ass ends up changing others' lives. I don't want to do that to you, to any of you."

"I know."

"Being here, seeing what this place means to all of you, knowing I have to sell . . . it sucks."

"Sometimes life sucks."

"And then there's you and me."

"No, there's not."

"We have to face it, Callie."

"Well, whatever *it* is, it's going to have to be willing to take its time," she said. "Because my head is full. So is yours."

"That'll be new, taking my time with a woman. How's the headache now?"

"Better, thanks to you." She stood and slipped into her shirt. "I'm sorry I yelled at you. I was embarrassed to be caught lying around in my underwear. It made me feel vulnerable."

"Everyone feels vulnerable sometimes."

"Even you?"

"Honey, I feel vulnerable every time I look at you."

"That's a pathetic come-on line."

"That wasn't a come-on line. It was the truth. And so was me being worried about you. Someone's screwing with you out here. I don't like it."

"Someone's screwing with the ranch."

"It seems more personal than that. How sure are you about the crew—"

"Extremely."

"Stone drinks. Lou's boss says he's a cheat. Amy won't look me in the eyes. How can you be sure about any of them?"

She finished buttoning herself, and put her hands on her hips. "Which actually brings us to another point," she said. "Have you noticed that this all started after you came here? Maybe someone's messing with *you*."

"No, that doesn't make any sense. Unless Tucker—"

"No," she said firmly. "You know your brother better than that."

"Actually, I don't. He won't let me in."

"He feels betrayed. Deserted."

"He told you that?"

"It's obvious. You dumped him here and never looked back."

"Yeah, that's what I did." He scrubbed a hand over his face, feeling his own headache coming on. "We used to be close."

"What happened?"

"I don't know." He let out a harsh breath. "That's not true. A lot happened."

"Like what?"

"When I was young, my mother traveled extensively."

"For her job?"

"You could say that. Her career was marrying men. She was gone a lot, even after Tucker was born. So I took care of him." At the time it'd been about survival, for the both of them. It hadn't been until later that he'd realized how much Tucker had meant to him. "Then I turned seventeen, graduated high school, and my mother got her fifth or sixth divorce. She had more time, and realized how close Tucker and I were. She hated that."

"I don't think I like your mother."

He laughed a little. "No, you wouldn't. Tucker was five, and pretty self-contained. So she kicked me out and replaced all the men in her life with Tucker. And he became the center of her world. I went to San Diego, and they moved around a lot after that. I kept track of them the best I could, but she made it difficult. When I called, she didn't want him to talk to me."

"So Tucker thinks you left when he was five and never looked back?"

"I don't know what he thinks."

"He's glad you're here now."

"Really? Because he just warned me to stay away from you or else."

Callie blinked. "What?"

"Yeah. He thinks I'm going to do this." He stepped close, bent his head and kissed her. "And this . . ." Pulling her close, he deepened the kiss.

With another of those sexy little sounds, she wrapped her arms around his neck, arched against him, and danced her tongue to his. And just like that,

Jake was a goner, a complete goner as he glided his hands up her body, holding her face still because he couldn't get enough. He was deathly afraid he could never get enough. Their bodies collided, shifted, and hungry for more he took it—until a shaft of pain shot through his shoulder.

"Sorry," she gasped, and tried to pull free, but he held on to her.

"It's okay, it's okay," he promised, thinking he'd take a thousand more hits like that, if she'd only stay close.

But she backed away. "You should go."

"What? Why?"

"Because I need to think."

"About . . . ?"

"About all this. About you. About me. The way I throw myself in heart first."

He stared at her, suddenly knowing where this was going.

"It's just me," she said. "Throwing myself in without looking. It's how I work, even knowing I'm going to sink like a stone. And I'd do that here, with you, but Jake, I can't be the only one."

She already knew him that well, knew he'd never throw himself in and follow his heart.

"I think your idea of taking our time was a good one," she said softly.

Caught by his own damn logic.

"Good-night, Jake." She smiled when he continued to stare at her, befuddled. "Say good-night back."

What choice did he have? He wanted her, so badly he could hardly see straight, but he couldn't promise to toss his heart in for the ride, and hell if he'd lie to her. His body came free, no vows, no ties. But even an untried heart such as his knew that love came at a price, a heavy one.

And he wasn't willing to pay. "Good-night, Callie."

She stood there looking at him, skin glowing, eyes soft. Her nipples were still hard beneath her camisole. He closed his eyes, stepped to the door. "Lock it behind me."

The sound of the lock tumbling into place echoed into the night.

12

The next morning, Amy made a large breakfast for the cheerleaders before their expedition out to some historic Apache sites. Having been spoiled by the Japanese businessmen who'd eaten every crumb she'd cooked, she was shocked when all the dishes came back with much of the food left over.

Marge laughed at her concern, saying it wasn't the food but the carb content in it. The cheerleaders were all fit and lean, so that made no sense to Amy, but the following morning she experimented with Marge's suggestions, and served eggs and lean bacon with no toast or muffins. It all vanished.

Seemed she'd have to be flexible. No problem, she'd been born flexible. She politely thanked Marge, who shocked the hell out of her by ignoring her hands-off aura and giving her a warm hug in return.

That night Amy stood in the kitchen cleaning up after a light chicken stew. Happy chatter came through the walls from the dining room. The guys had all made a point to be around for dinner the last few nights—big surprise given who their guests were, but she didn't mind.

Humming, she scrubbed the stovetop and the floor,

and whatever else needed a good cleaning. It took her a while to recognize that she was enjoying herself.

Callie had asked her to join the dinner group but she'd declined, and she didn't regret that. It gave her comfort to work in peace without having to socialize, while knowing the house was full and she wasn't alone. Plus, she felt partly responsible for those people enjoying themselves out there, and that felt good, too.

She knew when she turned to clean out the already spotless refrigerator that she was merely delaying the moment when she'd have to go back to her empty cabin. . . .

But that lingering fear made her mad, mad enough that she put down her sponge, straightened her aching back, and headed resolutely to the back door.

No more fear.

That had been her promise to herself, and she'd nearly forgotten it, damn it. She was eighteen, a legal adult. Sure, her father could find her if he tried hard enough, but he couldn't make her come home as he'd been able to all the other times.

Knowing that, she headed out into the night, but her feet faltered on the grass, and not just because Goose showed up out of nowhere looking to chase her. Her cabin was dark, too dark. And inside it, waiting for her, were her nightmares.

Lifting her chin, she turned and headed toward the barn instead. Goose watched her closely but since Amy stepped off the grass, the bossy creature didn't try to block her path. Amy rewarded her with a pat on the head, then let herself into the barn. She wanted to touch the horses, wanted to put her hand on a warm flank and be in the company of a living thing that couldn't talk, demand, yell, hit . . . couldn't do anything but just be.

She turned on the lights and smiled when a few of the horses blinked balefully at her. A few more stuck their heads out to see if she'd brought them a treat from the kitchen, as she'd done several times before.

"Shh," she said to her audience. "I'm not supposed to be here." She offered a sugar cube to Sierra, and then to Moe, who though quiet and a little distant, happily crunched on the treat. Homer, Tucker's much friendlier horse, bumped her arm with his nose. Smiling for the first time all day, she gave him one, too, then took a nice deep breath, feeling herself start to relax as his soft muzzle tickled her palm. "I wish I knew how to ride you."

"All you have to do is ask."

With a soft scream she whipped around, her entire handful of sugar cubes scattering at her feet. Tucker stood in the shadow of the doorway watching her, his hat low enough that she couldn't see his expression. "I'm sorry," she said quickly. "I wasn't doing anything, I just wanted . . ." She trailed off awkwardly when he took a step closer.

He was tall, built like an athlete, and as she knew, from the day she'd flipped him to the floor, beneath those jeans and T-shirt was a hard body complete with harder muscles and a strength that she couldn't come close to matching if he wanted to exert his. Remembering that morning still horrified her, but damn it, he'd scared her. He was scaring her now, too. She backed up a step and came in close personal contact with Homer's stall door. The padlock gouged into her back and her fists tightened.

"You just wanted what?" he asked.

She blinked at the unexpected smile in his voice, unable to speak with the fear and anger and frustration that was one big unswallowable lump in her throat.

"Amy?"

Why was his voice so gentle? He came close and she flinched back, but all he did was tip his hat back on his head as his smile faded. "Couple of things," he said quietly. "First of all, if you keep jumping guiltily every time someone so much as looks at you, someone's going to think you did something wrong."

"I didn't."

"Which is my point," he said patiently. "And second—"

A lecture. She was good at those. She studied her shoes and prepared to wait it out.

But he broke off and just looked at her for a long moment. "I don't expect you to believe me," he finally said. "But no one working here has ever hurt another soul. Not Callie, not Marge or Lou. Not Eddie or Stone. And not me. I never would. Sierra, stop it." The horse had stuck her head out from her stall and was searching his pockets. Absently Tucker rubbed her nose. "I didn't bring anything for you. I didn't expect to come out here."

"So why did you?" Amy asked.

"Saw the light. Was wondering who was where they didn't belong and why."

"I forgot you told me not to come out here."

"No, you didn't." He stroked beneath Homer's chin now, who snorted in pleasure. "You just don't like rules. You've probably had too many that don't make sense. I meant what I said about not getting hurt by anyone here."

She felt her face heat, and mortified, she looked away.

Leaving plenty of space between them, Tucker leaned back against the stall door next to her. Something crunched beneath his boot and he lifted it to see. "Ah." He bent for an uncrushed sugar cube.

Sierra's head stretched out as far as she could get it, and Amy let out a little laugh at the hopeful expression on the horse's face. Tucker fed Sierra the cube, but kept his eyes on Amy. "A laugh. I don't think I've heard that from you before."

Her heart, which had just finally slowed down its painful race, took off again. She looked away, wondering when he'd leave.

He didn't, nor did he say anything for a long time. "Life's pretty simple out here. We're a tight-knit group. Friends. We trust one another."

She let out another laugh, this one without mirth. "If you want me to trust you . . ."

"I'd settle for a friendship."

Bemused, she shook her head.

"Yeah, I felt that way when I came here, too. Shit, I was a handful, and pissed—at my mother, my brother . . . the entire world. Callie had a time with me." He turned his head and met her gaze with his steely gray one. "But she never gave up, not once. I'm pretty patient myself, Amy. I learned that from her."

She'd been holding her breath, and she slowly let it out, feeling a tightness in her chest. "I don't need a friend."

"I didn't, either. I was sure of it."

"I just want to be alone. With the horses."

He adjusted his hat again. "You know you're not supposed to be out here without a good reason."

"I didn't hurt Sierra, or take that money."

He looked at her for a long time. "Do you want a reason to be out here? Because Eddie, Stone, Lou, and I . . . we can always use some help."

"How do you know I'm not the one who tried to hurt Sierra, or steal the money?"

"You just said you weren't."

She stared at him, completely thrown off. He simply leaned back and let time go by, with a quiet ease she wanted to find fault with, and couldn't. She was where she shouldn't be, she'd been rude, and he didn't seem bothered. Even more unsettling, he didn't push her to talk.

Which suddenly made her want to. She leaned back, too, and stared up at the open-beamed ceiling. "Remember when I told you I wasn't a misfit? That I had somewhere to belong?"

"I remember."

What the hell. She turned her head and looked at him. "I lied. I am, and I don't."

"You mean you were, and you didn't." When he smiled, she had the most awful urge to cry, so she looked away.

She heard a crinkling, and then smelled chocolate.

"Mmm." He held out a candy bar with a good chunk gone. He was chewing it. "Want some?"

She wrinkled her nose and he laughed. "Yeah, I figured you'd be a candy bar snob, given how good your own cookies and brownies are." Unperturbed, he proceeded to eat the whole thing. He didn't say another word, just stood there eating, occasionally stroking Sierra, Homer, and Moe.

Was he ever going to leave? Apparently not.

"You're the strangest person I've ever met," she finally said into the silence.

"Really?" He looked rather proud of that, and she couldn't help it, she laughed. *Again.*

His approving smile was warm.

And so, she found, her own warmed a little, along with something deep inside her. She'd come here tonight needing to be with something alive, thinking the animals would do it, but somehow this worked, too. So she leaned back, too, and just breathed.

Later, when she entered her cabin and dead-bolted the door, she stared down at her bag, which she still hadn't unpacked. She nudged it with her toe and glanced up at the armoire in the corner, which stood empty. A yearning to actually unpack came over her, but then common sense prevailed. She never unpacked, anywhere.

Instead she went to bed.

The next few days proved to be quiet and rather easy for Callie. The cheerleaders had some good horsing experience. They worked a roundup and everyone participated, even Jake, who didn't seem to have too much trouble riding Molly. Of course, no one had trouble on Molly, but Callie gave him credit for trying.

On the cheerleader's third day, Eddie, Stone, and Tucker got up at the crack of dawn to take the women on a two-day mountain horseback expedition through the Dragoons, to hike among old, deserted mining camps.

Lou had spent the past few days cleaning and oiling all the riding equipment. Marge packed up all the sleeping gear. Amy prepared their food, and when she helped Tucker pack it into saddle bags, she went on and on with cooking directions for so long that his eyes glazed over and he pretended to snore.

Everyone laughed, and Amy smacked Tucker, then looked horrified at herself. But Tucker just laughed some more, then walked off completely uninsulted, leaving Amy staring after him for the longest time, as if waiting for the other shoe to fall, which of course it never did.

Tucker actually asked Jake to go with them on the camping trip, but Jake paled at the idea of camping and declined. When they'd left, Callie, Lou, and Marge divided all the chores. With a bucket of feed and an empty basket for the eggs, Callie headed toward the hen house.

"Whatcha doing?"

She didn't have to turn around and see Jake to get that odd, nameless feeling in her stomach. She forced herself to take a deep calming breath before turning to face him. "Working."

"Want some help?"

There was something in his eyes beyond the easy smile: a hint of pain and also a sadness that got to her. "You're going to help me gather eggs?"

"Now, see, *that's* what I'm talking about. Gathering eggs . . . why didn't Tucker give me that job?"

He was trying hard to be light and carefree, and she decided to let him have it. "Think it's easy?"

"How hard can it be?"

"Not as hard as running into a burning building, I'm quite certain." Inside she gestured to the row of hens. "Go for it."

He walked up to the first hen, eyeballed the thing sitting there so calmly. "Okay, I'm going in." He started to reach in with his right hand, winced at the movement of his shoulder, and pulled back. Before Callie could stop him, he tried again with his left—and got pecked hard. He jumped back with a yelp. "What the hell—"

"You've got to be quick."

He stared at her, and then tried again.

And took another hit.

"Here." The man was going to get pecked to death. "Like this . . ." She scattered some feed on the ground. The hens cackled and coo'd and leapt toward the feed, leaving their eggs wide open. She reached in and filled her basket, then grinned at him.

"Wow."

"Impressive, huh?"

"No, it's not the eggs, it's the smile. Love it, even though it's cocky as hell." He snagged her hips in his hands, pulled her close and lowered his head.

"Oh no." She slapped a hand on his chest. "We're working."

"I know." He touched his forehead to hers. "But I'm losing it here, Callie. Kissing you is about all I have left."

She cupped his face and looked into his serious one. Her heart slipped. "Oh, Jake."

Before the words were out, he kissed her, and for a long, delirious moment, she let herself sink into him, but finally managed to locate a few working brain cells. "If you're going to kiss me in between every hen, this is going to be a slow process."

"What's wrong with slow?"

"Because I have the goats, the cows, the horses, the puppies, and a million other things left to do after we finish here."

"Don't make me try again for more eggs," he begged, eyeing the hens with dread.

Shaking her head, he held the basket while she grabbed the eggs. "You ever going to tell me what's wrong?"

"I thought you already had it all figured out." He followed her into the pig pen with the bucket of kitchen leftovers.

She tipped it into their trough herself, feeling Jake's tension behind her at not being able to lift it for her. She looked at him. "It's not being able to get back to work, work that is your entire life."

"Bingo," he said.

"And being here on your father's land feels weird."

"Double bingo."

"I'm sorry, Jake."

"Sorry enough to sleep with me again?"

She laughed, and he shot her a small smile. "I guess not." But they stayed together to feed the cows and the horses. Last, they checked on Tiger and her puppies, who crawled in ecstasy all over Jake, and Callie had to laugh at the sight of him sitting on the ground being mauled by the puppies. "What?" he asked.

He was unexpectedly cute, that's what, and sleeping with him sounded damn good. She just shook her head and headed to the shed.

Jake followed her. "What next?"

"I need the rake to drag over the grass, that is, if Goose lets me." She grappled with the lock for a moment, wanting to grab last year's leftover fertilizer as well, for the flowers she would plant beneath the living room window.

Jake entered the shed behind her, so that when she turned around to block the door open, he was right there. He pressed her up against the wall, sandwiching her in with his body. "You're thinking about it."

Her breath caught at the feel of his hard, warm body against her. "About what?"

"Sleeping with me."

A bolt of white hot lust shot through her. "Still working here."

"Yeah, I know. Do you have any idea what watching you be all in charge is doing to me?"

Yep. She could feel it pressing low on her belly. "You're sick."

"Definitely." He'd made his way to her ear, his soft breath sending delicious shivers down her spine. "What color is your underwear today, Callie?"

"Jake—"

"Is it silk? Or lace?"

Clearly only one of them was capable of rational thought. She slipped free of his hold and slapped on the light.

In the sudden brightness, he blinked once, slowly, looking rumpled and adorable. She had to remind herself that it was all a look, that he could not possibly be so adorable when he had one foot out the door, the other crushing her future.

"You're doing it again." He lightly tapped her temple. "Thinking too much."

"Someone here needs to."

He just sighed and slipped his hands in his pockets. "I'm trying like hell, Callie, not to think at all. If you were at all kind, you'd help distract me."

She closed her eyes. "I'm not having sex with you in this shed."

"I meant talk to me." He grinned. "But if you're thinking sex . . ."

"What do you want me to talk about?"

"I don't know. Tell me about your parents."

"Nothing to tell." She shrugged and began to search for the fertilizer. "My mother isn't exactly maternal."

"And your dad?"

"Not into kids. I landed here like Amy. Eighteen and pretty much on my own."

"Richard took you under his wing." He scratched his jaw as he studied her. "But you said he wasn't exactly the warm, loving, parental type, either."

"He cared enough."

"Then your ex came along, right? Just another in a string of people who were around but not really *around*. Not attached to you."

She set her teeth. "I'm not a pity case."

"I didn't think you were. Tell me more about Matt."

Her frown deepened. "I was young and stupid. Nineteen," she admitted when he just looked at her, his eyes warm and patient. "I kept forgiving him, thinking he could change."

"Forgiving him for what?"

"You name it." She turned to the door.

With surprisingly gentle hands, he turned her back. Then stroked a strand of hair off her face, running his finger down her jaw. "Other women?"

"Well, I did say we were young and stupid."

"Sounds like he was the only stupid one."

"Funny, coming from a man who's never had a serious relationship in the two years I've known him."

"And have you?"

She closed her mouth.

"See, you say you follow your heart, Callie, but it seems to me like you've burned it out." He smiled. "I have a suggestion."

"I'm afraid to hear it."

"A good, long, hot spring fling. No strings."

"Gee, wherever would I find a man up for that job?"

He grinned at her wry tone as he lifted a hand. "I readily volunteer."

"How noble of you." Despite everything, she was more tempted than he could ever imagine. Desperately needing a distraction, she continued to search the shed and finally found the two bags of fertilizer. She tossed him the first, then bent for the second when she heard his low grunt of pain. She whipped around.

Eyes closed, face tight, he dropped the bag and leaned back against the wall, holding his shoulder.

"Oh my God, Jake, I'm sorry. I didn't even think—"

"Not your fault." This came out through his clenched teeth. Sweat had broken out on his brow as he sank to the ground. "I shouldn't have reached out to catch it."

She went to her knees beside him. "Let me—"

"No. I'm fine." He shifted away. "Just give me a sec."

The man had probably never shied away from a woman's touch in his life, but that was when the touching was on his own terms. Clearly he was humiliated at not being able to even catch something, and she felt like slime for putting him through it. "I'm so sorry—"

"Car," he said tightly.

"What?"

"Car just drove up."

She heard it now, coming up the driveway. She wasn't expecting anyone, and rose to her feet. "It must be Michael. He was going to come out for a ride. Wait here a sec, and I'll be right back—"

Jake grabbed her wrist. "He wants you."

"Jake."

"Just remember one thing if you're going off with him."

"I'm not going—"

"One thing."

She sighed. "What?"

"This." Tugging her back down, he cupped her face and kissed her, hard and wet and deep, making her moan low in her throat.

"Your shoulder," she gasped.

"Fuck my shoulder." And he slid his tongue to hers in a motion that melted her bones. Sliding her arms around his neck, she held on for dear life because when he kissed her like this, like she was better than sliced bread, she couldn't remember why it was a bad idea to fall for him.

He raised his head a fraction, looking at her with heavy-lidded eyes before coming at her again, with a roughness that shouldn't have excited her but did, beyond belief. There in the damp, small shed, she clung to him, tangling her tongue with his, pressing as close as she could get. She'd have climbed up his body if she could.

"More," he muttered, and changed the angle of his kiss, settling his mouth firmly over hers again, gripping her head as if he thought she might pull away. Not a chance. In fact, she struggled to get even closer, so that they fell, her spine pressing into the ground, Jake towering over her. His hands slid beneath her shirt, covering her breasts while his erection pressed hard at the juncture of her legs, his hips moving in a slow, tight, rocking motion that threatened to drive her right off the edge. She wanted to make the leap, nearly did—

But suddenly, he ripped his mouth free. Sliding his hands out of her shirt, he sat back on his heels. With a murmur of protest, she tried to draw him back but he shook his head, his breath coming out in pants. "Someone's here."

From outside came a honk, and she realized she'd forgotten Michael. "Oh my God."

He helped her up, her eyes dark and hot. "Can he do that to you?" he murmured, the pad of his thumb brushing over the pulse racing at the base of her throat. "Can he?"

"N-no."

"Good." Eyes lit with a fierce desire that made her weak, he kissed her one last time, his hand skimming down her throat, over her pumping heart, his fingers rasping over a hardened nipple. "Remember that."

She doubted she could forget.

Together they stepped back out into the bright sunshine, and looked at the red convertible Mustang. A gorgeous blond woman leapt out of it. Callie's first thought was that one of the cheerleaders was arriving late, but then the woman saw Jake and bounced up and down, waving wildly. "Jake! Jake, I can't believe it, I found you!"

Shocked, though not sure why, Callie looked at Jake. "That's not Michael."

He sighed. "No."

"Jake! Over here, over here!"

"She appears to know you well," Callie said dryly, while her heart took a dive. Her mouth was still wet from his, for God's sake, and she swiped the back of her hand over it.

"Yeah." He turned to her. "Callie—"

"Your blonde finally arrived." Good timing, too, she told herself. Because she hadn't fallen for him, at least not yet.

13

A piece of Jake's world had found him. A hot little piece he'd been with twice named Cici. He hadn't intended to ever see her again, but she was hugging up to him as he showed her around the ranch at her insistence. She wore a denim miniskirt and vest, complete with calf-high boots, matching hat, and glitter on her lips. Her idea of roughing it in the country, no doubt.

"Oh, Jake." She threw her arms around him, making him see stars when she jarred his shoulder. "I've been haunting the fire station since you vanished." They passed the pig pen, and several piglets raced to the gate hopefully. Cici scooted close to Jake, an alarmed expression on her face. "Oh, ugh. Anyway, finally one of the guys told me I'd find you on your own dude ranch, with the word *Blue* in the name, somewhere in Arizona." She laughed, and for the third time in as many minutes, set her head down on his bad shoulder. "You weren't hard to find after that."

Grimacing, he pulled free, even as he had to admire her tenacity at finding him. "Watch the shoulder, okay?"

"Oops, sorry. So . . ." She waggled her eyebrows at him. "How's the rest of you doing?"

Only a month and a half ago he'd have acted on that unmistakable invitation in her gaze. But seeing her out here on the ranch, so far out of her element and away from his, was far more disturbing than arousing.

They passed the hen coop. Cici squealed when she nearly stepped on a questionable looking lump of something that was definitely not dirt. The hens squawked and ran off.

Finally they came to the big house. Callie stood on the porch, shading her eyes from the sun as she watched them head toward her.

"Not exactly friendly, is she?" Cici whispered.

She had been, Jake thought, only a few moments ago. "She's busy."

Cici looked around her at the open, rugged country, at the rocky, dry mountains and the ranch around them. "What is it you people do out here all day long?"

How many times had he wondered the same thing? A hundred. A thousand. But now he knew differently, knew exactly the work it took to keep this place going. "The guests go on horseback expeditions, or hike. There are some historical monuments to visit, and—"

"Wow. You sound like a real cowboy." They came closer to Callie now, and Cici smiled up at her. "I'd love to go to my room and freshen up."

Callie's return smile could only be called such because she bared her teeth. "As Jake might have mentioned, we're fully booked."

"But it looks so empty around here."

"Everyone's gone right now, but the rooms are theirs for several more days."

Cici turned to Jake. "My flight out of Tucson isn't until tomorrow night. If I turn around now, I'll have to drive through the desert in the dark by myself."

Jake grimaced, then appealed to Callie. "Isn't there—" She crossed her arms, and he broke off. "No," he guessed.

"I'd think you'd at least try," sniffed an insulted Cici. "For your boss's girlfriend."

Oh boy.

Callie's gaze positively froze over now. "If, as the boss"—she said this in a carefully neutral tone that made Jake wince—"Jake wants to share his room with you, that's none of my concern."

And with that, she turned on her heel and headed back up the steps to the front door.

"I don't mind sharing," Cici said.

The front door closed with a finality that made him wince. He managed a weak smile. "Great." Out of the corner of his eye he saw Amy heading toward the barn, and an idea occurred to him. "Just a sec—" He ran toward Blue Flame's youngest and most enigmatic employee.

Amy watched him as he came to a stop in front of her. "Tucker gave me stuff to do in here," she said, gesturing to the barn. "So I'm not breaking any rules—"

"Can I borrow your cabin tonight?"

"Huh?"

"I had a friend come into town unexpectedly and I was wondering if she could stay in your cabin tonight."

Amy's gaze cut across the yard to where Cici stood, trying to examine the bottom of her high-heeled boots without falling over. "Is that her?"

"Yes."

"Are you going to fire me if I say no?"

"What? Of course not."

"Then no."

Dejected, he went back to Cici.

"Why don't you show me your cabin?" she asked, her eyes dark and sultry as she rubbed up against him.

Of all the nights for Tucker to be gone. He considered breaking into Stone's or Eddie's cabin, but in the end he opened his, managing to dodge Cici's advances only because the dinner bell rang.

Amy served the two of them in the dining room, a simple dinner of chicken and rice. It might as well have been dirt and rocks for all Jake could eat. Afterward, he excused himself and searched for Callie. He found her in the weight room, attacking a punching bag as if her life depended on it. She wore a sports bra and spandex shorts snug to her body. Her skin glowed, and he had the insane urge to lick her. "You missed dinner."

"And you have glitter on the corner of your mouth," she said, before resuming her massacre of the punching bag.

"I didn't kiss her, damn it." But he swiped at his mouth and looked at his hand. Indeed, he had glitter all over him.

"Go away, Jake."

"Yeah." But only because he didn't want this conversation—and there would be a conversation about it—to be interrupted by Cici, which would only make it worse. With a sigh he went back into the dining room.

"I'm ready for bed," Cici said.

"Dessert first." He had no idea if there even was dessert, but Amy served ice cream, and because she did, letting him delay another thirty minutes, he forgave her for not taking Cici off his hands.

"Now?" Cici asked when she'd finished.

"Coffee," he said desperately.

"No coffee." She stood, dragged him up. Smiled.

Unable to delay any longer, he took her back to the cabin, and they stared together at the bed and the futon. "You can have that one—"

"I thought we'd share." She slipped her arms around him, finally careful of his right shoulder. She snuggled up, nibbled on his ear, and he actually closed his eyes, remembering the last time she'd done that, and how well it had turned out for him.

But this time, nothing happened, not even a spark.

"Jake?"

He'd been so desperate and hungry for something from his world, and now look at him. He wished his world had stayed away. "Let's go to sleep, Cici."

She grinned at him, but it slowly faded at the look in his eyes. "You mean . . . ?"

"*Sleep*." He plopped down on Tucker's bed, leaving Cici his own. Closing his eyes, he sighed. He'd either entirely lost his mind, giving up a night with this woman . . .

Or he'd fallen for another. He didn't like either prospect.

The cheerleaders returned, happily declaring it'd been the best trip ever.

Callie was glad for it, even if she had to listen to stories from the boys about their escapades. Cici left, and Callie was glad for that, too. She hadn't been happy with the odd feeling that surged through her every time she'd looked at the woman, or late last night, when out the window of her cabin she'd seen the lights go off in Jake's.

She had a terrible feeling it was jealousy, and that was what bothered her the most. Since when did she want a man who drove her crazy at every turn? A man who wasn't planning on sticking around?

Just looking at him kick-started her heart, damn it. She'd spent too much of her life waiting for someone to love her. That wasn't self-pity talking, but fact. But the hell with that, she didn't need anyone but herself.

Only by diving into work and keeping everyone swamped with it as well did she manage to avoid talking directly to Jake for a few days. If she wasn't mistaken, he'd been just as eager to avoid her.

That was both a relief, and hard on the ego, but she decided to stick with relief.

On the morning of the cheerleaders' last full day, Michael showed up with donuts, and found her alone in her office. "Sugar fix?"

"Please."

He waited until she'd taken the box and was perusing her choice. "We've been friends for a long time," he said.

Smiling, she picked an old-fashioned glaze. She took her first bite and hugged him. "So long I can't remember what it was like before you."

His eyes were solemn when he pulled back. "I hope you mean that."

"Of course I do. You going riding?"

"In a minute. Callie, I can tell you what I think, even if it might hurt you, right?"

Her smile slowly faded. "Absolutely. Unless you're going to repeat yourself and tell me I'm putting too much of myself into this place."

"Well . . ."

Her donut stuck in her throat and she set the rest down. "I don't think I want to hear this."

"When Richard was alive, this place didn't consume

you. You were happy to just work here. You took more time for yourself. For me."

"Oh, Michael." She brushed off her fingers and put her hand on his.

"I miss you, Callie."

He'd been her first real friend, the first person to know her, to care about her. He'd been there for her through her marriage to Matt Lowell, and through its demise. He'd been there through Richard's death. She figured he'd always be there. "Everything is the same as it's always been."

"Everything, yes. But not you. You're putting it all into the Blue Flame, your heart and soul, everything. You've got nothing left over for anything else. Or anyone."

"It's my home."

"It's your job. You aren't your job, Callie."

"It's more than a job for me."

"Because you feel you have nothing else." He cupped her face. "But that's not true, you have plenty. All you have to do is look around and see it. See me."

"Michael . . ." She didn't know how to do this. She didn't want to hurt him. She loved him. "I can love the Blue Flame and give it my all, and still have the life I want. I'm living it."

"Yes, but at what cost?"

"At no cost." She put her hands on his wrists, trying to compel him to understand. "I thought you knew how much the Blue Flame means to me."

"I do know, but it *is* costing you. It's costing you happiness." He lifted his hands from hers, and shaking his head, backed away. "It's costing you me."

"No, it's not." When he just looked at her, eyes so solemn, she let out a disparaging sound, her throat burning as she lifted a finger. "Don't you make me choose."

"You've already chosen."

"Michael—"

He came back toward her, and once again put his hands on her arms, pulling her back into him. She expected a hug, so she was shocked when he kissed her, his lips warm and firm on hers.

With everything she had, she tried to feel something, anything. She would have welcomed it for a man who would never hurt her, but it didn't happen, and he pulled back.

She stared up at him, seeing everything he felt for her, the magnitude of it all over his face, and her eyes filled.

He closed his. "You felt nothing. Not even a tingle."

Her heart cracked. "Not nothing," she whispered, "But . . . not what you felt." And no tingle. "God, Michael. I—"

"Don't be sorry for what you don't have to give me." He looked at her for a long moment, his gaze running over her face, and then he walked out.

Callie couldn't get Michael's expression out of her mind. She stressed and worried over it for a good long time, until something happened late that afternoon to distract her. She was in the kitchen going over a shopping list for Amy to take into town. They had a big group barbeque planned for the cheerleaders, and needed some supplies.

"Stuff for s'mores?" Amy asked.

"Of course. Here—" Callie started flipping through her purse while Amy scribbled on the list. "I'll give you some cash." She looked into her empty wallet. She'd taken sixty bucks out of the bank machine the night she'd gone out to dinner with Michael, and hadn't spent a penny of it, but it was gone.

"What's the matter?" Amy had stopped writing and was staring at her.

Callie stared back. Not a single sign of guilt, and then Callie felt her own guilt for even looking for it.

Amy went stiff, then backed up a step. "You're missing money."

"I'm not sure." She shook her head. "No, I can't be." She forced a smile. "I'm just going senile. I misplaced it or something." Before Amy could question that, Callie made up an excuse about needing to get outside, and made her escape.

Eddie was coaxing a few of the cheerleaders into getting eggs from the hens. They were laughing and having a great time by the looks of it. Tucker had talked a few others into milking their two milk cows, which was also causing great amusement.

Stone and Jake were painting the shed, Jake using his left hand, the two of them egged on by yet another set of cheerleaders. She was glad to see Stone smiling. She knew he'd stayed out all night, staggering in at dawn that morning looking quite hungover. He looked fine now, thankfully.

So did Jake, in his jeans and T-shirt stretched taut across the muscles of his back as he worked. Callie had figured she'd come out here and tell him about the money missing from her wallet, but something held her back. A tall blonde something named Cici. She hated herself for the weakness of caring, for the stupid jealousy, but that didn't change a thing.

Callie didn't have any hold on him, and she didn't want one—or so she'd told herself a million times.

They hadn't spoken directly to each other in days, and she decided to keep it that way, especially since as of right now, men were the bane of her existence.

By nightfall, they had a bonfire going despite a steady wind, and were all working on making their guests' last night a smash hit. It was an organized chaos, with the cheerleaders wandering around, drinks in hand, flirting with the guys, and the guys each handling their responsibilities and enjoying themselves as well.

Vicki finally realized she was beating a dead horse when it came to chasing Jake, and adjusted her mission to Eddie. She had her hands all over him, laughing in apology when she accidentally dumped the contents of his denim jacket pocket to the ground. Lighter, keys, and three folded twenties scattered at their feet.

Three twenties, like the three twenties Callie was missing. Callie stared at him, but he laughed and scooped everything back up without one sign of distress or nerves, and she forced herself to relax. Eddie would never steal from her. None of them would. She hated that she'd even thought it.

The wind cut through her and she moved closer to the fire for the warmth. She tried to enjoy herself, but she was tired and her heart felt heavy. She looked around the fire to make sure everyone was having a good time, and realized one thing they'd forgotten—the long fire pokers they used to toast the marshmallows for the s'mores. "I'll be right back," she told Stone, and headed in the dark toward the newly painted shed, where they kept the bonfire supplies.

Pulling her pen-sized flashlight from her pocket, she

turned it on and put it between her teeth, freeing her hands to open the door.

She stepped inside and was immediately hit by the fumes. Her boot connected with a can and she looked down. Paint cans, paint brushes sitting in trays, rags, all the supplies they'd used had been hastily stored here. She remembered rushing Stone through his clean-up a couple of hours ago and sighed. "Damn it, Stone."

Suddenly the shed door shut behind her, and she jerked in surprise, dropping her flashlight. *The wind.* In the pitch black, she whirled around to open the door again, but it wouldn't budge. "No!" Paint vapors invading her lungs, she bent to feel around for the flashlight, grateful when her fingers closed over it and the thing clicked on again. Standing up, she reached for the overhead light. As it clicked on, she weaved, dizzy now. The fumes were bad. She put her fist to the door, pounding as hard as she could. "Hello? *Can anyone hear me?*"

It was useless and she knew it. She was a good hundred yards away from the bonfire, and with the wind kicking up, the sounds of the crackling fire and all the talking, no one could possibly hear her. She moved around the small space, looking for something to hit the door with, something to make a loud noise. She tried a broom, then the handle of a paintbrush. Nothing worked, and feeling sick, she sank to her knees. The wind whistled through a few cracks, but she also thought she heard something else. Footsteps? What if it hadn't been the wind to shut her in here? Her heart kicked it up a notch. Was that someone outside right this minute, listening to her scream?

Which begged the next question. How long she could stand here before her crew realized she was miss-

ing? Or before she suffocated? "They'll come," she told
herself, and leaned back against the door. Any second
now. She closed her eyes to wait . . .

Only to gasp in surprise when the door jerked
opened behind her, spilling her outside and into a pair
of strong, warm arms. *Jake's.* "Callie!"

Other voices crowded close, too. "Let me see her—"

"What's the matter with her?"

"—My God, the fumes— Is she breathing?"

Callie's head swam with both the fumes and the
voices of all the people in her life. Tucker, Stone, Eddie,
Lou and Marge. Michael, too. When had he come?

"Let me take her." That was him, full of fear.

"I've got her." This was Jake again, and his arms
tightened on her. "Callie?"

She opened her eyes, and found herself on the
ground in his lap, cradled to his chest, the faces of the
rest of her crew so close that she had to blink to put
them in focus.

"You rescued me again," she whispered to Jake. Her
throat hurt. "Damn it."

"What the hell were you doing in there?"

"I think the wind slammed the door shut on me. I
couldn't breathe."

"Of course not," Jake said fiercely. "Some idiot put
all the paint supplies in there."

Everyone turned to look at Stone. He seemed horrified. "We were in a hurry, I didn't think—"

"Didn't think? Or couldn't?" Michael snapped.
"Were you drinking?"

"No."

"I saw you," Tucker said quietly.

"Yes, but that was after," Stone said faintly. "We all
had a beer . . ." He looked around at each of them. "I

wasn't drinking this afternoon when I put the stuff in there, I swear!"

"We're just lucky the shed didn't burst into flames," Jake said. "Callie, why didn't you yell for us?"

"I did! I was screaming my head off for all of you."

Jake's hands tightened on her, his eyes never left her face. "We didn't hear you, everything was so noisy."

She tried to get up but he was holding her with a gentle grip of steel and he wouldn't let her go, even when she knew she had to be hurting him. "Jake—"

"Another minute," he murmured, hugging her. "Give yourself another minute."

"I'm fine."

"Then give me another minute."

"Give us all one." Eddie sat back on his heels, swiping at his forehead with his arm as he eyed his brother in concern. "My God."

Tucker touched Callie's face. "She's okay."

"We're calling the sheriff," Michael said. "No one touch that latch, we're fingerprinting it."

"All of us have touched that latch," Callie said. "And I don't want to scare the guests."

"Stone and Eddie, maybe you should go check on the fire," Jake said. "Tucker—"

"Yeah." Tucker surged to his feet, not arguing with him for once. "I'll check the guests." He touched Callie's face again and then was gone.

Michael didn't budge. "Callie—"

"I'm fine." She had no idea why she was still cuddled on Jake's lap, secure within his arms, as if she was hurt. She wasn't. With the fresh night air, her head had cleared. "I'm *fine*," she repeated, and to prove it, she stood up. She smiled at Michael, who didn't smile back.

He was still upset over what had happened earlier, and hurt, and yet everything he felt for her was in his eyes. God help her, she couldn't deal with that now. She turned and held a hand to Jake.

He struggled up, his face a mask of pain.

"You're hurt."

"I jarred it a little."

"That was from playing he-man with the jammed shed door," Michael said. He didn't add how stupid it'd been, though the implication was there in his tone.

Jake's jaw tightened, whether from more pain or annoyance, Callie had no idea, but she slipped her arm around his good side. "You need ice."

"Cal, you need taking care of, too," Michael said.

"I can take care of myself," she reminded him gently, but she gave him a hard hug, and found her heart softening when he hugged her hard right back. "Don't worry about me," she whispered. "Please?"

"It's a habit," Michael said, and when she took Jake inside, he sighed. "My heart's habit."

14

Callie took Jake inside the big house, and into the weight room.

"You want me to try to strangle myself again?" he asked, glancing at the bench.

"Another time." She opened the small room they used for massages. Twice a week Macy came in from Three Rocks to give massage therapy, and in fact was there that night. Callie had caught a glimpse of her outside partying with the guests. She already had her massage table all set up, along with some scented candles and oils. "Hot or cold pack, do you think?"

"Callie." Jake looked a little stunned. "You're the one who got locked in that shed with no air. I should be taking care of you—"

She pushed him down to the table.

He sat up. "You're still upset with me because of Cici, but I swear, I didn't invite her here."

She pushed him flat again. "Your life is your own. Now do you want a massage or not?"

"Are you kidding?" He blinked. "A massage would be . . . fantastic."

"Great. Macy'll be here any minute. You can go before the cheerleaders get their turn. Consider it an owner bonus."

He stopped in the act of pulling off his shirt. "Macy?"

"Well you didn't think I—" She broke off because she could tell from the look on his face that that's exactly what he'd thought. Cost of the candles, $10. Cost of the soft rock CD, $18. Cost of the look on his face, priceless. "That's a good one, Jake. You propose a wild spring fling with me, then sleep with another woman, and then you actually believe I'd touch you with a ten-foot pole."

"There are so many things wrong with that statement, I don't know where to start," he said softly. He got off the table and came toward her.

She backed away, holding up a hand to ward him off. "I have guests to see to."

"This is more important."

"Nothing's more important than the guests, and the money they bring in." Whipping open the door, she slipped out. She hurried through the weight room and down the hall.

Back out into the night, she took in the bonfire scene, and all the guests and her ranch hands sitting around, laughing, talking, singing, having a grand old time. So normal. It seemed like ages since she'd set out to get the fire pokers for the s'mores. Now someone else had clearly located them, and the s'mores were a huge success as always.

Macy stood among them, smiling and taking a bite of Stone's dessert. When she saw Callie, she waved and came over. "Hey. Bunch of perky cheerleaders, huh? Only three signed up for a massage." She shrugged. "Maybe they'll tip good. It'd have been nice if there'd been a few guys though. Guys can be cheerleaders, can't they?"

"I don't know, but I have a guy for you. He's one hundred and ninety pounds of solid hurting muscle."

"Ooh, goodie."

"He's not a cheerleader."

"Honey, you had me at the solid, hurting muscle."

Callie watched Macy let herself inside the big house, and forcing a smile on her face, joined the crowd at the fire.

Michael came up to her immediately, but then just looked at her.

"What?"

"I'm fighting the urge to grab you and hold on." He let out a low laugh and spread out his hands in front of him. "I don't want to be overbearing or pushy."

"Well, you're in luck." She leaned on him. "I could use a little TLC."

His arms came around her and he held on, resting his chin on her head. "You gave me gray hair today."

"The shed incident?"

"Yeah, the shed incident. Holy shit. But also because you're pulling away from me. I'm sorry I made you feel like you had to choose between me and the ranch. I'm sorry I overstepped the boundaries and kissed you like that."

"Michael, I can't stand it that I'm hurting you, but—"

"But this is how it is. I know. And this is all you have to give me. I know that, too." After another moment, he pulled away, offering her a small smile designed to hide his feelings. As he headed back to the fire, a pang went through her, because she knew that after today things might never be the same. It scared her because she didn't have that many people in her life, and the ones she did have were all important to her, so very important. And yet she couldn't give what she didn't have, she just couldn't.

She moved around the fire, making small talk with the guests, checking to see that everyone was happy and having a good time. Lou and Marge stopped her, with Marge clucking over her like a mother hen. After assuring them that she was fine, Callie kept moving. Eddie squeezed her hand. Tucker did the same, adding a long, searching look as if to make sure she was really okay.

She was on the far side of the large fire now. She wanted to be alone, wanted to check on Sierra, and then maybe hit the sack. It was early but she felt the weight of the day like a lead ball.

"Callie." Stone appeared at her side. His usual happy smile was nowhere in sight. "God, Callie, I'm so sorry. It's just that we were rushing to clean up, and I knew I had to hurry if I wanted to get all the chores done, so I just shoved everything in the shed. I meant to get back to it, clean it all out, I swear." His eyes were tortured. "If I'd known you'd get shut in there—"

"I know."

"I should have just let the animals wait for once, I never should have just walked away from paint, especially the rags. I know better, I do. And I wasn't drinking until later—"

"It's okay," she said quietly, reaching for his hand. "It was a mistake any of us could have made."

"I wasn't drinking," he said again.

"I know." She took his other hand and looked into his eyes. "But you are drinking at night. A lot. It's never been any of my business," she said when he would have spoken. "It's never affected your work here."

"It doesn't. It won't."

"Stone . . ." She squeezed his hands. "I don't want to worry about you."

"You don't have to."

"But I do. And so does Eddie."

He was quiet a moment, and then he grimaced. "Yeah." He lowered his voice. "I guess, to tell you the truth, sometimes I worry, too."

"Oh, Stone."

He tried smiling but it didn't quite reach his eyes. "I can fix this. I can stop. I will stop."

"You could get help."

"I'll be fine."

"But—"

"I'll be fine," he repeated, and let her hug him. And when he'd gone back to the fire, she continued walking the grounds, checking on the animals. She made sure Sierra was okay, petted the puppies, and then found herself, an hour after she'd left it, going back into the big house. Macy came down the hall. "You were right. One solid aching muscle, the poor guy. I put him right to sleep. You didn't tell me about his injuries. I'm going to go out and sit by the fire to give him a few minutes."

Callie waited until she was gone, then peeked into the weight room. Like a moth to a flame, she thought. The candles were still lit, the portable CD player still on so that the sounds of the ocean spilled softly into the air.

She had no business intruding, and she faltered a moment while her mind argued with her hormones, but it all backed up in her throat at the sight of Jake's big, beautiful body sprawled face down on the massage table, fast asleep.

Macy had pulled the sheet up to the small of his bare

back. His left arm was up, cradling his head, his right arm straight along his side. She could see his scar as it curved over his shoulder. His back was sleek with the oil Macy had used, except—

Except for beneath his right shoulder blade, where a healing burn marked the span of her two hands. She'd not seen him without his shirt from behind before, and he'd never said ... But the implications of his accident, of saving a kid, then falling three stories through burning floors, finally sank in.

Looking at him, she felt such an ache, such an inexplicable longing she couldn't explain it, even to herself. What was she doing? They had such different lives, and such different dreams ... and still she stood there watching over him, guarding his sleep, wondering and wishing.

Jake woke up the next morning to the scent of coffee. Since Tucker didn't give a shit about improving the quality of Jake's morning, he knew he had to be dreaming.

"Get your ass up, I'm not going to serve it to you in bed."

Jake cracked an eye and took in the sight of his brother scowling at the foot of the cot, which meant that Jake had somehow managed to stumble back to the cabin last night on his own. Vaguely he remembered doing so, and being chased across the grass by Goose.

Tucker wore only his boxers, hair wild, but God bless him, he held two steaming mugs, and was sipping from one. Jake sat up and braced for the usual shaft of pain to go through his aching body, but surprisingly enough, it didn't come. "Macy's a goddess."

"Yeah." Tucker nodded toward his shoulder. "Getting better?"

"Is that longing I hear in your voice?" Jake stood up and took the mug of coffee.

"Well, you did say you'd go back to firefighting as soon as you were fit."

A pang of nerves went through him. *When the hell would he be fit?* "Which would get me out of here, of course. And out of your hair."

Tucker just sipped his coffee.

"The love and caring in the room is overwhelming," Jake said dryly, and turned away. "Thanks for the coffee."

"Yeah— Holy shit."

Jake glanced over his shoulder. Tucker's gaze was locked on Jake's back.

"A burn?"

"Yeah."

Tucker let out a low whistle. "That fire really screwed you up."

"Not too bad. Don't worry, Tuck, I'll be gone soon enough." One way or another. He moved toward the bathroom, thinking maybe a shower would help improve his sudden bad mood. He took great pleasure in getting to the bathroom first for a change, where he planned on using all the hot water. On principal, he slammed the door behind him.

He took a good hard look at himself in the mirror. He was tanner than he'd been, and some of the exhaustion had left his face. Despite the two-day-old beard he looked healthier than when he'd first arrived.

And yet he'd been here, what, nearly three weeks? Amy still jumped when he so much as looked at her. Stone and Eddie went out every night and had never invited him, not once. His own brother couldn't wait for him to heal and go far, far away, and Callie . . .

Callie actually thought he could kiss her the way he'd kissed her, and then turn around and sleep with Cici. Flattering.

And worse than all that, he didn't have a frigging clue as to what to do with the rest of his life if he couldn't go back to firefighting, which was beginning to look like the case.

"Jake." Tucker knocked at the bathroom door.

"I'm not done." He grabbed his toothbrush, turned on the sink.

"About last night, when Callie got stuck in the shed with those fumes . . ."

Jake turned off the water. "What about it?"

"You realized before anyone else that she'd been gone too long."

"Jesus. I didn't shut her in there—"

"I didn't think you did. I'm trying to thank you, damn it."

Jake craned his neck and stared at the closed door. "Thank me?"

"Yeah. For the help."

"For the help," he repeated slowly, and set down his toothbrush. Polite, he'd give his brother that. "I don't want to be *thanked*, Tucker, like . . . like I'm some guest."

"You are a guest."

At that, he hauled open the door. "I have as much a right to be here as you do. Or maybe you've forgotten who brought you here, who owns the land and signs your paychecks."

Tucker's eyes flashed. "Don't worry, I've never forgotten who dumped me here."

"Dumped?" Jake gaped at him. "I didn't—"

"I was used to it by then though."

"Are you talking about when I went to San Diego? When you were five and—"

"I remember how old I was when you walked out."

"Tucker—"

"I missed you." On that furiously uttered admission, Tucker turned away, moving around the couch as he started hunting up clothes. He jammed a bare foot into a discarded pair of jeans that turned out to be Jake's. "*Shit.*" He threw them at Jake, who caught them just before they hit him in the face. "We're fucking slobs," he muttered, and hunted up a pair of his own.

Jake stood there still holding his jeans, shocked. "I tried to see you. But—"

"Mom wouldn't let you. Yeah, I've heard that before."

"You don't believe it."

Tucker buttoned up his jeans and looked at Jake. "Why would she keep us apart?"

Because she was a selfish bitch, was Jake's first thought. But Mary Ann had treated Tucker differently. He'd been her baby in a way Jake had never been, because when Jake had been born, Mary Ann had still been a baby herself.

"She said you took off, that you never looked back." Tucker stood there shirtless and barefooted. For once his expression was clear of derision or anger, just a need to know.

He wanted a real answer. Jake didn't know if the one he had was good enough. "If I'd never looked back, how would I have known you were in trouble?"

Tucker stared at him for a long moment. "You called us?"

Jake nodded. "It was hard to keep track of you with her moving you guys around, but I did the best I could."

Tucker looked confused. "She said . . ."

"That I'd left without a word? Yeah, she always was fond of playing the victim."

Tucker frowned, and after a long moment, turned away. "Save me some hot water."

"Yeah." Well, Jake wondered, had he expected Tucker to smile and hug him and say all was well? That was never going to happen. He shut the bathroom door and cranked on the hot water. When he came out, Tucker was gone and Jake had a message on his cell from Joe.

"No news on the lawsuit," Joe said on the message. "But there was a reporter at the fire station today wanting a press picture of you. So was a group of women who claimed to run your fan club. They wanted pictures, too." Joe's voice held amusement. "Maybe I should hunt up some from over the years and put them on eBay, raise some funds for the station . . ."

Jake tossed his cell phone to his bed. He left the cabin thinking it was all well and good for Joe to make fun, *he* could still do his job. *He* hadn't been forced out of a career he loved with all his heart.

And Jake hadn't been forced out, either, he assured himself. At least not yet. But his shoulder twitched and so did something deep inside. Knowing damn well it was the denial and fear, the same feelings that haunted his dreams at night, he walked faster, but there was no running from such dark emotions. They followed him everywhere.

The sun hadn't yet risen. He put one foot on the grass and, predictably, Goose came running. Jake lifted his foot off and she skidded to a stop in front of him, guarding, waiting for him to make a move.

"What do you do, have hate meetings with Moe?" he asked. He could almost see his father in the damn goose's dark gaze. *Look at what I built without you. Look at what you wanted no part of. Look at what I left you to screw up. . . .*

He turned his back on the damn goose. Tucker was in the pasture doing something with the horses there. He could see his blue silhouette as the first sunbeams flashed over the rocky, bushy mountains like flames. He hadn't asked anyone if that was how the ranch had gotten its name, and that bothered him. Suddenly he wanted to know, not that Tucker would tell him. Shivering in the chilly air, he kept walking. Voices came out of the barn, Stone's and Eddie's. The sun rose quickly now. Way out beyond the pasture, coming in from the hills like the opening credits of a western, was a horse and rider.

Even knowing it was Callie riding, Jake still wished he could switch the channel and find a good basketball game instead.

Goose let out a honk, probably to a bird who dared land on her precious grass, but Jake figured the sound for his father's spirit, laughing at him.

His stomach rumbled, reminding him he hadn't eaten dinner last night. Between Callie getting stuck in the shed and him hurting his shoulder and his subsequent massage, he'd missed the barbeque, and his mouth watered at the thought. The food had been surprisingly good out here but, damn, he missed drive-thrus. He missed Starbucks. He missed jelly-filled donuts on the way to his shift at the firehouse.

And that wasn't all. He missed surfing on lazy

mornings. He missed the roar of the waves. He missed the green rolling hills.

Beneath his feet he could feel the vibration of Sierra galloping closer. Callie wore her cowboy hat, long, red hair streaming out behind her as she effortlessly rode the rough terrain.

He'd never known a woman like her. She was tough yet soft, sweet yet hard. A challenge through and through. She rode Sierra in, slowed her down.

Sierra didn't like slowing down. Still raring to go, she trotted around, tossing her head, snorting her displeasure at having to stop. "Shh," Callie soothed, and looked at Jake. "You going to try to rescue me again?"

"Nope."

"Did the massage help?"

"Yep."

Sierra snorted again, then nudged Jake's chest with her nose.

"Sierra, stop it." Callie swung a leg over and hopped down. Hair a little wild, hat hanging down her back now, she stroked the horse's long neck. "She thinks all men around here carry treats."

"Guess she doesn't realize I'm not really one of you."

Callie stopped petting the horse for one telling moment. "Maybe it's not her who thinks you're not. Maybe it's you."

He looked at her, and she looked right back, silently daring him to say otherwise, but damn if she wasn't right, not that he'd admit it.

Eddie stuck his head out of the barn. "Could use some help this morning. Shep's girlfriend won't let me into the tack room again."

"Tiger?"

"Don't tell me the old guy has more than one girl-friend."

Callie looked relieved not to have it be more serious, and grabbed Sierra's reins.

"What are you going to do, go get yourself bitten?" Jake asked.

"Hopefully not."

Jake let out a breath. "I'll go."

"So you are going to rescue me again after all."

"Looks like it."

15

Callie decided to let Eddie and Jake deal with Tiger so that she could walk through the corral and visit the horses, spending a few minutes with each of them. Patches, one of their older mares, was limping, and Callie checked her hooves. "There," she soothed, picking out a little pebble. "That'll be better."

And so was she for not having to spend the time with Jake. Jake with the haunting eyes and sexy body that she couldn't stop dreaming of. Patches turned her head and eyed the young woman walking toward them. Amy came to a stop at the fencing with her black jeans, black boots, black hair spiked straight up, her face carefully blank.

Her expression reminded Callie of Tucker, and how he'd looked his first few months on the ranch, so desperately needing to be cool, and yet just as desperate for acceptance. "Hey." She added a smile to see if the girl would smile back. She didn't. "Everything okay in the kitchen?"

"Yeah." Amy shifted her feet. "I saw you out the window. I, uh, got breakfast ready early so I could come talk to you."

"Sure." She saw Tucker watching them from across

the yard, and then he started toward them. Amy saw him, then let out a slow, tense breath. "Is something wrong?" Callie asked her.

Amy wiped her hands on her apron, then shoved them in her back pockets. "I didn't take your money," she said. "But I'll leave if you want me to."

"No." Tucker had come close. "You're not going anywhere, not like this."

"Of course she's not going anywhere." Callie stuck the hoof pick in her back pocket and moved toward the fence. She hooked her hands in it and climbed over. "Amy, did anyone here act like they thought you stole money?"

Tucker made a sound low in his throat. "No one would."

"No," Amy admitted. "They didn't."

"Did someone ask you to leave?"

"No."

Callie looked at Tucker, then back to Amy. She'd tried softness, she'd tried compassion and understanding. What else could she do?

Tucker still stood there, his fists clenched, ready to take on the world for this girl, and it was just romantic enough to make Callie sigh. She didn't believe Amy to be behind the ranch's problems; she never had. She'd hoped to chalk it all up to strange coincidence, or bad luck, but she wasn't that naïve. Someone *was* responsible, and as far as the law or the sheriff went, Amy was a strong suspect. "If no one's accused you, and no one's asked you to leave, then why are you out here wasting both of our time?"

Amy stopped looking at her boots and met Callie's gaze. "I just wanted you to know I didn't do it."

"I already know that."

Amy blinked, looking so confused she broke Callie's heart. "How?"

"Because you're a part of us now," Tucker said simply.

"And because I figure a thief wouldn't stick around beating herself up about what people think of her," Callie said. "A thief certainly wouldn't ask me if I thought she'd done it, and a thief wouldn't be standing here right now trying to get me to fire her."

"I don't want to be fired."

"Good. Because you're not."

Amy stared at her for a long moment, and then her lips curved. Before the smile fully formed, she covered her mouth. "I've . . . got to get back to the kitchen."

"Sure, but Amy? The smiling thing? Keep that. It looks good on you."

"Yeah," Tucker agreed inanely, nodding, looking a little cupid-struck.

Amy's smile spread, and then she whirled and ran all the way back to the house.

Callie watched Tucker watch Amy. "Something going on with you two?"

"Are you kidding? She won't let me within five feet of her."

She eyed the longing on his face. "But you'd like there to be something going on."

He lifted a shoulder, the casual gesture belying the expression of yearning on his face.

As the days passed, Jake found himself far more active at the ranch than he ever intended, due to Stone taking off for some unexpected personal time.

Jake got more up front and personal with the pigs, hens, cows, and horses than he'd ever intended. Each day he finished work exhausted and filthy. Not all that different from firefighting, really, but when he fought fires, he didn't also smell like a manicure.

That, apparently, was just a little bonus.

Callie kept mum about Stone's disappearance, which didn't seem to sit well with the others. After lunch one day, he heard angry voices coming out of the barn.

"He's my own brother, damn it." This from Eddie.

"You think I've forgotten that?" Callie asked, an octave above polite.

Jake moved to the doorway to see what was up. Eddie's jaw was bunched, his eyes desperate. "You can tell me what's wrong," he said to Callie. "*Please* tell me what's wrong."

Her regret and sorrow conveyed in every line of her taut body, she shook her head. "I promised. Eddie, I promised I wouldn't tell anyone, including you."

"Callie—"

"Don't make me say it again. I'm sorry for it, but that's the end of it. Now leave it."

Jake stepped closer for support, but Eddie did drop it. The tension remained though, between all of them. Worse, they were still short-handed because Jake couldn't lead expeditions or do anything that required actual skill.

Their weekend guests—nine sisters, there for fun without their individual families—had signed up for a two-day trek, complete with tents, no electricity, and no beds.

Jake's personal nightmare, but Tucker eyed him. "You're in. You're joining the misfit posse."

"No way," Jake said.

"Yes way. We need you."

"Callie shouldn't stay alone for two days," Jake said, quite pleased with what he thought was a brilliant excuse.

Unfortunately Callie heard him, and came close. "What did you just say?"

"You shouldn't be here alone."

Tucker winced. "Dude, not a good idea—"

"I take care of myself," Callie said in a glacial tone.

Tucker shot him a *tried-to-tell-you* look.

"I'm not questioning your ability to take care of yourself," Jake said, exasperated. "I'm just saying there's been a lot of goings on, and I don't want you alone."

"I have Amy."

"Great. *Two* women."

Even Eddie winced at that one.

Callie narrowed her eyes. "Marge and Lou will be around as well, and I can always call for help." "Michael would come in a heartbeat, and anyway, you'll be on a radio. Have fun camping, Jake."

Have *fun*? Not a chance in hell.

Jake figured Eddie and Tucker had made him go on the trip because they needed a good laugh, but it turned out they really did need three men to handle all the horses, not to mention the rambunctious, flirty, over-the-top sisters, who ranged in age from nineteen to forty-two and turned out to be more wild than the cheerleaders.

For some reason Jake had decided to try to ride Moe instead of Molly. The big rugged tan horse drew him, mostly because he seemed to like everyone but Jake, but also because it was a connection to his father. He wouldn't have admitted that he needed that connection, but he did.

Moe did let him grab ahold of his reins, and even waited quietly until Jake had pulled himself up and seated himself.

Then he bucked.

"Whoa, *whoa*." Tucker ran over, soothing the animal with such ease that Jake just gritted his teeth and got down.

"You crazy?" Tucker asked Jake.

"Yeah." Moe seemed to smile at him as he stalked off to get Molly.

He got on the quieter horse, and half an hour into the ride, they'd entered a vertical labyrinth from which they could see at least fifty miles in all directions. Clear springs seeped from narrow canyons, falling from hillsides alive with mesquite and piñons and yuccas. Tucker came up close on Homer, then jerked his head to the sharp drop-off edge, marked by a series of high, jagged rocks that seemed to point to the sky. "Richard's Peak. It was his favorite place."

Jake slowed and took it all in, from the maze of rock formations to the incredible view. He tried to imagine his father standing on this very spot—it wasn't hard.

"It's where we came to spread his ashes," Tucker said. "Remember, you left the morning after the service? We all came out here that afternoon."

Jake looked out into the valley below and waited, desperate to feel something, anything, other than an aching emptiness and sadness for not feeling more. "What am I supposed to say? Sorry?"

"Not to me."

He opened his mouth to tell Tucker what he'd told Callie, that the street between Richard and Jake had

gone two ways, but suddenly that seemed like an excuse. Maybe Richard hadn't made a move, but Jake
could have. If for nothing else than to get rid of all this
useless regret and loss.

They stopped before sunset to make camp. Jake
looked at the hard, wide open land and wished for a
bed. Eddie set up the tents, smiling and flirting with
their guests when they all jumped in to help him, but
Jake knew him now, and for the first time, Eddie's easygoing nature was forced.

"It's Stone," Tucker told him quietly as they set up a
barbeque pit, gathering large stones to make a circle.
"He misses his brother."

Because that sounded a little like an accusation, Jake
picked up a larger rock than he'd intended.

"Christ, don't even try to help if you're going to go
all pale and pretend your shoulder isn't killing you,"
Tucker said, disgusted.

"It's not killing me." There were degrees of pain, as
he'd learned all too well. On a scale of one to ten, he
was only at a six, and that was saying something. And
actually, so was the fact that Tucker had noticed his
pain at all, and without a derogatory comment. "Can't
Eddie just call Stone's cell?"

"Stone isn't answering. Now Eddie's all bent that
Stone didn't tell anyone but Callie where he is. He's
worried."

And clearly, so was Tucker. "You guys are all pretty
close."

"We're family," Tucker said simply, and lit the fire.

And you're not. That message had been loud and
clear in the past, but he'd thought today the lines between the ranch and himself had finally seemed to blur
somewhat. Tucker, while not overwhelmingly friendly

by any means, had seemed to lose at least some of his antagonism.

Great timing. He'd finally softened, and Jake had spoken to his Realtor only yesterday, who'd assured him she could sell the ranch quickly.

He'd lived for that, and yet the truth was, he could have gone back to San Diego without waiting for the sale. He could take care of himself now, and while work was still out of the question, surely the media frenzy had died down.

But he hadn't gone anywhere. Learning to fit into this group of self-titled misfits no longer seemed so bad. Especially since at the moment no one wore the title of *misfit* better than he.

Tucker nodded in satisfaction at his blazing fire, then pulled out a sheet of paper filled with neat, precise handwriting. He read some of it and swore. "She should have come out herself, damn it. I'm not going to peel the cucumbers in little strips. And what the hell does she mean, toss the salad? We shouldn't even be having salad, that's not camping food."

"It is for women," Jake said.

Tucker's head whipped up, eyes lit with ready attitude, but then he caught the teasing light in Jake's eyes and let out what was the closest thing to a laugh that he was going to get. "Yeah, I guess."

Across the fire near the tents, Eddie had some of the women all over him while he put the gear into the shelters. The rest were waiting to jump on his every whim.

"Why aren't you joining him?" Jake asked Tucker. "That must be one of the benefits, right? Beautiful guests? Harmless flirting?"

Tucker was still reading his directions and muttering. "It's complicated."

"You mean it's a woman complicated. *Amy* complicated."

"Aren't they all?"

"Every single last one," Jake said fervently.

Tucker lifted his narrowed gaze and studied him. "You're not having women trouble, not here," he said flatly. "Tell me you're not. Because there's only Callie, and since you're leaving, there'd be nothing about her giving you trouble, nothing at all."

"Tucker—"

"You're painting. You're selling us out. And then you're leaving. In that order. Remember?"

"I'm not selling you out. I can't keep the ranch, I can't—"

"Yeah, yeah. I've heard this story, so save it." He shoved Amy's long note in his pocket and stalked off.

They didn't talk again, other than to communicate about what needed to be done. Callie checked in regularly by radio with Tucker, though she didn't talk to Jake.

Had he actually thought he might be fitting in? He'd been dreaming. That night and the next, Jake dealt with rocks beneath his sleeping bag, clinging women, and more bugs than he'd ever seen. Thankfully he lived, and two mornings later they finally rode out.

By that time, Jake couldn't remember why he was still there. He missed hot water and a bed, and it was likely his butt would never be the same after all those hours in the saddle.

All he wanted was a plane ticket home, whether he could be a firefighter or not, whether he'd sold the ranch or not.

Then they rode back onto the ranch, and he saw Callie standing on the porch of the big house. She wore her

usual jeans and tank with a blouse layered over it. No
hat today, which left her fiery hair blowing around her
face and shoulders. She stood tall and proud, and just
looking at her filled him with a longing he didn't fully
understand.

And suddenly the plane ride took a backseat to
being with her.

She saw him, he was certain of it, yet she didn't
react. Undeterred, he dismounted, threw the reins to
Eddie, then strode forward. He took Callie's arm and
pulled her off the steps. "Two things."

She looked around, making sure they were alone,
which frankly, he didn't care about. The guests had
gone inside with Amy to pack up for their departure,
and Eddie and Tucker weren't paying either of them
any notice.

"Forget everyone else," he said. "First, I'm never
camping again."

"That's a shame since you're finally walking like a
cowboy."

"If that means that I look like I've been in the saddle
for days, I have, thank you. I think I broke my ass, if
you're concerned. Now listen up, Callie, for thing number two, and this probably should have been first. Hell,
this should have been said days ago, but we're both
pretty damn bull-headed."

"Jake—"

"I didn't sleep with Cici."

"Yes, you did."

"She slept in my bed, I slept in Tucker's. And I
would have put her in another room, as far away from
me as I could get her, but the ranch manager wasn't
very accommodating."

She bit her lower lip. "Is that right?"

"Extremely right. In fact, she was mean and rude, and jumped to conclusions. Wrong conclusions." He took her hand. "Callie, I had just been trying to get into *your* bed. How could you think I would—"

"I don't know." She shoved her fingers through her hair. "You drive me crazy."

"Ditto. But no matter what you think of me, say that deep down you know that. I wouldn't sleep with another woman, not when I want you."

She stared at him. "You're telling me the truth."

"Hell, yeah, I'm telling you the truth."

He saw acceptance of that truth dawn in her eyes. "I'm sorry," she whispered. "I know you better than that."

"That's all right, I just figured out how you can repay me." He tugged her close and kissed her. He had no idea why exactly, other than he'd felt like an outsider for so long, and that hadn't changed much, but she was the one person out here who seemed to let him be whatever he needed to be, idiot or not.

She hesitated, her hands in the air, hovering above his shoulders. He lifted his face a fraction, staring into her eyes, and then changing the angle of his head, kissed her again. He'd meant only for a quick, hot connection but God, the taste and feel of her filled his head. He'd missed her so much, and hadn't even realized it until now. In fact, he was so blown over by the realization, he nearly pulled back again, but she startled him by pressing closer and touching her tongue to his.

It made no sense, but the odd sense of loneliness he'd experienced since he'd been there dissipated. It always did when he was with her. Maybe that was because of all the blood draining from his head for parts further south, but he had enough sense left to know it was more than physical. With a low, wordless murmur of need, he slid his hand down her slim back, fingers spread wide to touch all of her that he could, then fisted his fingers in the material of her shirt, anchoring her to him.

When he finally pulled back, she blinked up at him, looking a little surprised that they were still on the steps out in broad daylight. She looked over at Eddie and Tucker still removing saddles and brushing down horses, neither of them paying them any attention. "What was that?" she whispered.

"I was trying to get you to look at me like you're looking at me right now."

"Which is how, exactly?"

He stared into her eyes, absorbing the heat, the reluctant affection. "Like I'm not such a bad guy. Like maybe you missed me, too. Like maybe you even want me half as much as I want you."

"Those things are all true," she admitted. "But it doesn't mean I have to like it. Jake, you don't even want to be here."

"Right now I do." To avoid argument, he kissed her again. Her mouth was open a little, in surprise no doubt, and he took full advantage of that, sweeping his tongue in, dancing it to hers.

An "mmmm" rumbled in her throat, and when they came up for air this time, her eyes were slumberous and just a bit wary. "What are we doing?"

"I haven't a clue. But I'm game. Say you are, too."

"For that spring fling?"

Was she offering? Before he could ask, Stone came out of the barn, and joined Eddie and Tucker in removing saddles.

"He's back," Jake said, glad to see him.

"He's back. I need to go help."

"Yeah, in a second." He turned her chin back to face him. Her lips were still wet and he wanted to kiss her again. "Nothing out of the ordinary happened while we were gone?"

"Other than I relaxed for the first time in nearly a month?"

"Because I was out of here?"

She smiled, touched her nose, then moved down the steps. Crossing the driveway, she entered the corral and walked up to a dark mare whose name he couldn't remember. He followed, knowing enough of the routine now to automatically help. Coming back after a trip, there was always a lot to do. Eyeing the mare with caution, he moved around it to stand next to Callie, then reached for the saddle.

She brushed him away. "Too heavy for you."

"I can take them off, I just can't put them on." He stepped in front of her and this time she let him. "You're getting so much better," she said, and he heard the rest of the unspoken sentence.

You'll be leaving soon.

"How was camping?" she asked. "Tucker told me you complained about everything."

So she didn't want to talk about his leaving. That made two of them, since he'd have to face the fact that when he left, he had nothing to go back to. "I did *not* complain about everything."

She lifted a brow.

"Okay, I might have said we should have thicker pads to sleep on, ones that actually work. For the guests' comfort."

"How are you and Tucker doing?"

"Well, there was no blood shed."

She rolled her eyes and pulled a few pink phone messages out of her pocket, slapping them in his hand. "Your cell phone wasn't working out there. You got some calls at the house."

The first was from his real estate agent. *Got a preliminary report for you on selling. Call me when you're ready and we'll set it in gear.*

Callie watched him read it, then without waiting for him to look at the two other messages, picked up the saddle and walked away.

Jake finished his phone call and sat back in Callie's office chair. His lawyer had been message number two. Billy's mother was looking for them to offer her some sort of settlement, a huge monetary one, which they wouldn't do. He couldn't.

And even though he knew Joe would already know, Jake picked the phone back up and returned his third message.

"Sucks," Joe said.

"Yeah."

"You'll beat it."

Maybe. But it was going to break him first.

"Just got back from an industrial fire in Del Mar," Joe said. "Three warehouses down to the ground, no fatalities. They could have used you there today. Half the station's out with the flu. How's the shoulder?"

Jake rolled first his left shoulder—no problem—and then his right. Problem. He could toss down a saddle, he could ride for days, but he had no lifting strength and little finesse or arm control. "Much better," he lied.

"Define better."

Well, he didn't want to cry at every little movement. "Good enough to come back." At least in his dreams.

"Thank God. I thought maybe you were enjoying yourself a little too much out there."

Jake pictured Callie's smile, could still taste it on his lips. He *was* enjoying himself too much. In fact, he was just a little afraid of how much.

"Jake? Call your doctor, get approval. I know it's only been two months since surgery, but if you're better, you're better, right?"

There was no chance in hell he could fool his doctor. But the thought of staying here, of never going back, of never getting into his gear and back in his life made his heart kick painfully. "I won't be shimmying up any ladders or hanging off any ledges," he admitted. "But there's other things I could do."

"Jake—"

"I could train." He'd never really thought about it before, never had to. But he had to get out of here before he fell for that cowgirl Joe had asked about. Before he convinced himself his life was over if he couldn't get back to work. And actually, now that the impromptu idea had blossomed, why not train? If he couldn't actually fight fires, why not teach others to do it?

"Yeah, training. That could work. There's an entire new class of recruits coming through in three weeks, and you're qualified for it. Certainly no doctor could object to a little teaching, right? Are you really up for it?"

Jake tried rolling his shoulder again, and felt the color drain from his face. "Three weeks, I'll be good as gold." He disconnected, then looked out the window into the day that had glorious written all over it. Wide blue sky with only the occasional white puff of cloud.

Rocky, jagged mountains in the distance, standing as tall and proud as the people here at the Blue Flame. Callie was still out there working with the guys, giving her usual one hundred and ten percent, the way she always did, the way he suspected she always would, in every single aspect of her life.

A life he didn't belong in anymore than Cici did. Granted, he'd miss the people; he'd miss Callie. More than he wanted to. But it was time to concentrate on his own life, not his father's and what he'd left behind.

He thought about that as he fingered the message from the real estate agent. He returned her call. "I'm ready."

16

The sisters left, and their next group came in, eight college students on spring break. Callie looked at the young guys, all of whom had lugged in their own stash of beer, and shook her head. Nowhere in their brochure or on their website did it promote college break, wild parties, or anything to remotely attract such a crowd. But they'd paid good money to work the ranch for three days, and here they were.

They wanted to take an overnight trip into the hills to see ancient Indian grounds and anything else spooky, so that's what the Blue Flame would provide.

She was going to lead them, with Tucker and Eddie. She didn't often go out on the overnights, preferring to stay with the ranch and watch over the animals and land, but she had a very good reason for replacing Stone on this trip.

He'd just taken three days of personal leave to go home to his father, an alcoholic who'd been dry ten years now. Stone wanted to know how his father had given up drinking. Callie had spent some time with Stone since he'd come back. He appeared to have a handle on things, but she knew appearances could be deceiving, and she couldn't in good conscience send him out into the wilderness for two days with a bunch of party-hardy guests his own age. So now she stood in the barn with Stone, delicately trying to get around this without hurting his feelings. "I was thinking you could stay here," she said casually. "And I'll take this one. I haven't been out in a long time."

He looked at her doubtfully. "You want to go out with a bunch of drunk college punks?"

"They're not drunk."

"Not yet, but it's only six in the morning."

"We'll go around the high canyons instead of through them." She smiled. "They'll definitely be drinking by then, and I don't want to lose anyone over the edge."

He shook his head and took her hand. "I can handle this, Cal."

"Of course you can. I just need to get outside, that's all."

"We both know why you're offering, and it's not for you to get outside."

"Does it really matter, Stone?"

He stared at her hand in his for a long moment. She expected an argument. Instead he sighed and pulled her close in a tight hug.

She hugged him back, and closed her eyes. God, she loved these guys, every last one of them. If Jake sold to someone who didn't want to keep them all on—

Footsteps and voices sounded just outside, and Stone pulled back to look into her eyes. "Thank you," he whispered, and kissed her, right on the mouth. He grinned just as Eddie and Tucker entered the barn. "And that's how you revive the cow if she stops breathing."

Eddie and Tucker stood there gaping. "Why are you kissing Cal?" Eddie demanded.

Stone smiled at Callie. "Because she's pretty damn cool."

"Oh." Eddie blinked. "Well, I want to kiss her, too."

Tucker shoved him, then came closer. "What's going on?"

Stone looked at Callie, his heart in his eyes. He didn't want them to know, and she wouldn't be the one to tell them. "He was showing me cow resuscitation techniques," she said primly. "And he'll be happy to show either of you, as well. But hurry, because we've got to get these college studs out on the trail if we want to get there before dark."

Tucker stared at her for a long moment, then at Stone, but he didn't say another word while they saddled up the horses. A little bit later, Jake met them outside, his hands shoved in his jeans pockets. "You're going?" he asked, reaching out to help her lift a saddle.

"Don't." She shouldered him away. "You'll hurt yourself."

He pulled back with the irritated look of a man used to taking over, used to being in charge, a man who kept forgetting he no longer could do that. "The weather is going to turn bad."

She glanced at the admittedly cloudy sky and shrugged. "That's part of the life out here."

"No, I mean really bad."

She strapped on the saddle. "How do you know?"

"My ribs hurt."

Her fingers went still on the horse. "I didn't know you'd hurt your ribs in your fall."

"Not that fall. I broke four of them in another fire, several years ago."

"Rescuing someone?"

"A staircase gave way while I was trying to get to a woman on the floor beneath me."

"What happened to her?"

"I got her out."

"With four broken ribs?"

"And a gash on my head." He put his finger on the inch long scar above his left eye. "There's a storm coming, and it's going to be a wet one. Trust me."

"We can't cancel, the guys are too excited. And anyway, a little rain never bothered me."

"Thought you'd say that." He squinted at the sky, then sighed grimly. "I'm coming, too."

"Fond of getting rained on, are you?"

"No. I'm fond of you." And upon delivering that shocking statement, he walked away, calling out to Eddie to say they needed one more horse.

Fine. Who was she to argue with the man? But she stepped close to Sierra and hugged her, needing the contact. "He's fond of me, damn it."

Tucker had just finished packing up the horses when he saw Amy walking toward him with a bag in her arms. Her dark hair glinted in the sun. She wasn't smiling, but he found himself wanting to at just the sight of her.

He'd never had much of a problem in the female department, but this woman was different, and though extremely resistant, he couldn't seem to help himself. He wanted to know her more.

"Here's the last bag. I added some popcorn for the bonfire tonight," she said.

"Thanks." He took the bag, touching her fingers with his as he did. He took it as a good sign when she didn't jerk away or slam him to the ground. "I've got all your directions." He patted his pocket. "You didn't ask me to make the carrots pretty or anything, right?"

"Not this time. But you do have to be careful with the chili—"

"I can handle it." Probably. "Trust me."

She just looked at him, and it was the oddest thing, but just looking right back at her somehow broke his heart. There was just something about her, something about her eyes, her tough attitude and soft center. He really did want to know her, and he had to say, it was unusual not to have that feeling returned.

She wore her black jeans and boots again. When she'd first come to the ranch, he'd figured they were all she owned, since she'd had only a small duffel bag. But she'd had a few paychecks now, and could have bought herself something else if she'd wanted. Maybe she was saving for a rainy day.

She leaned in past him and inspected the way he'd packed everything. Her hair fell forward, revealing the sweet spot on the back of her neck. She had a small tattoo of the sun there, and he winced as he reached out and touched it.

She jerked as if she'd been shot, and whipped around.

"Sorry." He lifted his hand in the air. "I was just thinking how that must have hurt on such a tender spot."

She put her hand to the back of her neck. "It was a long time ago."

"It's pretty. It is," he said when she arched a brow. "You are."

Now she let out one bark of a laugh and turned to leave.

He moved in front of her. "So how long ago could it have been? You're only . . . what, eighteen?"

"Six years."

"Jesus." He whistled softly. "What kind of a mother let her daughter get a tattoo at twelve?"

"The dead kind."

Ah, man. He was an idiot. An idiot with a big old boot in his mouth.

She started adjusting the pack on the horse, even though they both knew he'd done a fine job. "Don't say you're sorry," she said when he opened his mouth. "I was just a baby when she died. I never knew her."

"Who raised you?"

"My dad." She shrugged and shifted some of the food around. "Sort of."

He put a hand over hers. "Sort of?"

"He wasn't around all that much."

"And now?"

"And now . . . he's still not around that much." She pulled her hand from his and put the horse between them. "He's a trucker."

An angry one, Tucker guessed, and very carefully he stepped around the horse and closer to Amy. "It must have been rough for you without a mom."

"Stop it." She moved back a step, her breathing coming out a little too quick. "I don't want your pity."

"It's not pity I'm feeling."

She searched his expression with a scowl, and he purposely put an easy smile on his face when what he really wanted to do was touch her. Hug her. But she was on the edge of panic over revealing too much, over his nearness, pick one. "Going to miss me while I'm gone?"

She gaped at him as if he were crazy.

He offered her a hopeful smile.

She shook her head, but if he wasn't mistaken, suddenly there was a small little sparkle of good humor lurking in her dark eyes.

"I'm not that bad of a guy, Amy. Maybe you could even give me a try sometime."

She looked at him for a long, long moment. "Maybe." And with that shocking word, she turned and walked away, leaving him staring after her.

"See you when I get back!" he called out.

Without looking back, she lifted a hand as if to say *yeah, yeah, whatever*, but still, a hopeful grin split his face.

They rode all day. The Dragoons were a maze of yawning crevices, abrupt precipices, and granite spires. Boulders the size of the ranch's barn were balanced with smaller rocks, sprinkled across steep hillsides from which deer, raptors, snakes, and coyotes made their home. On the valley floor lay wheaten grasslands, dotted with bush and huge oaks wide enough to conceal whole packs of coyotes.

Above them the skies churned and burned, going from blue to slate, and then nearly black, but not a drop fell. If it had started to rain, Callie might have been able to turn them back, but the guys were into it, and she had to admit, it felt good to ride.

By noon, seven of the eight Washington State students had hit on her.

She took each come-on in the same manner, that is, with great amusement. Smithy was the most aggressive one, the twenty-one-year-old basketball star and all-around God's gift to women—just ask him. He didn't like being turned down, and afterward, when

Callie had said no to him—twice—he made a point of riding the fastest and being the most outrageous. He pretty much toed the line on everything they did, leaving her with the urge to throttle him.

"There's one in every group," Eddie said in disgust after lunch, when Smithy had tried jumping his horse, Tongue, over a small creek. Tongue—named for his love of licking everything—ran along with Smithy as asked, until his hooves got wet. Then he stopped so short that Smithy sailed over the top of him, landing in the water.

He'd been furious, made all the madder when his buddies howled with laughter. But his fury hadn't matched Callie's. With steam coming out her ears, she'd started forward but Eddie and Tucker had each put a hand on either of her shoulders, holding her back until she calmed down. When she'd swallowed most of her anger, she had a long talk with Smithy, and only after threatening to send him back with Eddie, did he apologize and promise to be good.

"You always have this problem?" Jake asked after they'd continued on the trail.

"Which? Leading idiots, or dealing with the ridiculous come-ons?"

"The come-ons, mostly."

"No," she admitted. "Never."

"Please."

"Seriously, I don't. It's not that often we get a group of single males like this." She shot him a wry glance. "They usually bring their own women."

He frowned. "Funny."

"I thought so."

"So tell me why I feel like smashing some heads."

She studied the darkening sky. Jake had been right,

they were in for a doozy of a storm. "They're just stupid kids."

"They're not much younger than you, and I can't see you ever acting like this."

"You know me well enough to make a statement like that?"

"Yes," he said boldly. "Just like you know me. Whether we like it or not."

They rode in silence for a while, along the valley floor, surrounded on either side by towering canyon walls and wild, spinning clouds. They began to hear thunder in the distance, but still no rain. "I didn't want to know you," she finally said. "That way, when you left, I wouldn't care."

"Every day I think about leaving."

"You can't wait to go."

He looked at her. "Most of the time. But once in a while like now . . . I don't want to ever go."

She didn't know what to make of that, so she said nothing. They descended down to the valley floor, moving along on the dry river bed.

Ahead of her now, Jake handled his horse well. He'd gotten quite proficient for a man who'd rather be moving of his own accord. He held his reins with authority, his body at ease in the saddle. He was definitely a chameleon, whatever he thought of himself, fitting into any different arena, no matter how foreign.

Eventually the last of the eight students, the only one who hadn't yet hit on her, fell in line beside her.

"Problem?" she asked him.

"Oh no." Wes grinned the grin of the wild and crazy youth. "This is great."

"Uh-huh." She lifted a brow. "Want to just cut to the chase?"

"Which is?"

"You have to come on to me. The others expect it. I
know it, and you know it. You also know there's not a
snowball's chance in hell you're getting anything the
others didn't. So whatever line you've come up with,
how about you just save it for another woman?"

"But now see, that's the problem. There are no other
women out here."

"But you had to know there wouldn't be. You guys
came out here for fun, then you saw me and thought
I'd be an easy mark, so—"

"None of us thought that," he rushed to assure her.
"We just had to try."

"And it's out of your system now, right? Good," she
said when he nodded. "Then go have the fun you came
for." She sighed in relief when he rode off, but the relief
was short-lived when a resounding crack of thunder
split the air above them, accompanied only a few seconds later by a blinding flash of lightning.

One big fat rain drop landed on Callie's nose. It was
only the very beginning, she thought, and glanced back
at Eddie who was looking straight up into the sky.

"Uh-oh," he said as the clouds slammed into each
other violently, covering every inch of visible sky.

Even as she watched, they tumbled and churned,
lowering until she felt as if she could reach up and
touch them. "Okay, listen up, everyone! We've had a
great time today—"

"Ah, man, you're going to make us head back," one
of the guys groaned.

"Up to you. But the rain is coming. Either way, we
have to get back off the valley floor to the canyons
above in case of flash flooding. But if we leave now, we
could gallop a good part of the way and make it to the

ranch in two hours tops. Plenty of time to get a roaring
fire going inside and sleep in warm beds."

"So we make the choice between warm"—Wes
looked around them even as the sky opened up, as another resonating shuddering boom of thunder vibrated
the ground beneath their feet, followed immediately by
a blinding flash of lightning—"or wet and wild.
Hmm . . ." Eyes lit with adventure, he looked at his
friends.

"Wet and wild," voted all the other guys, with
whooping and cheers.

Eddie looked at Jake, who shook his head. Smithy
pointed northeast to a rock formation not too far off,
beyond the dry riverbed they stood in. "Looks like a
naked chick. We need a picture of us beneath it."

"All right," Callie said. "But after we get there and
take the picture, we go up."

They rode on toward the rock formation, Callie
holding her breath, knowing they had to still go down
the valley a half mile or so before catching the trail to
the higher elevation, where they'd be safe from a flood.

Halfway to the rocks, a series of lightning strikes hit
close and the world went bright white. The rain turned
to buckets of water, and within seconds, they were all
drenched. This was more rain than even she'd counted
on. In fact, it was more than she'd seen come down in
years. They'd had a dry spring until now, and the
parched, cracked earth couldn't absorb it fast enough.

The flood she worried about became an all too real
possibility, and they still were in the narrow valley between nothing but sharp, rocky cliffs. She had to yell to
be heard. "We're sitting ducks in this dry river bed!"
Which was already beginning to fill. "We make a run

for the trail to the top, then head back, taking the high route this time. It'll take longer, but we'll be safer."

The guys started to moan and groan but Jake moved forward on his horse, until he was at Callie's side. "She said we go back. We go back."

"Fine!" Smithy yelled. "Just as soon as I get my picture." He pointed to the rocks still to their north, barely visible now in the driving rain. Without waiting for anyone else, he kicked Tongue, who leapt into a canter.

"Goddammit." Callie turned her horse around. Shielding her eyes so she could see through the pouring rain, she sought out Eddie, Tucker, and Jake. "Take the guys and head to the trail. I'll go after Smithy. We'll be right behind you."

"I'm coming with you," Jake said grimly.

"It's going to flash flood," she said urgently. "Just get the guys back—"

"Eddie and I can take these guys back." Tucker nodded to the suddenly humble group of guys, all looking wet, bedraggled, and extremely young. "Capturing Smithy might take both of you." He exchanged a long look with Jake, who nodded. "*Go!*"

Callie nodded curtly and urged Sierra ahead into a gallop, knowing Eddie and Tucker would get the guys up the canyon walls, then head back to the ranch. Jake was right at her side as they rode after Smithy. They could just see him up ahead. There, at the next bolt of thunder, Tongue reared up.

Callie gasped, fear becoming one big ball in her belly, but Smithy managed to hang on to the now terrified horse and keep going. "*Smithy!*" she yelled, her voice lost in the drumming rain. Seconds later, she lost sight of him entirely. "Jake! Do you see him?"

"We're catching him."

Jake wasn't wearing a hat, so she had no idea how he could see anything. His hair was plastered to his head and water streamed down his face. But believing in him, she kept riding in the same direction.

Sierra jerked at the next crack of thunder, and the immediate flash of lightning, but stayed in control. Thankfully Molly did the same for Jake. Callie had seen some spring storms before but never one as fast and violent as this one. She hoped to God no one got struck by lightning, and even as she hoped it, the sky lit up again, a series of bolts that seemed to go on forever. She thought she saw Smithy and Tongue again, only several hundred feet away now. He'd nearly made it to the other side of the valley floor, where he'd be safe enough if he held still. She nearly sagged in relief but then it backed up in her throat.

Because from the dry riverbed, the path they'd just ridden the past few hours, came a huge, thundering roar, and Callie knew what that meant. Water, tons of it, falling from the sky, from the sharp precipices, onto the dry riverbed, rushing at them.

And when it hit, they'd be carried downriver with it.

17

"Don't look!" Jake yelled at her as the wall of water rushed at them. "Just keep going straight across, not toward Smithy! *Hurry*, Callie!"

"But Smithy—"

"Go, goddammit!"

The rain blinded her, and the ground rumbled, not from the thunder now, but the rushing, tumbling flash flood coming their way.

Ahead of her Smithy stopped Tongue and turned around, squinting into the pouring rain. Seeing her, he waved.

"No!" she shouted. "Keep going, keep going!" She waved at him, tried to warn him to get completely across the riverbed.

He craned his neck, saw the rushing flood. He opened his mouth in surprise, and then leapt off his horse.

"No!" Jake yelled just as Tongue, freed now, took off, instinctively galloping north toward the rocks on the far side.

Jake slid down off his horse, too, and thrust the reins up to Callie. "Go to Tongue. Go!" Then he started running toward Smithy.

Callie gripped both horses' reins and urged them to move. She kept glancing back, but the rain blocked her vision. When she reached the rocks safely, she jumped off Sierra, grabbed Tongue's reins as well, and whipped around, just as the riverbed flooded. Suddenly there was three or four feet of dirty, tumbling river running past her.

"Jake!" Callie searched madly for a sign of him, but saw nothing. She stumbled to the edge of the flowing water. A crack of thunder rocked her back a step.

And then, in the next flash of lightning, she saw them, Jake staggering through the chest-deep water toward her, dragging Smithy along with him. Whirling around, she ran to a tree and tied up the frightened horses, then raced back to the water's edge. This time she plunged in, sucking in a breath as the cold water hit her like a punch in the chest.

The current nearly dragged her off.

"No. Callie, no!" Jake jerked his head toward shore. "Go back!"

Doing that, waiting, watching him struggle to fight the current and hold on to a flailing Smithy nearly killed her, but the last thing Jake needed was to have to rescue her, too. So she stood her ground for what seemed like an eternity before he got close enough that she could plunge in and help. She grabbed Smithy's other side, and together the three of them stumbled out of the water, plopping down to the muddy ground.

The rain still came down, and Callie shoved her hair out of her eyes to see. Then she did the same for Smithy, looking down into his face. "What's hurt?"

"Nothing. Just . . . can't . . . swim," gasped Smithy.

Jake had dropped to his knees, his chest rising and

falling with each harsh breath. "Then you should stay the hell away from water. Jesus, you weigh a ton."

"Yeah." Smithy sat up, looking shaken. "Sorry about that."

Callie couldn't believe it. "You put us all in danger with that stupid stunt." She sagged back on her heels and stared at him. "I don't even have words for you." She crawled over to Jake and put her hands on his arms, blinking through the rain to see his face, which, as she'd imagined, was full of pain. "Oh, Jake. Tell me what to do."

He shook his head. She'd have sworn he was sweating, though the air was cold, the water even colder, and they were all soaked to the bone. "Can you ride?"

"Yeah." He staggered to his feet with her help while Smithy just sat on the ground still looking stunned. "Help me," she hissed at him.

But once Jake was on his feet, he shrugged them both off. "I'm fine." He strode to the horses, and with a scathing look at Smithy, Callie followed him. Tongue was terrified, and it took her a moment to calm him down enough so Smithy could mount.

Callie had a wool blanket in her backpack, which she got out. Jake mounted his horse before she could help him and then refused the blanket. Stupid male pride, she thought. Smithy apparently had no pride and quickly wrapped himself in the blanket without asking if there was another one for her.

Disgusted, she mounted Sierra. All the horses were snorting and puffing, and stomping uneasily. She didn't blame them. She took one good long look at Jake through the curtain of rain but his face was a mask of stone. Good enough, she thought. She turned to look at

Smithy, who looked miserable, huddling in his blanket as the rain pelted him. *Not good enough.*

"Careful," Jake said to him. "It's going to be slippery going."

"And rocky," she added. "You'll stay in the middle and do as you're told."

"Yes," Smithy said meekly. "Uh, you don't by any chance have a beer— Or not," he muttered when she glared at him.

They rode back with the wind and slashing, freezing rain beating them up. Halfway there, darkness fell, an utterly complete blackness relieved only by the rapid flashes of lightning that seemed to be right over the top of them. Though she could ride back blind-folded, and so could the horses, Callie pulled out her flashlight so she could keep checking on Jake and Smithy.

"I'm fine," Jake told her every time she blinded him with the light, and she figured he wouldn't sound so irritated if he wasn't fine, so that eased her worry a bit.

"I guess the guys are all warm and dry by the fireplace," Smithy muttered at one point.

"No doubt," she said. "Probably eating a hot meal, too."

He looked so sad at this news, she almost felt sorry for him, until she once again glanced at Jake. No matter what he said, his jaw was tight with pain, his body tense. Smithy's stupidity had cost him the most. He could have dislocated his shoulder, or been swept downstream. . . . People died out here every year being as stupid as Smithy had been today.

"I'm sorry," he said, making her realize she'd spoken aloud, and this time, she could tell he meant it.

When they got out of the canyons, they no longer had to ride so closely together. Jake nudged his way close to Callie, letting Smithy get a little ahead. "You okay?" he asked quietly.

"I was just going to ask you the same thing. You holding up?"

"I'm good."

She studied his face but it was dark, and he was giving nothing away. "Close call, huh?"

He let out an agreeing grunt that said she didn't know the half of it.

"You saved him, Jake." She voiced the fear she'd been dwelling on. "What if you weren't used to such heroics, or if you couldn't swim? Or if you hadn't been so quick? I don't know if I could have done what you did."

He reached out and touched her wet face. "You could have. You would have."

She stared through the dark at him. Today had created a bond she hadn't counted on, and deepened the one they had, whether she liked it or not. "You're really not hurting?"

"Actually, yeah. I am."

Her heart stopped. "Want to stop so I can massage it?"

His teeth flashed. "Wouldn't you like to know where I'm hurting first?"

That should have pissed her off. Instead, she laughed. "You know what? Maybe I don't."

Again the flashing teeth, and then he shifted in his saddle. "Christ, how do you do this day in and day out? My parts are so chafed they're going to fall right off."

Unbelievably, she laughed again, and when Smithy shot her a hurt look, apparently thinking she was laughing at him, she only laughed harder. "I'm sorry," she gasped.

"Stress," Jake said to Smithy, who nodded seriously.

Callie just shook her head, the laughter having relieved much of it. Jake's presence did that, too, she realized. Finally, they came out of the hills, crossed the plain, and saw the lights of the ranch wavering through the night. The three of them stopped side by side to look at it together. "I've never seen a more welcome sight," she said.

Jake didn't say anything, and she remembered—it wasn't a welcome sight to him, and what had happened today had in all likelihood just cemented that for him.

Eddie and Tucker were waiting for them in the barn and took care of their gear and horses. Stone escorted the exhausted Smithy inside and saw to it that he got a hot shower and food.

"You, too," Tucker told Jake and Callie. "We'll finish up in here. Go." He gestured with his chin to the open barn door. The light spilled out into the night, highlighting the glittery silver curtain of rain that still came down.

Jake didn't argue. He took Callie to her cabin. She opened her door, then put her hand on his chest. For a moment his heart leapt, thinking she would invite him in to take care of him—not that he needed it, but a little fawning would cheer him up considerably. She blocked his way, however. "Go get warm," she said, then shut her door.

He stood staring at it for a moment, then sighed.

In his cabin, he took a long, hot shower, letting the steaming water beat off his various aches and bruises.

Damn, working the land and playing host to a variety of new people, some smart, some not, week in and week out was infinitely more exhausting then he could have possibly imagined.

He wasn't sure when it had sunk in—possibly when Smithy had nearly drowned them both—but this ranch was more demanding than any job he'd ever had. In fact, this was more than a job, it was a way of life.

He'd have sworn he had the most demanding, unpredictable, difficult job he could think of, but a month out here, and he had to admit he'd been wrong.

He'd always assumed if he ended up here because he couldn't work, that would make him a loser, but the only thing that made him a true loser had been assuming that the ranch's way of life was somehow less than his.

The hot water finally dispelled his bone-deep chill and he got out of the shower. He took a good long look at the narrow, hard cot waiting for him as he pulled on warm, dry clothes. Outside the storm raged. He figured only an idiot would go back out. He stepped into the pouring rain anyway and went to Callie's cabin. He could tell himself she'd been pale and shivering, and he wanted to see that she'd gotten warm and dry, but that was bullshit. He didn't want to be alone.

She didn't answer his knock, and when he opened her door, no one was there. "Damn it, Callie." He headed toward the big house, getting wet and cold—again—crossing the grass because it was faster. Through the rain, Goose came running at him, honking her alarm and annoyance, but he just bared his teeth.

She stopped so short she nearly tipped onto her back, then gave a confused little flutter of her wings, having apparently no experience with being challenged.

He walked right past her and let himself in the big house. The college guys were all in the huge living room, in front of the fireplace, eating and drinking as if they didn't have a care. Smithy sat in the middle of them all, completely dry and recovered. He waved.

Jake would have liked to wring his neck, but he refrained and headed down the hallway, making Amy squeak in surprise when he barged into the kitchen. She stood at the stove stirring something with a delicious scent wafting from it that made his mouth water.

Tucker sat on the counter across from Amy, eating out of a bowl. "Hey."

"Hey. Have you seen Callie?"

Amy shook her head.

Tucker looked him over. "You okay?"

Clearly Jake was more tired than he'd thought because that had sounded like real concern in his brother's voice. "I'm fine. Where do you think Callie is?"

"Hopefully in her cabin asleep," Tucker said, and Jake nodded, not wanting to set off an alarm, because he intended to find her and put her in bed himself.

He looked in the weight room, thinking maybe Macy had come to give her a massage, but Macy was working on one of the college guys. Jake left, wondering where the hell Callie had gone, when he saw the light coming from beneath her office door. He opened it without knocking, took one look at her sitting behind her desk, and shook his head. "You are shitting me."

"I'm just—"

"I don't care what you're just." He came around her desk, pulled her to her feet. She'd lost her hat. Her long, red hair had partially dried in loose curls down past her shoulders. She'd taken off her wet sweatshirt and shoes, but was still in her jeans and blouse, which clung to her in a way he might have enjoyed, if he hadn't been so pissed. "So you took care of everyone but yourself?"

"I was just checking the petty cash, which I'd locked in a different drawer this time."

"Let's go." He tugged on her hand.

"Don't you care if it's all there?"

"I'll care tomorrow. Tonight, it's you. You're wet, tired, and still shaking, damn it." He felt the tremor in her chilled limbs. Shrugging out of his jacket, he put it around her, waited until she shoved her feet back into her boots and led her out of the office and out of the big house.

It was still raining, coming down in long shiny rivers, as if Mother Nature was making up for lost time. And the noise. It was unbelievable how loud the slapping of the water on the parched earth sounded. He figured he'd seen enough rain today to last him a lifetime. "I'm going to kill Goose if she— Damn it."

Once again Goose came running through the rain honking at them.

"Go night-night, Goose," Callie said, and unbelievably, the goose walked away.

Jake gaped at her, rain running into his eyes. "How do you do that?"

"I don't threaten to eat her for Thanksgiving." She kept moving, her boots striking the puddles on the rain soaked ground.

"I think of her as my father's spirit. Yelling at me."

"Ever think maybe she's just squawking at you, wondering what took you so long to get here?"

He stared at Goose's butt waddling away. "No," he muttered. "I don't." *But now he would.*

When they got to her cabin, she opened the door, and would have walked in alone if he hadn't kept his hand on her arm.

"I can take it from here," she said through her chattering teeth and blue lips.

"Uh-huh." He shut the door behind the both of them, then slipped his arms around her and drew her into him. "Humor me," he whispered.

"I don't need help."

"We've already established that. This is for me, not you."

She shivered again, but put her hands over his, stopping him from removing her blouse.

"I want you to take a hot shower and warm up." He tunneled his fingers through her hair, clamping her face very gently between his palms. "Go." When she didn't move, he shifted closer. "You know what? Never mind. I'm here now, I'll just warm you up myself."

And he covered his mouth with hers.

18

"Jake."

With a sigh, he pulled back and stroked a long wet curl out of Callie's face.

"I'm not quite as emotionally challenged as you," she whispered. "I can't separate sex and emotion like you can."

"Hey, give a guy a handicap." His finger rimmed over her ear now, and her breathing went shallow. Quite a satisfying reaction. "I'm just a little slow, but I'm catching on."

"What does that mean?"

"It means that even I, an emotionally challenged male, can figure out this isn't just sex. Not between us."

She stared at him, eyes wide.

"Yeah. Terrifying, I know." Jake drew her hands down to her sides, then slipped his jacket off her shoulders. It fell to the floor. "Worse than running into a burning building, I'll tell you that."

Thunder rolled. In the ensuing flash of lightning, her eyes were luminous. He knew she was afraid of getting too attached. Well, damn it, he was already attached, far more than he wanted to be, so she should suffer the same as he. He dropped to his knees and tugged at a foot until she lifted it. He slipped off one boot, and then the other, tossing both over his shoulder.

"We can't do this, Jake."

"Why not?" His fingers went to the button on her jeans. Pop. The rasp of her zipper came next. In the open wedge of the denim he saw sheer black lace and groaned.

"For a million reasons."

"Name one."

"Okay." She hesitated. "I had you already, and I still want you."

"I want you, too." He ran a finger over the lace. "I want you a lot."

"Yes, but you're . . ." She seemed to have trouble speaking, so he surged back up to his feet, took her hand, and directed her into her bathroom. There he flicked on the shower and waited for it to start steaming. Turning to her, he put his hands on the buttons of her blouse. She covered his fingers with her own shaking ones. "You're bigger than life, Jake. You're wild and adventurous, and everything I'm not."

"Are you kidding me?" He had to laugh at that. "I've been here, what, a month now? Every single day you're either racing across the rough ground on the back of a twelve hundred pound fickle animal, or you're shimmying up the hay barn on a rickety ladder, or you're taking a bunch of stupid kids out into the wilderness. Jesus, Callie. Are you really going to try to tell me your life out here isn't as wild and adventurous as it gets?"

"It's real," she said simply.

"And what, mine isn't?"

"Your life as a firefighter is real, intensely so. And dangerous, and admirable, too. You're a hero."

"But? Because I sure as hell hear a big *but* at the end of that sentence."

"But when you're not working, your life is city. It's women. It's just having a good time in between shifts."

"Callie—"

"And if that's not enough, if you need another reason, then fine." She crossed her arms. "You're not my type."

"Well, if that's true, then you'll be left completely unmoved by this." He slid his arms around her wet body and dipped his head.

"Jake—"

"Shh. It's just a kiss." A bigger lie he'd never told. "You're not afraid of a little kiss, are you, Callie?" He settled his mouth against hers. Deep, wet, and instantly hot, he had her clinging to him two seconds in, but actually, the clinging might have been mutual. Pulling back a fraction, he looked down into her surprised, aroused, frustrated face. "If I'm not your type, then why do you melt all over me when I do that?"

She let out a sound, but didn't stop him when he reached down to unbutton her wet shirt. She was breathless, and the pulse at the base of her neck leapt wildly. "Damn, you're soft," he said. "Sexy as hell, too. I can't keep my hands off you, Callie."

Another sound came from deep in her throat, and eyes closed, she slid her fingers into his hair and held on.

Enjoying that, he dragged more open-mouthed kisses down her throat as he slid the blouse off her shoulders. "All you ever wear are jeans and work shirts, and all I ever think about is what you have on beneath them." He stroked a finger over the black lace bra that matched her panties. Her nipples pebbled against the lace.

Her hands slid from his hair, fisting on his shirt right above his heart, holding on for what felt like dear life.

"Love it when you do that," he said roughly. "When you make that little sound . . ."

She made it now, breathing heavily over the sound of the driving rain hitting the roof. He loved that, too, that he affected her so strongly, but he wished he didn't have to coax her into these hot embraces, into admitting she felt something for him. "Should I point out here that you clearly *are* enjoying my type?"

"Shut up and kiss me." But she kissed him first, with all she had, while steam rose all around them. Thunder rattled the small bathroom window, and he held this amazing woman and wondered how it would feel when he'd gone home, without her in his life on a daily basis. He looked up at the same time the lightning flashed, looked right into her eyes as she gently touched her mouth to his with a questioning light in her gaze. "You okay?"

He kissed the line furrowed between her brow, then the bridge of her nose, feeling an almost overwhelming sense of tenderness. "Yeah." He wanted to scoop her up, but that was beyond him after dragging Smithy through the raging water, so he took her hand and opened the shower door. "Get in."

She dropped her bra and panties, and stepped in. He watched her silhouette as the scent of the soap she ran over her body teased his nostrils much like her outline was doing. When she turned off the water, he tossed her a towel over the glass. She came out wrapped in it. He took her hand again, led her to her futon couch, not yet opened into her bed.

They sank upon it. Callie tugged at his shirt, and he obliged her, lifting his left arm. "Can't lift my right all the way yet," he whispered.

"Then let me," she whispered back, and rearing up, kissed his right shoulder before carefully, slowly, maneuvering his shirt off without disturbing his shoulder. She stroked a finger over his bare flesh and then kissed the long incision scar before lifting her gaze to his. "I don't want to hurt you."

"You're not." She was only killing him.

She went to her knees, having to straddle him so she didn't fall off the futon, and went to work on the buttons of his Levi's, concentrating hard, the tip of her tongue resting on her upper lip. Finally, she managed to rid him of his rain-spattered clothing. He pulled off her towel, tugged her down over the top of him, and kissed her. Her breasts bore into his chest, the heat between her legs rested on the part of him desperate for a repeat performance of a night from all those weeks ago. Unable to take it anymore, he reared up, and when that didn't hurt, he tumbled her over, tucking her beneath him.

"That's an improvement," she gasped.

"Isn't it?" He settled between her sprawled legs and gently took her face between his hands. "I have several condoms this time."

"Well by all means, get one."

She helped him put it on, by which time he was trembling like a damned baby. He couldn't wait to experience the almost unbearable erotic sensation of her wet flesh tugging on his every time he thrust into her.

She ran her hands up his arms. "I need a time frame on this thing, Jake. A beginning, a middle. An end."

"Well, we've had our beginning." Lowering his

head, he took a nip out of her throat, which caused a satisfying reaction to her pulse. "We'll have our middle tonight, *all* night." He kissed his way over her collar bone, and cupped a breast. She was having trouble breathing again, which sent a surge of possessive pride and heat right through him.

"And the end?"

"It's not tonight," he promised, his thumb making several passes over her nipple while he watched it react to his touch.

She hummed deep in her throat and arched up. "Spell it out for me, Jake."

"All right, but I'm not very good at spelling things out." He kept his hands on her warm, gorgeous body. "I like you. I like you a lot." Her eyes darkened, and he touched his forehead to hers. "And I'm scared shitless it's more than like."

Her fingers sank into his hair. "How much more?"

"I've never wanted another woman like I want you. Never," he said, tracing her mouth with his thumb. "But as for where it's going, or what we'll do with it, I don't know. I'm facing a lawsuit, the possibility of never being able to fight fires—" Horrifying him, his voice cracked, and he shook his head.

"Oh, Jake."

"Look, I have no future to offer you. You can either live with that, or walk away."

Her eyes were huge on his, and wet. "I can't imagine being told I can't do what I love anymore. I'm so sorry—"

"Don't," he said softly when a single tear spilled over. "Don't."

"You have so much to offer," she said fiercely. "No matter what you end up doing. So very much."

"If you really believe that, then of the two options, I hope walking away isn't the one you pick."

"But what about when *you* walk away? When you go back?"

"There's this new-fangled contraption called an airplane." He heard the words come out of his mouth with some surprise. Alien concept, a future with a woman.

"You're not going to want to come back here."

"Maybe you'll come to me."

"Maybe."

"So does that mean you're in?" he whispered.

"No." Callie watched the disappointment flash across his face, then slipped a hand down his belly, wrapping her fingers around him, guiding him to her. "*You're* in."

The bathroom light spilled into the room, the only light in the place. It silhouetted him towering above her, pushing into her slow and deep. Then his wide shoulders were blocking the light, and she could only feel, and she let herself fall into the immense pleasure of his eyes on her, his scent, the weight of his body.

His expression was a tight grimace of intense pleasure; a low, raw sound ripped from within his throat. His hands slid down the backs of her thighs, urging them open even more. All day she'd been cold, a bone deep cold, but as he began to move he vanquished it, until she was hot, burning up, from the inside out.

How could it be like this again, she wondered wildly, so intense, so mind-bogglingly intense? It was as if every moment they'd ever spent had been leading toward this— every word, every look, every touch had all culminated into this unrelenting ball of fire inside that threatened to consume her if she didn't let it out.

She gripped his arms, then gently slid her hands down his damp, hot, sleek back, past his healing scars, feeling his muscles flex as he sank deep inside her again, deep and slow, so very slow, as if he meant to stop time, to do this forever, binding her to him . . .

He rolled his hips to hers. "I can't tell where you end and I begin."

Nothing had ever been like this, like she was going to die if he didn't keep on holding her, thrusting into her. That alone might have terrified her, but she knew by the look on his face that he was every bit as lost in her. He surrendered to it utterly, to her, to them, and she couldn't help but do the same. "Jake—"

"I know. God, I know—" He broke off and kissed her. Their rhythm increased, and she got lost in the heat of his skin, his hard thrusts, and when it was over, when they'd both taken the plunge, neither of them moved for the longest time. Callie thrived on that, on the utter repletion, the closeness. She loved the way he stayed over her, muscles quaking, his breath harsh and choppy, and she held on tight, soaking it all in. Finally he pressed his mouth to her throat, then lifted his head. "Hey."

She smiled. "Hey."

"Good?"

"More than."

He kissed her again, then got up. A terrible sense of déjà vu came over her. She didn't want him to go, not like last time, but she didn't possess the courage to say so, or to stop him from walking away from her again. Too many damn times people had walked away from her. Just for once, she wanted someone to *want* to stay.

He stood by her bed, naked. A beautiful man at total ease with himself.

Holding her breath, she lifted the covers, and this time he slid in, drawing her close. "I wish we had a road map on this," she whispered, and he let out a rough laugh, but drew her even closer.

"Worried we'll get lost?" he asked.

"A little." But the truth was, she already was lost. In him.

Callie woke before dawn to Jake worshipping her body, and as she lay back and let him have his way with her before returning the favor, she dreamily figured she could wake up like this every morning. But eventually they had to get up. Much as she didn't want to, she had to face reality—and being with Jake like this wasn't it.

The rain had moved on, and after breakfast, so did their guests, leaving Callie breathing a sigh of relief as she went about her day. She helped with the morning chores, played with the puppies for a few minutes, surprised and flattered when Tiger actually greeted her with a tail wag. Soon, they'd be giving the puppies to whichever guests wanted to take one, but not Tiger. They were going to keep her.

Another misfit.

When she got hungry, she grabbed a muffin from the kitchen and went into her office. Stone met her there, grim-faced.

"Oh no," she breathed, taking in the shadows beneath his eyes, the tension in his body. "Now what?"

"I need another few days."

"What's the matter?"

"I need to start an AA program, and there isn't one in Three Rocks. I have to go to Tucson."

He was shaking. She got up and pushed him into a

chair. He sank without a fight and drew a trembly sigh. "I thought I could handle the frat boys and their partying no problem, but last night they got especially rowdy, and kept asking me to join them. At midnight I was still pacing my cabin, fighting with myself. I knew if I went—" He shut his mouth and shook his head.

"Stone." She dropped to her knees and hugged him hard. "I'm sorry."

For a moment, he clung. "I went," he whispered. "And woke up on the floor of Homer's stall. I don't remember much."

"Oh, Stone."

"I know it's a bad time to go," he said into her shoulder.

"We'll manage." She sat back on her heels. "Go do what you have to do."

"A few days, that's all. I'll be back."

"Just do what you have to do. We'll be here waiting for you."

Choked up, he nodded and went to the door. "Thanks," he said to the wood. "You're great to work for, and a friend, too. And not a bad kisser."

She laughed and watched him go before letting the worry take over. He didn't remember much from last night, and now she couldn't help but wonder if with him gone, the odd little mysteries would end.

A few minutes later, Tucker came in, followed by Michael who'd come for a morning ride, which he often liked to do. She smiled at them wearily, not quite recovered from Stone's news. "No more guests we have to baby-sit," she told Tucker.

"Deal," he said, watching her carefully. "Now tell me what's wrong."

"Stone's gone for a little while."

Tucker let out a breath. "To get help?"

"Tucker—"

"You can't say." He nodded. "I know."

Michael handed her a cup of coffee and looked over her shoulder as she read over the forms for the incoming group, a bunch of novelists looking for a retreat and a chance to do some fun research.

"At least everyone's ridden before." Tucker joined in on flipping through the forms. "That's good."

"And they're not young, idiot, keg-dwellers," Michael noted. "Tucker filled me in on yesterday's events."

And he'd rushed right out here. Thankfully *after* Jake had left her cabin. She didn't intend to hide anything from anyone, but nor did she want to flaunt a relationship she didn't fully understand herself.

"We have two days before they get here." She drew a deep breath. Stone would be okay, she assured himself. He would.

And so would she. She stood up, rolling her shoulders, stretching a little. She was stiff as a board, and would have liked to attribute that to riding through the storm after Smithy, but she knew the truth. It was from making love all night long with Jake.

"Sore?" Tucker asked, and her gaze flew to his.

He wasn't looking at her, but down at the paperwork in his hands, so she had no idea what was going through his head. "No," she said slowly. "I'm fine."

His eyes met hers then, without judgment or cynism. "Stay that way," he said simply.

"I plan to."

Michael's face was volleying back and forth between them. "What's going on?"

"Besides the usual shit around here? Nothing." But Tucker didn't take his gaze off Callie's.

"Well, the usual shit is enough to give me gray hair," Michael said.

She patted his arm, surprised to find him so tense. Tense for her. The knowledge gentled her voice but she still had to say it. "I'm not going to ever be happy behind a bank desk, Michael. You'd be forced to fire me within a week."

Tucker laughed. "A day."

"Hey," she said, but had to laugh, too.

Michael ignored their amusement. "I know you'd be so much happier if you'd just—"

"No." She slipped her arm around him. "*You'd* be happier. I'm good here. At least for now. You're going to have to face that."

"Yeah." But he didn't look like that would be any time soon.

"Jake's meeting his real estate agent out here today," Tucker said.

Callie looked at him in surprise. "So you and Jake are talking to each other?"

Tucker shrugged. "If you can't beat 'em . . ."

"But he is selling," Michael reminded them both. "Focus on that."

"I wouldn't have to if you'd finagle a loan for me," Callie said.

"Cal . . ." Michael looked tortured. "I can't do it unless you qualify on your own."

"I know. It was only wishful thinking. Don't worry, I'd never ask you to do anything to jeopardize you or Matt."

"He's my business partner and my best friend. I can't just—"

"I thought *I* was your best friend," she said, trying to lighten the mood, but given the look on his face she hadn't succeeded. She smiled and pretended everything was okay. "Don't worry. Maybe Jake'll change his mind."

He stared at her. "Say his name again."

"What? Why?"

"You sighed when you said it, a dreamy kind of sigh."

She felt her face flush. "I did not."

"Oh my God." His mouth fell open as the shock spread across his face. "I thought you were just playing around, flirting with the guy for something new and exciting, but he's the one. The one who makes you tingle."

"Michael—" She let out a laugh that didn't sound so convincing. "Stop it."

"You're passing me over for him, a guy who'll tear your heart out and stomp on your world. Are you already sleeping with him?"

Tucker looked pained. "Jesus, why don't you just get right to the point?"

"*Are you?*"

"Last I checked, that was my business," she said, but then rushed to snag his hand when he would have stormed out. "Michael, please, don't be angry."

"Angry?" He looked down at their conjoined hands. A spasm of hurt crossed his face. "That's not quite it." He shook his head then managed a smile though it didn't reach his eyes. "I've got to get to work."

"Michael—"

"I'm okay, Cal. And you will be, too." But he didn't look at her when he left.

She tried to maintain her composure but it slipped. "Damn."

"He already knew you weren't ever going to be his. He just needs to deal with it," Tucker told her gently.

"Yeah."

"I guess he thought that with Jake selling, he still had a shot."

She sagged to her chair. Somehow, somewhere, she'd lost her anger about Jake selling, but a sorrow filled her, so much so that for a moment she couldn't breathe. "How did this all get so out of control?"

He looked out the window, to where Amy was fussing with the vegetable garden, and shook his head.

"He can't afford the ranch, Tucker," she said quietly.

"I know that. Or we wouldn't be in this position."

"You know what I think?"

"No, but I have a feeling you're going to tell me."

"I think you're starting to like him."

"Yeah? Well, why don't you look in the mirror, boss, because I've got the feeling you are, too."

Callie stood there long after he'd left, trying that on for size. She and Jake . . . no doubt when they were together, they simultaneously combusted, both in bed and out of it. But could they really be more? He belonged hundreds of miles away, in a world so different from hers that she couldn't imagine them meshing, couldn't imagine him wanting them to.

Damn it. Why did it have to be so difficult? She didn't want to yearn and ache like this, but even more than that, she didn't want to yearn and ache like this for him. But not wanting it to be so changed nothing.

Fact was fact, and Tucker was right. She liked Jake. She liked him a hell of a lot.

19

Tucker was in the horse corral working with Moe when Amy drove up in Callie's Jeep and began unloading groceries. Tucker hopped the fence to help her.

"I can handle it," she informed him in that lofty voice he was sure she thought scared people off, when in fact, it made him a little hot.

He scooped up four of the bags. "Sure you can, but why should you when I can help?"

"I'm fine."

He smiled at her. "Yeah, you're extremely fine."

She had four bags in her arms, too, and she just stared at him. "Why do you say such things?"

"Because they're true."

"So you always speak the truth?"

"Always," he said.

She started walking toward the house. He followed her. In the kitchen they set down the bags, and she turned to him. "I'm not like the girls you hang out with at the bars in Three Rocks."

"Those girls are just friends."

She shot him a disgusted look, and he laughed. "They are." He moved close to help her empty out the bags. "We all hang out together, Eddie and Stone, too, and none of us really hook up, if that's what you're thinking." Since he had no idea where to put the things he pulled out of the bag—fresh fruits and vegetables, meats—he just began stacking them all on the counters. "Wish you'd come with us sometime."

"I wouldn't fit in."

"How do you know?"

"I know." She turned away. "I've got stuff to do."

"Come with me tonight."

"I don't date."

"Then we'll go out as friends, with the others."

Her hands stilled. With a can of tomato sauce in each palm, she looked at him. "Not a date?"

"Just fun. A bunch of us. No pressure, no anything. You'll eat, talk, smile . . . hell, you might even forget yourself and laugh."

"I don't know."

"Think about it."

"Maybe. You have to go now."

"Why?"

"Because I can't think when you're in here."

He grinned. "You know, I think that's the nicest thing you've ever said to me." Whistling, he strolled out of the kitchen, and spent the rest of the afternoon chopping wood, making sure to stay in view of Amy's kitchen window as he did.

Amy shocked herself that night by going with Tucker into town. They sat in the Last Stop Bar and Grill with a bunch of his friends, laughing and talking and—she had to admit—having a decent time. She'd worn the least faded of her three pairs of jeans, and a new T-shirt she'd gotten with her last paycheck. The music rocked, the food was good, and she actually found herself smiling for no reason at all.

"Now *that's* what I've been waiting for." Tucker drew her to her feet and toward the dance floor. "Don't forget you're having a good time."

"Oh no." She dug in her heels. "I'm not having that good a time— Tucker!"

He let go of her hand and started dancing, if you could call arms flailing and legs dancing—good Lord, what was he doing with his legs? He was easily the worst dancer out there, and she clamped her hand over her mouth. Was he kidding?

"Come on." He gestured she should do the same.

He wasn't kidding.

Eddie was also out on the floor with two girls. The rest of the group they'd been sitting with was there, too, all dancing together, none quite as dorkily as Tucker, but no one seemed to care what they looked like, only that the music was good.

"If you think I look silly," Tucker said over the music, "then you should see how you look just standing there with a scowl on your face."

"I'm not scowling." But she was, so she smoothed that out first. Then with Tucker still wobbling and hopping and bobbing all around her as he smiled into her face, looking so cute and happy, she rolled her eyes. "Fine." She swayed. "See? Dancing."

He laughed. "Is that it? That's all you've got?"

"Shut up." But she moved a little bit more, using her arms this time. She knew how to dance; she'd spent hours doing so late at night after her father passed out cold on the couch. She'd sneak into his closet and put on the one thing of her mother's he'd kept, a long, flowery sundress. She'd twirl around in it to the music from her little AM/FM radio, pretending she was a fairy-tale princess locked away in her castle waiting for her prince. It'd been the only time she'd ever been happy.

So when she closed her eyes now and let herself go, let herself dance—much better than Tucker, she might add—the same emotion came over her.

Happiness.

Callie stood in front of the sink in her bathroom wearing a sea green lace camisole and matching shorts, neither of which even attempted to hide much of her body. Another online impulse buy. Of course the model had been long, leggy and lean as a whistle, but Callie had to admit, having curves suited the set as well.

She knew wearing pretty things beneath her work clothes was a pathetic attempt at feeling feminine in a decidedly unfeminine world, but figured she deserved one little concession to being a woman.

When the knock came at her door, her heart jerked.

"Callie?"

God, just his voice, a little thick and husky, wound her up. Not sure how she felt about that, she reached for her robe, slipping into it before opening the door.

Jake filled her vision, his good arm holding up the doorjamb. "Hi."

"Hi." Suddenly a little unsure, she crossed her arms. "You had a busy day."

"I wanted to introduce you to the real estate agent but you vanished."

"I was busy, too." She'd avoided them on purpose. Childish, definitely, but she'd needed the distance. "How did it go?"

"People are pretty spooked over the gossip. They're

saying we've either got a mischievous ghost, or someone is after giving the ranch a bad name."

"None of the incidents are that bad . . ."

"Missing money." He ticked off the others on his fingers. "Injury to a horse, injury to horse's owner, more missing money." He shook his head. "It's just enough to scare people."

"I'm sorry, Jake."

"Are you?"

She leaned against the opposite side of the door. "I'm sorry it's giving you trouble, yes. I'm not sorry you haven't sold yet."

A smile touched his lips. "I can always count on you for honesty."

"Always. You got your message from Joe."

"He said you sounded pretty." His smile widened. "I told him you were."

"And he said you'd promised to come and train his next group of recruits." She didn't let any emotion tinge her voice, even though she felt plenty. "I told him to expect an ugly puppy along with you."

His smile faded. "Callie—"

"I don't want to talk about it." Honest to God she didn't because nothing would change. "Can you live with that?"

He ran his gaze over her face for a long moment. "I can. For now."

She moved back. His body brushed hers as he came inside and shut the door, holding her to his side as he lightly drew his knuckles along her cheek. "I thought about you all day. I'm going off the assumption you gave me at least a passing thought."

A laugh almost bubbled out of her. A passing

thought? Try a hundred. "Yeah. You could assume that."

His other hand skimmed up and down her back over the smooth robe. That warmth he always caused within began deep inside, and she lifted her hand to his chest.

"Another assumption I had was that we'd share your bed tonight." His voice was nothing but a rough whisper. His eyes were lit with hunger, and more, so much more that it took her breath away.

She ran her hand back and forth over his chest. Beneath his shirt he was warm, hard with strength. "I think that's a good assumption."

"What's beneath the robe?" he asked hoarsely, then unbelted it himself, sweeping it off her shoulders, letting it fall to the floor. He took her in with one sweep of his eyes, and groaned. "That's incredible. Now take it off." That said, he took care of it himself.

She had every light on in the place, and for a minute felt bare and vulnerable sandwiched between the closed door and his fully dressed form. "The bed?"

He kissed her, then lifted his head. "Too far." He kissed her again and then again, until she forgot about feeling vulnerable and open. When he scraped his teeth over a nipple, then soothed it with his tongue, she writhed against him while his busy, clever, and extremely talented hands skimmed up the backs of her thighs, exploring between. "Jake." She let out a shaky laugh. "My legs won't hold me."

He eyed her kitchen table, which was only a few feet to the left, then slid his good arm around her waist, lifting her against him as he headed toward it.

"No," she gasped, laughing. "It won't hold."

So he set her down on the counter instead. Stepping

back, he began to strip out of his clothes, and she blessed the light she'd just cursed because he had such a glorious body. He pulled out a condom, held her gaze while he put it on. Settling his big palms on her thighs, he pushed them apart. She'd barely taken a breath before one powerful thrust brought him home. And he *was* home right here in her arms, just as she was in his, which was both simple and terrifying.

Or maybe just simply terrifying.

Two days later, the next group arrived, an eclectic mix of romance authors who from the moment they stepped foot on the ranch were a dream group—happy to be there, happier to help, and happiest grilling the ranch hands for research.

They'd asked for an overnight camping trip, and as Callie liked to do when she had the time, she rode out with them for the day, planning on riding back to the ranch just before nightfall. She loved the interaction with the guests, but loved even more the two hours of sheer freedom she'd get galloping home as the sun set.

Tucker was coming along for only a few hours as well, but he planned on riding back before Callie, wanting to be around the ranch for two of the cows that were close to term. He didn't want to miss the births.

Jake came along, too, for reasons that were his own. With Stone gone, Amy stayed behind with Marge and Lou, who'd made himself so useful around the ranch fixing and repairing and maintaining, they'd upped his hours to full time.

The day was a glorious marvel. They rode along the top of the canyon walls, a set of rocky sheer cliffs rising up to majestic heights, and far below ran the river, still and calm now, as if last week's storm had never happened. The sky was a startlingly pure azure blue, without a single cloud. As the day warmed, Callie shrugged out of her long-sleeved denim shirt, leaving her in a tank top and jeans. Eddie had stripped out of his shirt entirely, trying to get a tan, and maybe a romance author all in one shot.

Jake wore one of his firefighter T-shirts and his jeans and, she had to admit, was looking good in the saddle. "It's so beautiful," she said.

"Breathtaking." He hadn't taken his eyes off her.

"I was talking about the day."

"And I was talking about you."

She smiled. "You don't have to give me those come-on lines, I'm already sleeping with you."

"Not that there's been much sleeping, but I wasn't giving you a come-on." He studied her curiously. "Hasn't anyone ever told you that you were beautiful before?"

"Sure. But I divorced him."

"The guy was an idiot."

"No, he wasn't. He just couldn't keep his zipper up."

"Like I said, idiot."

She laughed. "Count for count, I'd bet you've brought home more women than Matt ever did."

"But I never put a ring on a woman's finger and promised to be true to her." He reached for her hand when she looked away, waiting until she brought her face back around. "I don't make promises often, Callie, but when I do, I keep them."

She had no idea why that brought a hard lump to her throat. Maybe because, somehow, she'd come to want exactly that from him. "What kind of promises *do* you make?"

He smiled. "How about as many orgasms as you want tonight?"

She rolled her eyes. Inexplicably let down and annoyed at the both of them, she shifted Sierra so that he had to let go of her hand. "If the subject was getting too serious for you, you could have just said so." Urging her horse into a trot, she moved to catch up with the other women, where maybe, somehow, she could get her mind off the men who alternately brought her to new heights, and new lows.

Jake watched her go.

"Women." Tucker patted Homer as they fell in place next to Jake.

He looked over at his brother. "Are we actually agreeing on something?"

"Bro, on the subject of women, all men agree. They're nuts."

Jake laughed. And perhaps best of all, so did Tucker. "I thought you had a problem with Callie and me."

Tucker lifted a shoulder. "I did. Now I don't."

No explanation, and Jake knew he wasn't going to get one.

"Just don't screw her up."

Jake looked at Callie ahead of him, smiling and laughing with the other women. He didn't know how to respond, because he didn't know how not to screw up.

"And don't screw you up, either," Tucker said. On that surprising statement, he said his good-byes to everyone and turned back for the ranch.

The rest of the day went fairly smoothly. Jake helped Eddie and Callie get the women all set up for the night. When Callie prepared to ride back to the ranch, Jake joined her. "What are you doing?" she asked.

"Eddie can handle the women on his own. I'm going back with you."

"I can come up with my own orgasms tonight, thank you," she said dryly.

"Yes, and imagining that will go a long way toward keeping me uncomfortably hot on the ride back, thank you."

"You just want a bed tonight."

"That's right. I'm not sleeping on the cold, hard ground when I can have a too short, too narrow, cold, hard cot." *Or you*.

She snorted her opinion of that, and he began to understand that once again, he was going to have to talk her into wanting him. He hated that, but it wouldn't stop him, not when he had to have her so badly. He had no idea what that said about him.

They rode in silence. There was a tension in the silence though, and a growing heaviness in the set of Callie's shoulders that clued him in to her mood, though he had no idea what to do about it.

Night fell as they rode the darkness, relieved by millions of twinkling stars that never failed to stun him. They just didn't make skies like this anywhere else. Without a city light or house in sight, he and Callie were completely, utterly alone, surrounded by flowing rivers and wild bush and rocky canyons, watched only by the coyotes and whatever other creatures habited this area. It was awe-inspiring, and more than a little unnerving. He was finally coming to terms with this place, and now he was going to leave it.

After an hour, Callie suddenly slowed to a stop, then dismounted. She tied Sierra to a tree and touched her forehead to her horse's.

Jake dismounted, too. The only sounds were water

rushing somewhere off to their left and the crunch of the ground beneath his feet when he came up behind her. "What's wrong?"

"I wish you hadn't come," she said.

"On the ride?"

A choking laugh escaped her. "To the ranch, Jake."

He'd lifted a hand to stroke down her hair, but it went still, hovering in the air as the words sank into him like a knife.

Then she lifted her head and her eyes were swimming with tears.

"Ah, Callie," he whispered, and he let his hand touch her after all.

"Before you, I was happy here." A tear slipped down her cheek, and broke his heart. "I knew what every day would bring," she choked out. "I knew what the future would hold. Now—" She broke off abruptly and closed her eyes. "This is useless. Forget it."

"No, I won't forget it. I can't." He cupped her face. "I never meant to hurt you."

The gentleness in his touch devastated Callie as his thumbs stroked away her tears. She couldn't speak.

"We agreed to see this through," he said softly as the night breeze blew over them. "Through me not being able to work at what I do best, through Tucker and I struggling to be brothers, through you fighting for this ranch and facing all the changes ahead. Just because you're scared now—"

"And you're not?"

"Not when we're doing this." Leaning in, he kissed her, tenderly at first, then deeper, nibbling at her with hungry bites that took her right out of herself. What happened then shocked her. She felt an overwhelming hunger, a blinding need, and before she knew it they were fumbling for each other's clothing, hands grappling for purchase right there in the dark with only the running creek for company. He tore open her shirt, she slid her fingers beneath his. Then he had her jeans down, and she had his open.

Bracing her between his hard body and the even harder tree, he lifted her up and sank into her. He sighed her name like a curse, a prayer, and she clung to his neck, pressing her face against his throat, feeling as if she was going to die if he didn't hurry, if he didn't take her now, hard and fast. None of it could be rationalized, not the way she abandoned all sense of shame, nor how much she needed him. She held on while he slid an arm behind her back, protecting her back from the tree, while his other hand gripped her hip, holding her open to his thrusts. It made no sense to feel so out of control, so wild for him, but she was, and with a shuddering sob, she came. He was only seconds behind her, and then his body trembled over hers as he held them both upright with the tree's help.

Heart pumping against hers, he lifted his head and stroked the damp hair from her face. "You okay?"

She was now. For whatever reason, her anger and frustration and fear had melted away, leaving in its place a warmth and languor that made movement difficult. He helped her right her clothing, and then put his attention to his. They got on their horses and headed back to the ranch, Callie still basking in sated glow. She knew it would fade when the ranch came into view, but for now she selfishly held on to it and pretended the glow was hers to keep.

20

Tucker and Amy sat on the porch watching the night go by. He felt good, damn good. He'd watched two brand-new baby calves come into the world and he had a relaxed Amy—at least a little—at his side. Only moments ago, Jake and Callie had ridden in, disappearing into the barn to put their horses away before coming back out.

"Interesting," Tucker said.

"What's interesting?"

Jake put a casual hand low on Callie's back to guide her toward her cabin. It wasn't so much a possessive hand as a protective one, and once upon a time that would have pissed Tucker off, but now he could remember how pretty damn great it had felt to once have Jake feel that protective about him. "They don't argue nearly as much as they used to," Tucker noted and picked up his soda.

"That's because they're doing it," Amy said.

Tucker nearly choked on his soda.

"Does that bother you? Or make you jealous?"

"Not jealous . . ." He studied Amy in the moonlight, looking so pretty she took his breath. "Maybe a little envious."

She snorted. "Please. You could be getting laid tonight if you wanted."

Carefully he set down his soda. "Really?"

"There were at least three girls in the bar the other night who'd have jumped you in a heartbeat."

"But I didn't want any of them."

"Why not?"

Because I want you. "Don't *you* ever feel envious, Amy?"

"Hell, no." She shuddered, and wrapped her arms around her bent-up legs, hunching over herself.

His smile faded. Earlier suspicions about her past took root deep in his belly, and he took her drink from her hands and set it down, keeping her fingers in his, even when she tried to tug free.

"I've got to go," she said.

"Not all men are assholes." He stroked his thumb lightly over her knuckles. "I'm not."

Her eyes were shiny, reflecting the starlight and none of her thoughts.

"Are you ever going to talk to me, Amy?"

"I talk to you."

"About you. About your past."

"I've told you some."

"Tell me more."

She stared down at their joined hands. "I filled out the employee forms. You could read those."

"Those are confidential, and as a ranch hand, I don't see them."

"Oh." She seemed surprised to find out her privacy had been kept.

Surprised, and touched, and his heart ached for her so much, but he didn't know how to reach her. "Where were you born?"

"Memphis. I told you my father's a trucker."

"Who wasn't around that much."

She said nothing to that, so he pressed a little. "When he was around, did you get along?"

Her mouth twisted. "Hard to get along with a drunk."

Her fingers were so cold, and though he suddenly felt chilled to the bone himself, he sandwiched hers between his two hands. "Did he—" He winced, unsure how to proceed.

"Are you trying to find out how he treated me? He likes to blame me for my mother's death. With his fists. Is that what you wanted to know?"

No. He'd wanted her to tell him she'd had a princess life, even though he'd known that hadn't been the case. "Amy."

"When I got older, he didn't blame me so much as . . . try to pretend I was her." She pulled her hands from his as if shocked to find them there, and fisted them tight. "That was the worst part," she whispered. "You know, fighting him off." She put her forehead to her bent knees.

God. His heart felt as if it'd been laid wide open, slashed with a butcher knife. He scrubbed his hands over his face, afraid he was in over his head here.

"Sorry you asked, I bet."

He looked at her bent head, at the sun tattooed on the back of her delicate neck. "No, I'm torn between wanting to hold you, and kill your father," he said very quietly.

She surged to her feet. "It was a long time ago."

"How long?"

"I haven't been home since I was fourteen."

Four years. Slowly he stood up, too, lifting his hands to put them on her shoulders, but letting them hover, afraid to scare her off. "Where did you go? What did you do?"

She shrugged her narrow shoulders. "Found my way into kitchens, mostly. I was happy in Dallas for a little while, but then the boss found out I'd lied about my age and canned me. I went to New Mexico then. Taos. Loved it there, but the winters were too cold . . ."

"So you made your way west. Here."

She was staring at her scuffed boots, apparently fascinated by them. "Yeah." She hugged herself tight. "So now you know about me."

Screw not touching her. He wanted to touch her, and he wanted her to like it. To like him. Gently he took her arm, drew her around to face him.

"Why aren't you running?" she whispered, her arms still tight around herself. "Didn't you hear what I said, what's in my past? I'm a basket case."

"No." Leaning in, he kissed her softly, and then pulled back. Her eyes were wide on his, her breathing shallow with what he hoped to God was arousal, not fear. "You're the strongest, most amazing woman I've ever met."

She blinked, slow as an owl. "I'm going to bed now. Alone."

"I'll walk you."

"I'm not going to invite you in."

"I know."

She blinked again. "Won't that . . . make you mad?"

"No."

"Disappointed?"

"Hey, I just kissed you and you didn't slug me. That's enough progress for one night."

She just stared at him. "You're crazy."

He held out his hand, waited.

She shook her head. "Scratch that. I'm the crazy one." And she took his hand.

Callie woke up to a glorious sunrise shining through her window. She hadn't set her alarm, knowing that Eddie and their guests wouldn't be back until mid-morning. What that meant for her was that instead of rising at five, she could wait until close to six, as half the horses were gone, which considerably shortened her morning routine.

Her body felt rather amazing, and it took her a moment to figure out why. Jake was currently wrapped around her as if he was her own personal blanket.

She scooted free and sat up, hooking her arms around her knees. Without waking, Jake flopped to his stomach, hogging the entire bed with the body she never tired of looking at. What was it about his sexy, mind-melting grin? Or the way he touched her deep inside with just one soulful look of those gray eyes? Last night she'd thought she'd been so in control of herself, and yet all he'd had to do was back her up to a tree and she'd abandoned any restraint.

She took her gaze off him and watched the early sunrise glow outside her window. Sierra walked past, just sauntered right on by. No bridle, no saddle, just the horse, casual as could be. Leaping out of bed, Callie ran to the window.

"What?" Jake sat straight up, groggy.

"The horses. Someone let them out of the corral and the stalls." Swearing, she whipped around and began to dress.

Jake had been angry plenty of times before, most recently the day he'd realized little Billy was going to try to ruin him. But that anger had passed because he couldn't maintain fury at a kid clearly being manipulated by the adults around him. He felt only sorrow for Billy now.

But someone had deliberately put eleven horses in danger, all in the name of yet another prank, and that got to him. He walked up to the huge, ugly tan horse that used to belong to his father. Moe stood nibbling on the grass, and not even Goose had the nerve to chase this big, bad guy off. Jake had a bridle in his hands, and he knew how to use it, but he sure as hell would rather be scaling the side of a burning building. "What do you say we get you back inside your nice stall?"

Without looking at him, Moe danced sideways, away from him.

Jake sighed, painfully aware of Callie on the other side of the yard, catching three horses to his every one. "Come on, now. All you have to do is put your head in this thing and then I'll lead you back home. What do you say?"

With a snort, the horse trotted away again.

"He says you're a pushover." Tucker grabbed the bridle from Jake, walked right up to Moe and bridled him, expertly avoiding his teeth when Moe snapped at him. "Stop it, Moe. You're just trying to scare him now." He glanced back as the sheriff pulled up the driveway. "By calling this in, you're going to have even more trouble selling."

"Don't know what else to do." Jake made sure to give Moe plenty of space. "It has to be stopped."

Tucker nodded and started to lead Moe away, but then he stopped. Kicked the dirt. "You know there's not many suspects, right? Other than us?"

"I'm hoping like hell there's someone else. A neighbor, a kid from town, *someone.*"

"Yeah." Tucker stroked Moe's face, who snorted in pleasure, looking nice and friendly.

Jake just sighed.

"Look," Tucker said. "I know I'm a prick to you most of the time, but I'd never—I mean, I wouldn't . . ."

"I know."

Tucker nodded, looking so touchingly relieved, Jake actually stepped closer, with some old, burning desire to do something stupid, like touch him.

But Tucker led Moe away before he could.

Tucker didn't go far, just to the nearest phone. He did what he'd been meaning to do for five weeks now, and called his mother. He was shocked as hell when he actually got her on the first try.

Mary Ann wasn't usually readily available. When she was after a guy, she faded out of his life, only coming back into it—like a freight train—when things soured in her relationship. He'd accepted that as a child. He'd had to. From the age of five, she'd been all he'd had. He'd accepted a lot of things that he wondered about now.

"You caught me in the middle of a manicure," she said.

She didn't waste time with greetings, even though they hadn't spoken in a few months, so he didn't, either. "When Jake left, did he ever try to contact us?"

"What? My goodness." She laughed. "That was so long ago."

"Did he?"

"Oh, you know your brother, baby. He had other fish to fry. He rarely had time to call."

"You told me he *never* called. That he walked out the door when I was five and never called again."

"Listen to that awful static. We have a bad connection. I'll call you another time—"

"I want to know the truth."

She sighed. "How many times do I have to tell you, the truth is always overrated."

"Mom."

"Fine. The truth is he walked away from you. You know that."

"He came back when I needed him."

"Yes, so he could throw it in my face that I'd ruined you."

"You told me you had to beg him to come." Tucker rubbed his temples, trying to absorb it all in. "That he only came at all because he had this ranch and needed another hand."

"I can't hear you. . . . Gotta go—"

He stared at the phone when she disconnected him, knowing the truth, that Jake had spoken it, and that Tucker had been nothing but an ungrateful, spoiled bastard to him in return. He slammed the kitchen phone down, glad Amy couldn't see the violence in him now or he'd scare her to death.

He drew a deep breath and looked around him, out the window at the wide open space he loved, at the people who ran it. These people were his real family, Jake included. And nothing could take that from him.

That evening, Callie rode out on Sierra. It was an hour before sunset, and another storm brewed. Clouds swirled and danced above her, the sky churning like the blue flames the ranch was named for. Their novelist guests were back, happy and talking animatedly about their overnight adventure. Amy had fed them a meaty lasagna, and they were all getting ready for a big bonfire that evening. Except for Jake, who was right this minute walking his Realtor and a prospective buyer around the ranch.

Callie urged Sierra into a gallop. The sheriff had come by again. He was concerned, and so was Jake.

And so was she. Not that she believed she was in any real peril. No, her danger came from losing her heart. *God*. She was tough enough to handle this thing between her and Jake. And whatever jerk was messing with the ranch. She could handle anything but losing the only place she'd ever considered home.

And yet she *was* going to lose it. Tilting her head up, she took a deep breath and watched the sky change as she rode the trail. The clouds grumbled overhead, moving swiftly, violently. She lost herself in it for a long moment, then at the sound of a horse behind her, turned and watched Jake ride toward her on Molly. "I want to be alone," she said.

"Callie—" He broke off at an odd flash of light in the hills. He cocked his head, searching the horizon. "Someone's behind the rocks over there."

A sudden loud pop startled them both as the rock on the other side of them pinged as if it'd been shot—

"Jesus. *Get down!*" Jake leapt off Molly, hauling Callie off Sierra before she could move, shoving her ahead of him. "Run for the rocks!"

"The horses—"

"Go!" He shoved her again and she ran. It was only about ten yards but it might as well have been a wide-open football field. Her skin prickled every step of the way, anticipating the burn of a bullet. She dove behind the rocks, ducking as another shot resounded over her head, raining dirt and rock down over her. She scooted over as much as she could, expecting Jake to dive in right on her heels.

He had the reins of both horses in his hands as he ran toward her, trying to rush without spooking them. But the next shot did just that, and Sierra reared up, ripping the reins from his hands, her hooves pawing at the air, inches from Jake's head.

"*Jake!*" Callie surged up to her knees, horrified as Sierra bumped into Molly, and then both horses were rearing as Jake fell backward to the ground. Callie ran out from behind the rock and threw herself between Jake and the horses, standing still and calm while her heart stuck her in her throat, crooning to both horses in a soft voice she knew would reach them.

"Callie, goddammit." Jake growled, struggling back to his feet.

"Hold on." She murmured to the horses again, sweating with each passing second, just waiting for the bite of a bullet in her flesh, but it didn't come. The moment Sierra's hooves hit the ground, Jake grabbed her reins, thrust them at Callie, then grabbed Molly's reins. They all moved around the rocks. They stood there, chests heaving in shock, staring at each other. Jake shoved Molly's reins at her. "Stay here."

"Where are you going?"

"To see who the hell's taking potshots at us."

"Jake, no."

But he was gone.

21

Jake was not a tracker, at least not out here with the sun nearly gone and mostly blocked out by the dark, thickening clouds. The rocky canyons were wide open in front of him and utterly, eerily silent. Damn, what he'd give for his cell phone and an entire squad of cops to swarm the area.

Whoever had shot at them was gone now; he knew it. He studied the rock area where they'd heard the ping of the bullet, and discovered something interesting. From where the shooter had stood, the distance hadn't been that great, one hundred feet tops.

And yet they hadn't been hit. So the shooter had terrible aim . . .

Or he'd been *trying* to miss them.

Something shimmered on the ground and he picked it up. A tiny round metal ball. A BB.

Callie came around the rock. "What?"

He opened his hand and showed her.

"A BB?" She looked as baffled as he felt. "But a BB gun wouldn't have killed us."

"It'd have hurt like hell, but no, it wouldn't have killed us, or the horses."

Their gazes met, and she looked no less unnerved by the knowledge. "Who the hell . . . ?" She closed her eyes and shook her head. "It doesn't matter, it's working," she whispered. "I'm officially scared."

He shoved the BB in his pocket and reached for her. She moved right into his arms, her body fitting to his as if she'd been made for the spot. Burying his face in her hair, he gave himself the luxury of holding her for a long moment, while his heart gave one slow roll in his chest at what might have happened out there to her if she'd been alone. "We've got to get back."

"Oh my God, you're right. He might go there next." She grabbed her radio and called the ranch, warning them. Then she mounted Sierra. "Hurry, Jake."

She didn't have to tell him twice. What had seemed like such a beautiful spot only a moment ago, with the wide-open canyons and little else beneath a flaming darkening sky, now seemed too big, too wide open. The entire ride to the ranch, he imagined them both in someone's gun sights, and he rode just a little bit behind Callie, desperate to watch her back, to keep her safe, hating that it was entirely out of his control. He wasn't used to that, things being out of his control, and it was one hell of a long fifteen-minute ride, with his spine itching the whole way.

Two days later, the novelists left, thankfully none the wiser about the ranch's increasingly aggressive stalker. Jake knew their next guests were coming right on their heels, a family reunion, with sixteen members arriving from all over the country.

He wanted to cancel them, and even Callie had agreed, but unfortunately, more than half the guests had already begun their travel, so the decision had been made to let them come.

The sheriff and a few of his men had scoured the

area where the shots had originated. They'd questioned all the ranch hands. They'd questioned their neighbors. They'd put out the word in town. No one knew anything.

In spite of that, Jake's agent called with an offer for the ranch from the New York millionaire, who'd decided she liked the idea of a tax break and a new lifestyle. She'd offered 90 percent of his asking price, and was willing to guarantee the employees one year of employment.

It was all Jake had wanted. He'd be stupid not to jump on it, and yet he hesitated.

It made no sense. He had a little over a week before he had to get back to San Diego to train recruits. His shoulder was so improved he wished he could get back to firefighting, but even "so improved" wasn't good enough. He knew he couldn't handle a hose, he couldn't climb a ladder with speed and efficiency, and he couldn't guarantee he could lift and carry a victim, much less his own gear for any length of time.

But that's not what really bothered him. He was learning to accept the fact that firefighting might be in his past, for the most part. What he was suddenly having trouble with was imagining leaving the Blue Flame. He liked to pretend that was because he worried about the ever-escalating danger, and leaving Callie to face it alone. Or that he'd started a new and different sort of relationship with Tucker, and that it was working for both of them.

But even he knew it was far more than that. He just didn't know what to do about it.

They had an overnight storm that left everything clear and glistening. The weather turned warm, almost hot. Stone came back, looking relaxed and much happier than he had when he'd left. And when their next guests arrived, the family members spent the first afternoon getting reacquainted with each other and handling the evening chores with gusto, falling in love with the puppies, two of which they claimed.

And late that night, when the guests retired to their rooms, Jake stood in the yard in the dark spring night, restless and unsettled.

"How are you holding up?"

He turned. Callie stood there looking at him. "Better now," he said, and she smiled.

But then it slowly faded. "You only have a week left," she said.

"I know."

She searched his gaze for a long moment, as if trying to make a decision. "You might not realize this, but there are still a few things you haven't experienced out here."

"Is that right?" Suddenly feeling a little less restless, certainly a lot less alone, he put his hands on her hips and pulled her close. "What's that?"

She hoisted the fishing poles she held in her hand.

He laughed. "That's definitely not what I had in mind."

"You have something against fishing?"

"Uh . . . not specifically."

"Okay then." She handed him a fishing pole. "Let's hit it."

He wanted to talk to her about the offer for the ranch, about how he felt about leaving, but he looked into her face and asked, "Where to?"

"Funny thing about fishing, we need water."

"You mean the river?"

"Well, I don't mean my shower."

"That's not a good idea."

"We're not going to get shot out there tonight, Jake. Look, I'm not going to be afraid and nervous and pissed off all the time. I want to live how I want to live, and so much is changing—" She pointed at him with the fishing pole when he opened his mouth. "I know, I can't stop change, but I sure as hell can be in charge of my own destiny. And tonight my destiny is fishing by moonlight, which I don't think is asking too much. So." She drew in a deep breath. "Yes or no?"

"Yes. To whatever you want."

"Now *there's* a dangerous promise." She led him past the hay barn and turned right, toward the first low rocky hill across the pasture.

"No horses?"

"I need to walk."

So they walked. The way was lit by the incredible sky, which felt so close and bright, Jake wanted to reach out and grab a star. Soon they came to the trail he'd taken on horseback many times now, so he knew exactly where the river curved alongside it, running parallel.

They walked side by side in the warm evening, their fingers brushing together. He took hers in his and smiled down at her. "You going to take advantage of me out here?"

She eyed him over. "I don't know. It's dirty and the ground is hard. There are *bugs*."

He laughed. "I haven't given you those complaints in a while now."

"You ever been skinny-dipping?"

"Oh, yeah." He sighed with remembered pleasure. "Me and Emma Peters. Good times." He laughed again when Callie yanked her hand out of his, and he grabbed it back. "We were thirteen."

Slightly mollified, she gave him a cool look as she left the path and headed down to the river's edge. "I'm not thirteen."

"For which I'm eternally grateful." They sat there, surrounded by rocky hills and bush, utterly isolated and alone, and yet unlike the last time they'd been out here, he felt no danger. The opposite, actually. This place, which he'd often thought so strange and stark and other-worldly, now felt as good a fit as the woman next to him.

She pulled a small jar of bait from her pocket and loaded her hook. The smell made his eyes water. "Baby," she called him, and loaded his hook for him, then rinsed her hands in the water. She stuck her pole in the damp, soft earth, between her knees, lay back on the ground, and stared up at the sky.

He did the same. They stayed like that for a long time, their bodies touching, the night all around them, and a peace filled him, a warm, soothing, soft peace. A little startled, he turned his head and found her looking at him.

Turning on her side, she propped her head up with her hand. "What's the matter?"

He turned on his side, too, having just realized the truth. He was falling for this amazing, different landscape. He was falling for the ranch and the people on it. And he was falling for the woman in front of him. It was just enough to make him momentarily speechless as the blood roared in his head and his bones liquefied.

"Jake?"

He started to shake his head—couldn't she see he was having a heart attack?—but she leaned in and kissed him softly on the lips. "Don't feel like talking?" she murmured. "That's okay. I have something else we can do to pass the time." She set aside the fishing poles, and slid into his arms. He closed them tight around her and held on like she was his next breath, his lifeline. Because she was.

They walked back, talking, smiling, and in Callie's case, feeling much more relaxed than she'd been before she'd jumped Jake's bones on the riverbed by moonlight. Their clothes were a little rumpled, and she was fairly certain she had river sand in places where there shouldn't be any, but she could live with that given how good she felt.

When they came into the yard, the big house was quiet and dark. Oddly enough, Michael's truck was parked behind Callie's Jeep, and her cabin lights were on. She frowned. "I wonder what's wrong for him to come out here this late."

Then her door opened and Michael stepped out onto the small square porch. He lifted his hand to shade his eyes from the glare of the porch light and looked across the yard to where they stood. "There you are," he called out. His voice was filled with relief, and a forced good cheer. On his face was a misery that tore at her.

She turned to Jake. "I'd better go see—"

"Yeah." He took her fishing pole.

"I'm sorry."

"Not a problem." He leaned into her and gave her one soft, warm kiss. He pulled back, looked at her for a long moment, then kissed her again, just a little longer this time. "Thanks for the fishing. And everything else," he added silkily.

She bit back her dreamy smile and watched him go,

then walked to her cabin. "Hey you," she said to Michael. "Everything okay?"

"Come talk to me." He held open her door. "Please?"

"Sure." She stepped inside, where she stopped and gasped in shock and surprise. There were candles everywhere, along the floor, on every countertop, on her coffee table, and in each windowsill, all lit and flickering fiercely. In addition, rose petals had been scattered on every surface of the small cabin, filling the air with their strong scent.

"For you," Michael said, and shut the cabin door.

She turned in a slow circle, absolutely stunned by the amount of time he'd spent putting everything together. He took her hands, looked down at them, at her fingernails still lined with fish bait. "It was the only way I could think of to tell you what I should have told you the day we met, and every day since."

Oh, God. "Michael—"

"Callie, I love you. I've always loved you, through your entire short and stupid marriage to Matt, a man who never appreciated you, through you working your fingers to the bone for that tyrant Richard—"

"He wasn't a—"

"Through all this fantasy you've had of buying this place—"

"Wait a minute." She tried to tug her hands free but he held firm. "What do you mean, *fantasy*? Michael, I'm serious about buying this place. I filled out your loan papers—" She stared at him, a funny feeling deep in the pit of her stomach. "I filled out your loan papers and kept asking you about them, and you've been vague. Terribly vague."

"Yes."

"Because . . . you didn't process them?"

He gave her a sad smile. "Do you really think I would do that to you?"

She tried to relax but couldn't. Nor could she tug free because his grip tightened, painfully so now. "No, I didn't think you would do anything to hurt me," she said carefully. "But maybe that's the problem. I didn't think at all. Michael, you're scaring me."

"I'm sorry." He leaned in and kissed her. "Don't flinch from me," he murmured, still holding her hands too tight. "It's just me."

"Yeah." She stared at him, thoughts racing along with her heart. "I've been thinking about all the mysterious incidents."

"Have you?"

"It could have been Amy," she said, watching him carefully. "Or Lou."

"Stone gets my vote." Michael shook his head. "An alcoholic."

"Right. But Stone was gone when someone took pot-shots at Jake and me, and Lou couldn't have had access to my office because he never comes in the big house."

"Eddie, then?"

"Eddie has an aim like a sniper."

"Maybe he missed on purpose," Michael said, and shrugged.

Her heart was in her throat now, pounding so hard she thought she might throw up. Or *you* missed on purpose. "You didn't process my loan, did you."

He stared at her for a long moment. "If you'd gotten that loan, you'd never see how much you need me. I was beginning to worry you'd never see."

Goosebumps broke out on her arms and the back of her neck. She stood there frozen in shock as he smiled, calm and sweet as always. "I tried patience," he said. "That didn't work. I've been trying to scare you into my arms for months now. You never so much as budged."

"Scare me." She was shocked he couldn't hear her heart drumming. "Like . . . letting out the horses. Like taking my coil wire."

Another long moment while things flashed in his eyes that terrified her. "It was time to take matters into my own hands," he finally said.

She tried to back away, but his hold prevented that. "It was you. The stolen money, Sierra's saddle—"

"I nearly came back the next night and killed that horse for hurting you," he said in a friendly, easygoing voice. "I let the pigs out, I stole the money. I have it set aside for you, of course, I only meant to rattle you a bit."

"The shed. How did you know I'd go to the shed?"

"I didn't. It was just a stroke of luck that you were walking into it as I was arriving. I smelled the fumes from my truck for God's sake. You really should fire Stone."

"Let go of me, Michael."

When he just regretfully shook his head and pulled her against him, she shuddered. The fear and anger surged together into a powerful fury. "Let go."

"Can't."

She kneed him as hard as she could, and with a sharp cry, he dropped to the floor.

She bolted for the door, but he lunged for her with surprising speed and agility, grabbing her foot and yanking it out from beneath her. She went down hard, hitting her head on the coffee table. Her vision filled with bright stars. The table tipped, and so did the candles, raining down hot wax and lit wicks near her face. The throw rug beneath her caught on fire, and she felt her eyebrows singe, and her shirt. Frantic, she slapped at the smoking material and tried to scramble away from the flickering flames now around her, but Michael still had her foot.

Then the front door burst open, and Amy stood there. "Callie? I heard you scream—" She took in both Michael and Callie on the floor, locked in battle around the fire starting to rage. *"Callie!"*

With a roar, Michael hauled himself to his feet and backhanded Amy across the face. She dropped, hit the leg of the upturned table, and lay unmoving.

"No—" Callie broke off when Michael turned toward her.

Chest heaving, face damp with sweat, he gave her a gentle smile. "Now. Where were we?"

22

Jake turned on the shower, took a glance at himself in the mirror, and realized he was frowning. He and Callie had had a beautiful night on the riverbed, where she'd thoroughly distracted him from all his problems. She had a way of doing that, of making nothing seem as important as the moment.

He loved that. In fact, he'd had high expectations for the rest of the moments left in the evening, but Michael had ruined that.

Callie hadn't seemed unnerved by Michael's late visit, but Jake sure as hell was. He claimed to be Callie's best friend, and everyone else liked and trusted him, but Jake had looked into his eyes that night and seen something new, something just a little ugly.

The guy wanted Callie, badly. And if Jake had been a good man, an unselfish one, he might have encouraged that relationship. After all, he was leaving, and he wanted Callie safe and happy.

But he wasn't unselfish. He turned off the shower without using it, and stepped out of the bathroom. He didn't want to think about Callie with another man. He wanted her safe and happy . . . with him. "Damn it."

In his bed, already fast asleep, Tucker stirred. "What?"

"Nothing." Callie was going to yell at him for interrupting, he was damn sure of it, but too bad. He'd already stripped out of his shirt and boots. Finding either in the dark mess of their cabin would take too long so he went to the door without. The moment he opened it and drew a smoke-filled breath, he jerked in disbelief. "*Jesus*. Tucker, call 9-1-1." Then he started running, because Callie's cabin was lit with fire from the inside, the windows a brilliant yellow and orange. "*Callie!*"

Her front door stood open. He leapt onto the porch and grabbed the doorjamb, taking in the sight before him like a snapshot. Callie was on the floor, with Michael holding her down while she struggled and kicked at him. Above them, the couch was on fire, and so was the coffee table, as well as the throw rug right next to them.

And on the floor a few feet away, far too close to the burning couch and coffee table, lay an utterly still Amy, with blood seeping from her head and mouth.

His heart nearly stopped. "Callie!" But he went for Amy first. He had to, she was out cold and the flames were too close to her hair. Scooping her up, he ran to the front door, nearly plowing into Tucker. "Take her." He thrust her in Tucker's arms, then whirled back.

Callie and Michael were rolling across the floor now, panting, fighting in eerie silence. Barefoot, he ran toward them, jumping over the fire that spread from the rug to the lace curtains. Flames leapt toward the ceiling. He reached the two of them just as Callie managed to stop their momentum with her on top. She fisted her hands in Michael's hair and slammed his head to the floor.

Michael's eyes rolled back in his head and his hands fell from her. Panting, Callie slouched over him for one second before Jake hauled her up and into his arms.

"Extinguisher," she rasped, grabbing her throat as if it hurt to talk, and he could see why. The bastard had tried to choke the life out of her, leaving bruising handprints on her skin.

"Kitchen. The extinguisher's in the kitchen." She struggled to pull away to do it herself.

"I've got it." He pointed at her as he started running. "Outside now!"

He found the extinguisher and turned back to find her struggling to drag Michael outside. Her shirt was torn off one shoulder. She had a bloody lip and a nasty scratch above one eye but she was tugging Michael's limp body for all she was worth. He rushed to her, picking up Michael himself, gritting his teeth at the burst of pain in his shoulder.

Outside, Tucker had just set Amy down and was heading back in. "Here," Jake said and dumped Michael on the grass next to Amy. "Watch him."

Back inside he went right for Callie, who was fighting with the extinguisher. He took it from her and with his shoulder screaming, started attacking the fire. It came second nature to him, thank God, because his usual calm was nowhere to be found. This was Callie's place, Callie who'd nearly gotten killed, and nothing about this felt like fighting a fire usually did.

And he knew right then and there, it wasn't just Callie. It was him. Something within him had changed. As that thought settled over him, a stream of water shot past him. Callie stood just behind him with the hand-held faucet from her kitchen sink on full blast.

Looking at her fierce protective expression, at the blood seeping from several cuts, her torn clothes, at how she was giving everything she had, he nearly sank to his knees with the force of emotion he felt for her. "Get outside," he said hoarsely.

"Not until you do," she said, continuing to send her small stream of water on the fire.

"Callie—" He broke off when he heard sirens racing up the drive. Thank God. "They're here—" He broke off when she put her hand to her head and swayed, and he dropped the extinguisher to grab her.

"Your shoulder," she murmured in protest when he carried her outside, but he didn't put her down. He couldn't, he discovered, not even when Eddie, Stone, and Lou came running. Not even when one of the paramedics came forward and wanted to check her.

The guests had all come outside, too, in various stages of dress, but Marge was with them, calming everyone down. Tucker held Amy in his lap again, while keeping a foot on Michael, who he relinquished to the sheriff. They could hear Michael moaning about his family jewels and how Callie had kicked them into next week.

Jake still couldn't believe it. There'd been an emergency, a *fire*. His own element, but Callie had saved herself. She'd saved herself, and maybe, just maybe, as he stared down into her face, heart pounding, blood still frozen in fear, she'd saved him as well. Not an easy admission for a man extremely used to being the hero.

He still couldn't let go of her. For nearly six weeks now, he'd told himself this odd and desperate need for her was just lust, but that was turning out to be pure bullshit. No matter that he didn't want to be falling for her, no matter that he didn't do love, things were happening inside him that he couldn't stop.

And he no longer wanted to.

Hours later, after the fire had been put out, after all the questions had been answered, after Amy and Callie had both been checked out by the paramedics, Amy let Tucker into her cabin. It was the first time she'd done so, and she stood by her little couch looking at him as he shut the door behind him.

In another place and time his doing so would have panicked her, put her into full defense mode, but at the moment she was either too tired or . . . or she'd come to trust him.

He turned to her, weariness and lingering fear etched in the lines of his face as he slid his hands into his pockets. "You sure you're okay?"

"Yes, but Callie—" Her voice cracked a little at that. She'd never forget the sight of Callie trying to crawl away from Michael. "She's hurt far worse—"

"Jake'll take care of her."

She knew a little about the tension between the brothers. "Is that okay with you?"

"Yeah." He rubbed a weary hand over his face. "I was wrong about Jake. And if he and Callie have found any happiness together, more power to them."

"But where will she sleep? I should have told her to come here—"

"I gave them my cabin for tonight, though surprisingly, Callie's cabin isn't that bad off."

"Where will you sleep?"

"I'll find a spot." He shrugged. "It's you I'm worried about right now." He walked toward her slowly, with his crooked, rather endearing smile in place, clearly not wanting to frighten her.

For some reason, she felt like bawling. "I'm okay."

He shook his head. "I'm not. I want to just look at you. God, I could look at you forever." He lifted a hand, and she stared at him unflinchingly. He let out a breath and ran a finger gently, so very gently, over the cut on her head. The paramedic had closed it with Steri-strips. He'd thought she could be mildly concussed and should go to the hospital.

But having a healthy fear of hospitals, she'd refused.

Now Tucker made a low, rough sound in his throat while he touched her. "When Jake put you in my arms, I just about died. You were so still—"

"Just knocked out for a second. I hit the corner of the coffee table."

He nodded, and his gaze dropped to hers. "You have got to have a helluva headache. They said no aspirin. Can I get you some Tylenol?"

She'd been through so much worse than this in her life, she nearly laughed, but he was still touching her, and her whole body was on alert. "I'm okay," she whispered.

"Yeah." His finger trailed down her temple, along her jaw.

"I'm so glad for all of us," she babbled quickly. "Stone, Lou. Me."

"None of us ever believed you'd done anything wrong. Amy—"

She caught his hand in hers, then closed her eyes. "I want you to know something." She opened her eyes and brought their joined hands to her chest. Still watching him, she spread his fingers over her heart. "I unpacked."

His smile was slow and heart-melting. "That's good. That's real good."

"Yeah. Tucker, I've not spent much of my life feeling wanted or even particularly liked. Certainly never cherished."

His smile faded, a tortured look crossing his face. "Amy—"

"No, listen. Please. I have to get this out. The way you try to be so careful with me makes me feel those things." Her heart had started pounding hard and fast as she spoke, and she knew he could feel it. "I've never done this before, never opened up like this, but life is too short." She drew a deep breath. "Tucker, I really like you. I just wanted you to know that."

"I like you, too, Amy. So much I can hardly stand it." His other hand skimmed up her back, lightly, not pulling or pawing, just touching, just holding, and slowly, so painfully slowly that her entire body tingled and melted in anticipation, he leaned in. "I'm going to kiss you now."

"Um."

"Say yes. Please say yes."

She wasn't going to let an old fear, one that couldn't hurt her now, ruin this, and as she stared up into the face so close to hers, waiting patiently, with warmth and affection and hot, hot need in his eyes, she thought, Oh my God, he's beautiful. "Okay," she whispered.

His mouth touched hers. An electric shock seemed to bolt through her, but his hand, light and sure and easy skimming up and down her back, grounded her. She sighed, in relief, in pleasure, and shyly touched her tongue to his.

He groaned, low and rough, and danced his tongue to hers for one glorious moment before pulling back.

Not breathing all that steadily anymore, he backed to the door, fumbled for the handle behind him.

"You're leaving?"

He closed his eyes, then opened them. "This is new for you, this opening up thing."

"Yes."

His entire heart was in his eyes when he smiled. "It's new for me, too. So for the first time in my entire life, I'm not going to rush a good thing. A great thing. Possibly the best thing that's ever happened to me." He opened the door, swore, then came back, and cupping her face, kissed her one more time. Then he let out a long breath. "Leaving now."

She stared at him. He was really going to go. He wasn't going to pressure her to sleep with him.

He opened the door, started to step out.

"Tucker?"

"Yeah?"

"I have both a couch and a cot." Her heart started to pound again, because she couldn't believe she was offering this to him. "You could, you know, use one. For tonight. Not the one I'm on, but—I mean—"

He came back to her, and very lightly stroked a strand of hair out of her eyes. "Are you sure?"

Unable to trust her voice, she reached for the extra blanket on the foot of her cot and offered it to him. He took it and smiled. "It'll be much nicer than the hay barn."

She didn't quite smile back, and his faded. "You know I can do this, right? I can sleep *waaaay* over here"—he stretched out on the couch, leaned back and closed his eyes—"without attacking you."

"Logically, yes." She stayed where she was and swallowed hard. "I'm working on everything else."

"Go to sleep," he whispered. "I'm going to check on you in a little while, don't be scared. I'll just say your name and you just answer. Okay?"

"Okay." She climbed onto the cot and laid down. She immediately popped back up to look at him.

He hadn't moved.

He wasn't going to. He'd promised.

She lay back, but once again popped up. He was still there, still not moving. She repeated this two more times, with the same result.

He never even twitched, though surely he had to hear her every time she jumped up like a lunatic. Then, for the first time in her entire life, she curled up and fell asleep . . .

With a smile on her lips.

After all the craziness, all Callie wanted was a shower. She used the one in Tucker and Jake's cabin, and Jake waited for her, knowing she was concentrating on the feel of the water, the scent of the soap, the sting of it on her various cuts and bruises, so that she could keep her mind blank of the evening's events—such as Michael's overwhelming betrayal.

When she stepped out of the shower, he held out a towel for her, which she walked into. He held out another towel for her hair, which she silently took.

Then she tipped her head up and looked at him.

At the misery, pain, and lingering fear in her gaze, his heart broke. She let him dry her off, another sign of how bad off she was.

"I'm okay, you know," she said quietly.

"Yeah." But the image of her lying on the floor, locked in battle with a man she'd loved and trusted, while fire rained down all around her, would haunt him for a long time to come, so he could only imagine what it was doing to her.

"Look, I should have seen it coming, okay?"

He put his hands on her shoulders and waited until she looked at him. "Tell me you know this was not your fault."

"Wasn't it?" Her eyes were shiny and far too bright. "My God, Jake, I brought danger to everyone here by letting him come around, by letting him be near—" She broke off and shuddered, then covered her face.

He took her hands and forced her to look at him. "No one is responsible for what happened tonight except Michael."

"He's sick, Jake."

"Don't defend him."

"I'm not. He's gone to jail. He's going to have to pay."

"Yes," Jake said grimly, thinking of what could have happened to her tonight. "He is."

Her hands, still in his, spread wide. She looked so exhausted a small breeze could have knocked her over. "I just can't believe it."

"I know. Bed," he decided when she wobbled on her feet. He led her to his cot. "Want one of my T-shirts?"

"Please."

She dropped the towel as he settled a shirt over her head, smoothing it down her body. Having his hands on her would have been a pleasure if tonight's fire and the weight of the offer he'd received on the ranch hadn't combined to make him as exhausted as she. He pulled the blankets over her and stepped back but she grabbed his wrist. "Where are you going?"

"You need sleep."

"I need you." She lifted the blankets. "Please," she

whispered, her eyes and voice so hollow it broke his
heart. He stripped down and slid in, carefully pulling
her against him. Her bare legs tangled with his. He tunneled his fingers through her hair, his other hand drift-
ing up and down her back in a gesture he hoped was
soothing her, but was having the opposite effect on
him. The T-shirt had bundled up around her waist.
Panty-free, he palmed her extremely palmable ass and
snuggled her in closer so that the heat of her cupped
his groin.

"Mmm," she mumbled when she realized he was
hard, and cuddled in closer. "Nice."

He rocked his hips to hers, then forced himself to
stop. "Callie?"

She tucked her face into the hollow of his neck and
sighed shakily. "Hmm-mmm . . ."

He kept running his fingers up and down her back,
waiting for her to look at him. "With all that's happened, maybe it'll be easier for us to talk about the offer
I got on the ranch."

She said nothing, but she didn't pull away, either,
which he considered a good sign. "I'm sorry, Callie. So
damned sorry, but I have to make a decision, and I
really wanted to talk to you first."

Nothing.

"Callie?"

A soft snore shuddered out of her, warming his
neck. He pulled away and looked down into her face.

She was fast asleep.

23

When Jake woke up, Callie was gone and he was alone. "Damn it." He got up, dressed, and went outside.

Callie's cabin looked shockingly normal, though the scent of burning wood still permeated the air. He took the extra few minutes to peek inside the front door to make sure everything was okay, and that there were no hot spots, but the firefighters had done their job well.

He looked at the burnt floor, couch, and coffee table, remembering the utter horror of seeing Callie and Amy in the middle of it all, and felt tense all over again.

He crossed the grass without thinking, and Goose came running, eyes fierce as she honked her alarm. He tried Callie's method and reached out to pat her on the head.

She nearly took off his fingers.

"Thanksgiving," he muttered to her, and jogged up the porch steps. He went straight to Callie's office and found her sitting behind her desk, propping her head up with one hand, the other on a steaming mug of coffee, staring glumly at an open checkbook. "Hi," she said, and wearily pushed away the paperwork.

"Hi yourself. How are you?"

She shrugged.

In her eyes was a sadness that broke his heart. She was cut and bruised, and yet here he was, about to make it worse. "I need to talk to you."

"You took the offer," she guessed.

"No," he said, and watched her sag with relief. "Not yet anyway."

Her eyes flew back to his, and he sank to a chair. "Hell, Callie, I don't know what to do."

"The offer is good."

"Yes."

She let out a long breath. "Well. We all knew it was only a matter of time."

"They'll keep all the employees on through the end of the year minimum. That gives everyone lots of time to figure out what they want to do."

"And you'll go back to San Diego."

"My new job starts in one week."

"Okay, then." Callie got to her feet and moved to the door.

"Where are you going?"

"I want to buy this ranch, Jake. I've wanted that for-ever, but I have no collateral for a loan and no credible financial history to speak of. Any real bank would laugh me right out of their building."

"Trust me, there's no one I'd rather give it to. But I need to recoup the money I've sunk into it—"

"I know."

"And I was hoping to set Tucker up with a fund from the profit, and—"

"Jake, *I know.* I know you have to get rid of it. Look, I'll be back. I need to ride. *Alone,*" she said when he got up. "Please, Jake. Just let me go."

The door shut after her and he let out a shaky breath. Let her go? How the hell was he supposed to do that?

He was still standing there when Tucker poked his head in the door. "How is she?"

"Gone for a ride. I need to talk to you."

"Ah, fuck. You're taking the offer."

"It's a good one, and I'd be stupid to turn it down. With the profit, I can get out of debt and have enough left over for the both of us to be comfortable—"

Tucker's eyes flashed. "I don't want your money."

"I want you to have—"

"What I want, Jake, is this job."

"You've got it. The jobs are guaranteed until the end of this year."

"And then?"

"And then you'll have a nice nest egg, you can take your time finding another ranch—"

"I told you, I don't want another ranch."

Jake winced when the door slammed. "Well, that went well." Feeling more alone than he had when he'd first gotten here, he sank back to the chair and rubbed his tired eyes.

Callie flew down the front steps of the big house. She'd told Jake she wanted to take a ride, and that she wanted to be alone, and she'd meant both, but she didn't get on Sierra. She got into her Jeep and drove to town.

She went straight to the offices of Lowell and Dawson and toward the receptionist, her sights set on seeing Matt. She should have gone to her ex-husband first instead of Michael, but she'd thought, mistakenly, that dealing with Michael would have been better for all the concerned parties.

She'd never been more wrong, but she could try to repair that error now. She *had* to repair that error now, because Jake was selling the ranch to someone else if she didn't.

The receptionist, a pretty, perky little blonde, stood up, quivering indignantly as Callie walked right past her. "Hey, you can't just—"

Callie didn't stop.

"You're supposed to stop and sign in, right here in my little book! *Hello*, he's on the phone with his ten o'clock meeting!"

Callie opened Matt's door. He was on the phone, and looked up at her, executing a comic double take.

She assumed this was because after she'd divorced him, she'd stood outside the courtroom and warned him to stay out of her path for the rest of his life or she'd make him a eunuch. Clearly he'd taken her seriously, as he'd made sure to never run into her.

He'd known that she and Michael were close— something deep inside her pinged at the thought of Michael—but Matt had respected that closeness—and his penis—and had steered clear of any mutual gatherings.

Still talking on the phone, he lifted a finger to indicate she should wait a moment. Callie took a seat and studied him. He was still way too gorgeous, with that dark, bed-tousled hair and those sleepy bedroom eyes that could seduce a nun from across the room. At five foot ten, he wasn't overly tall, or even gym buffed out, but his body looked damn fine in clothes, and he knew how to dress. Women still fell all over him, she was quite certain, but inside that beautiful exterior beat a fickle heart.

He hung up the phone but didn't look directly at her. "You wouldn't believe the shit Michael got me into. It's all falling down around me. The business is screwed. I'm screwed."

"Yeah, he only tried to kill me. I'm fine though, thanks for asking."

"Uh . . . yeah." Matt winced and met her gaze, with apology in his. "Are you really fine? Because you look like shit."

"I'm going to live. Look, I'm sorry about Michael, and the business."

He sighed. "Yeah. Me too. You didn't come here to tell me you're sorry I got hosed."

"No, I didn't."

"I'm not going to like this, am I?"

"You hosed *me* once, remember?"

"That was a long time ago—"

"You hosed me bad."

"Not that bad—"

"On our wedding night I went out to get us pizza because you begged me to, you said you were too tired to drive. I came back and you were banging the desk clerk. In our honeymoon suite."

"Yeah." He grimaced. "Uh, this isn't a great day for a trip down memory lane—"

"And then the next day, I came home—"

"Unexpectedly," he pointed out.

"—And you had the mail lady in our bed!"

"Do we really need to talk about this?"

She crossed her arms. "You owe me. You know you do."

"All right!" He tossed up his hands. "I made a terrible husband. I knew I would, it's just that you were so different from the others, I really thought I could—" He shook his head. "I was sorry then, and I'm sorry now. But, Callie, how long do I have to be sorry?"

"Until you remember telling me that if there was ever anything you could do . . ."

"I meant it."

"Good. Give me a loan."

"For how much?"

"Half a million dollars."

Matt laughed. He laughed good and hard, then stopped abruptly when she didn't so much as crack a smile. "That's . . . not a joke."

"No."

His smile faded. He looked a little worried. "You know I love you, Cal—"

Now *she* laughed.

"Hey." He actually seemed hurt over that. "I know I was an ass, but I really did care about you."

She shook off any momentary softening she might have had because she knew he had a way of turning things around to suit him. "I know today sucks, Matt. You want me out of here. No, don't shake your head, you do. Your current bimbo—er, your receptionist—is already pissed. You want me gone. Michael let me think he'd give me a loan. He strung me on for a month and a half. You get me a loan today, and I'll leave."

He looked at her for a long time, then sighed. "Shit."

"You can do this for me. I know you can."

"*Shit*," he said again, but reached for his pen and a pad.

Jake paced around on the ranch, unsettled and unhappy. When Joe called, Jake didn't feel like talking. "I'm sorry, Joe, but it's a bad time—"

"I know. Just listen, you got to hear this." Joe sounded jubilant. "We just found out Billy has a fascination with fire, a fascination that predates you. In fact, over the past two years, the kid started no less than three fires at his school. Can you believe it? No way will any case against you or the department or anyone stand up to that. Celebrate, man, cuz it's over."

Jake stared at the phone. "Are you serious?"

"As a heart attack."

Jake didn't quite know what to do with himself after that. He pocketed his cell phone and paced around some more. He wanted to be excited, but he also wanted to share it with someone. With Callie. But two hours later, she was still gone.

She'd called in and talked to Amy, saying she wasn't going to be back in time to do the meet and greet for the new guests, or even the afternoon ride, but the crew would show Amy what to do.

Amy had looked so proud to be given this job that Jake had to swallow his frustration when Amy had hung up without finding out where Callie was.

And why she couldn't come back.

And why she'd taken the Jeep for a ride, instead of Sierra. He managed not to hassle Amy, but he didn't have to be so gentle with his own brother. Jake grabbed Tucker and pulled him aside. "Where the hell is she?"

Tucker didn't speak for a moment, and when he did, his voice was utterly void of the derision and sarcasm Jake expected. "She's probably upset, and doesn't want to upset us. She'll stay away until she has it together."

Jake stared at him, searching for any sign that Tucker was lying, that maybe he really knew where Callie was, but his words sank in, as well as his sincerity. "Damn it."

Tucker actually looked sympathetic. "She'll be okay."

Yeah, but would he? "She's got guests coming."

"I know." Tucker scratched his jaw. "She's never missed a meet and greet before, not even after Richard died."

But she missed this one, and as he pitched in and helped, working with the entire crew, he realized how much he'd learned over the past two months. He knew how to coax the guests into enjoying themselves, he knew what and how much to feed each of the animals. It was all second nature.

Now he stood in the corral with Stone, Eddie, and Tucker, getting the horses ready for an afternoon ride with the guests. At two o'clock on the dot, Eddie and Tucker both looked at their watches, then patted Stone on the back.

Jake looked between them, confused, and Eddie said proudly, "He's gone two weeks without a drink."

Stone nodded. "Fourteen days."

"That's . . ." Tucker stopped to count. "Over three hundred hours."

"Three hundred thirty-six," Stone corrected, and snagging his arm around Eddie's neck, kissed him noisily on the cheek.

Eddie swiped at the spot with the back of his hand. "What was that for?"

"For being my brother." Stone grinned. "Love you, man. Love you all."

"Jesus, you sure you're not drinking?"

"Tell me you love me back," Stone said with a grin.

"Shut up."

"Come on, tell me." Stone made kissy face noises near his brother's ear until finally, laughing, Eddie shoved him away. "Fine, you idiot. I love you. Now you'd better remember that cuz I'm not going to repeat it."

Tucker laughed, too. "You'll repeat it, soon as you need to borrow some money."

Jake smiled, but, damn, he'd really wanted this place to be nothing more than a plot of dry land filled with a bunch of animals that ate too much, and a big house that drained him dry.

But there was more, so much more. A family lived and breathed here, a family and a group of people he cared about deeply. While he stood there absorbing that, his cell phone rang. "Jake," his real estate agent said, "you have another offer. A bigger one." When she rattled off the terms, he stood there, dazzled and stunned. "Jake? All it takes is a yes from you and I'll get the paperwork going."

Eddie and Stone were now helping two of the guests get on horseback. Everyone was laughing, taking pictures. Tucker showed yet another guest how to put on a bridle. Marge and Lou were handing out hats and gloves. Amy had come out, too, and sat on the fence watching, smiling. *Smiling*.

"Jake? You there?" came his agent's voice.

This place had come to mean more to him than he could have ever dreamed, and if he felt that way after only six weeks, he could only imagine what Callie and these guys all felt after spending years here. This was their home, their life. "I'm sorry," he said into the phone. "Turn the offers down. Both of them."

Callie sat staring at Matt in shock. She was still in his office. She'd planted herself there, refusing to leave until he secured her the loan she wanted, and then called Jake's Realtor on her behalf to make the offer. "What did you just say?"

"I'm sorry, Cal. He turned down the offer."

"Why?"

"The agent said the ranch was already sold."

"He really did take that other offer." She dropped her head into her hands. "How could he?"

"He can do whatever he wants. It's his place. Look, you gave it your best shot, but it's over. Fini. The end."

Stunned, she shook her head. "It . . . can't be."

"Maybe you should have let me tell him who was making the offer."

"I told you, I didn't want him to know it was me, because I wanted to do this fair and square. Without emotional debts or attachments."

Matt sighed. "You and I both know it's far too late for that. If he's in your life, you're attached. Just as you're attached to that godforsaken piece of land, and all the people on it. Everyone knows this about you, baby, so it's time for you to admit it. You leap with your heart, and just let your brain along for the ride."

She stared at him, horrified to find her eyes filled with tears.

"No." He shook his head and pointed at her. "Don't do that. *Shit,*" he said when she didn't—couldn't—stop, and thrust a box of tissues at her. "Christ, dry up, would ya? You didn't even cry when I screwed around on you."

"Shut up, Matt." She blew her nose. Sighed. Leaned back and studied his ceiling.

Matt came around his desk and sat next to her, tentatively putting a hand on her shoulder. "It's too late for tears now."

She sniffed. "I know."

"Good." He snatched his tissues back. "You should also know, my emotional debt to you is now paid in full."

"Yeah." She sniffed. "Hope I didn't put you out."

"Hey, can this be about *me* now? My entire life is falling apart, and you've taken up hours of my time." He sighed. "What do you think the chances are that people won't notice that my partner is a raving lunatic?"

Amy stood in the kitchen creating dinner. Thick, meaty sandwiches on bread she'd baked earlier, with a side of fresh coleslaw. She was humming to herself and having a good time when Tucker came into the kitchen.

He walked right up to her, pulled her away from the counter, and turned her to face him.

She held a knife in one hand, a celery stalk in the other. She took in his expression, which was tense and grim, and felt her stomach drop. "What is it?"

"I'm going to kiss you," he said.

The breath shuddered out of her lungs, and it wasn't fear or revulsion that did it, but sheer shock, and . . . a trembly sort of anticipation so foreign it took her a moment to recognize it for what it was.

"I know you don't like to be surprised," he said. "So I thought I'd warn you." His head lowered slowly, his eyes steady on hers. "Ready?" he whispered.

Her entire body quivered it was so ready. "I think so."

"Good." Then his warm lips were on hers, warm and easy. The knife and celery clattered to the floor.

Tucker pulled back, his eyes darker now, his mouth just a little wet—from hers, she thought with surprise. And something else surprised her, too. He looked a lot less grim. She'd done that for him, and the power of that was an incredible rush. Suddenly she wanted to kiss him again and erase the rest of the tension from his body. "So what was that for?" she asked unevenly.

"For trusting me with you last night."

She stared at him. "I think I'd trust you with anything."

"Good, because you can." Gently he pulled her into him for a hug. A hug. Her eyes burned. Her hands didn't hover this time, but touched his shoulders.

"Mmm," rumbled from his chest. "Love your hands on me. I trust you, too, you know. With anything. Even my heart. Which you have by the way. In the palm of your hand."

She concentrated on dragging air into her lungs; not easy. "What do you mean?"

"I love you."

Nope, breathing was impossible. "Is that supposed to be some kind of a joke?"

"No joke." He touched her face. "It's a gift, freely given. You just sit on it a while, see how it fits." Then he kissed her again and walked toward the door.

She stared at his back. "Where are you going?"

"Taking the guests on a ride."

She put her hand to her lips, still tingling from his touch. He loved her.

He wanted her to get used to that.

She smiled. She thought maybe she could.

24

Callie made the drive from Three Rocks to the Blue Flame on autopilot, numb to the core.

She had no one to blame but herself. If she'd told Jake from the beginning she wanted to buy the ranch, if she'd swallowed her pride sooner and gone to Matt a month ago . . .

She could go over the reasons and excuses until the cows came home, it didn't matter. The ranch wasn't hers. It never would be.

When she pulled up the driveway, she could see that most of the horses were gone, which meant that Eddie, Stone, and Tucker had the new guests out.

Good. She could have this out with Jake in privacy. And they *were* going to have it out. Because though this was her own fault, she was pissed. He couldn't have waited one hour to accept that offer? Gathering more and more righteous indignation as she went, she searched for him, hoping he hadn't gone riding, too. He wasn't in his cabin, nor the big house. To her shock, she found him in the barn brushing Moe. She stared at him in confusion. "What are you doing? You hate that horse."

At the sound of her voice, he jerked around. "Jesus,

where have you been? I've been going out of my mind."

"Really? Why?"

He came out of the stall and toward her. "*Why?*"

"Yes." Stepping back out of his reach, she crossed her arms. "I would have thought you had plenty to do around here without wondering where I'd run off to, what with selling the ranch and all."

He looked confused. "Who told you I sold the ranch?"

"You did."

"I told you I had an offer."

"Don't play games with me, Jake. You sold the place. It's over. When do you leave?"

"Callie—"

"When do you leave?"

"Sunday."

My God. Sunday. Just three days away. . . . The air escaped her lungs, and to her horror, she felt her eyes fill. "Fine. Great." She turned away, but then whipped back toward him. "I can't believe it, I just can't. You couldn't wait one more hour. I guess not, seeing how desperate you've been to get away from here. All the wide open space and country lifestyle was just dragging you down, right? The lack of nightlife, the lack of women—"

"Callie, I didn't sell the ranch."

"Then maybe you could tell me why the hell I swallowed all my pride and went to Matt, begged him for a loan, and you *still* turned down my offer?"

Jake looked shocked. "You went to Matt for a loan? So *you* were the second offer? The one that came through a couple of hours ago?"

"And all I had to do was relive his transgressions

one by one, watch him squirm, and remember how it felt to have my heart sliced in two. Not too much humiliation, really, when I compare it to this." She laughed harshly, swiped at her eyes, and turned in a slow circle in the barn she'd imagined as hers. "You never wanted this place, or all that went with it, and I understood that. But to come so close, so damn close—"

"Callie, I didn't sell. In fact"—he pulled a piece of paper out of his pocket and thrust it at her—"I was busy this afternoon myself."

She stared at him. "What's this?"

"Read it."

She did, and her eyes nearly popped out of her head. "A quitclaim deed?"

"In your name."

"You're"—lifting her head, she stared at him—"*giving* this place to me?"

"Yeah. Good luck with it." He shoved his hands in his pockets and offered a smile.

She let out a baffled laugh. "You can't just give me the ranch."

"Look, the lawsuits are all going to be dropped. I'm not going to be swept through the gutters financially like I thought."

"The suit was dropped?"

"Yeah. I'm going to be okay."

"Oh, Jake." She put a hand to her aching heart. "Oh my God, I'm so glad. So you can keep the ranch now."

"I've got to get back to San Diego, you know that." He strode up to Moe. "You let me brush you," he said to the horse. "You damn stubborn animal. Now I'm riding you. Do you hear me? I'm riding you once before I leave. Don't kill me." He grabbed the reins and mounted, and rode past Callie and right out of the barn.

"Damn it." Callie saddled up Sierra. By the time she rode out into the early evening, both Jake and Moe were long gone. But she figured she knew Jake far better than she'd ever intended to. He was saying goodbye, and there was only one place for that. Urging Sierra into a gallop, she headed toward Richard's Peak.

When she got to the top of the canyon, near the rock formation where they'd scattered Richard's ashes, the wind ripped right through her. She turned a little to the west, and against a slowly sinking sun, she saw the stone they'd marked for Richard. Jake stood before it, his back to her as he stared down at the stone, the valley sprawled out in front of him. The wind plastered his shirt to him, ruffled his hair. Moe was tied to a tree, far enough away that he couldn't take a bite out of Jake.

Callie dismounted Sierra and came close.

"I thought I might feel Richard here," Jake said without looking at her. "I thought maybe the answers would be here." Hunkering down, he brushed some dirt off the stone. "I keep wondering how this all happened, how he could have let my entire childhood go by without bringing me here even once. Maybe if he had, I would have seen—" He ran his fingers over his father's name on the stone. "I just don't get it. How could he so easily accept the rebuke of a twelve-year-old, without ever trying again?"

Her anger drained. Heart aching, she moved closer. "I don't know."

"I just threw the firefighting thing at him because my ego was hurting, and after his reaction, it stuck with me. Good thing I loved it, huh?"

"Jake—"

He shook his head. "At the end, when he had his will drawn, do you think he remembered he hadn't spoken to me in years? And if he did, then why the hell did he leave me everything he owned?" He let out a disparaging sound. "So many damn questions, and not a single answer."

He surged back to his feet. "I don't know what I expected. Maybe the answers to leap out at me?" He shook his head. "But the only thing up here is the setting sun, and"—he looked at her—"an odd sense that it's okay. It's okay because in spite of everything, he did the best he could. And in the end, just like in the beginning, this was all he had to give me."

"It's a hell of a lot," she said quietly.

"Far more than I knew. He gave me everything. *Everything*," he said softly, and took her hand, turning them both so they could look out into the valley together. "I don't want to fight with you, Callie."

"That's too bad, because we have one good one left." She pulled the deed out of her back pocket, then ripped it in half, slapping the two halves against his chest. "I want to buy this place from you, Jake. Not have it handed to me."

"You never take the easy route, do you."

"Not often."

He looked so confused. "I thought I was doing the right thing, giving you the ranch."

"No."

"What do you want from me, Callie?"

"To hear what's going on." She put her palm over his heart. "In here."

"Isn't trying to give you a half million dollar property a big enough statement?"

"I see you with your brother, and there's such longing in your face. Do you ever tell him? I see you brushing your father's horse even when it would bite you on the ass if it could, and still, you keep trying with the stubborn thing. I see you look at me, and I've got to tell you, Jake, there's so much in one look that you take my breath, but you don't say anything. When we're in bed at night, our bodies sing together, and I . . ." She closed her eyes and felt a dreamy smile cross her lips. "I've never felt happier." She opened her eyes and looked at him. "But you never say a word about how you feel about us."

"I'm leaving—"

"Yes, I know. But as you've said, there are planes. Cars. Phones. E-mail." She touched his face, wanting so badly to reach him. "I just want to hear what you're feeling," she said again, more softly, and held her breath. "About the ranch, the people in it. *Me.*"

He looked at her, then closed his eyes. "I remember what it was like to have Tucker in my life. I mean *really* in my life. God, I miss that. And that damn ornery horse over there, my *father's* horse . . . looking at him I feel such regret that it's like a stab in my chest." She still had her hand over his heart, and he covered it with his. "How am I doing?"

Through a veil of tears, she nodded. "Good. Now me."

"And you . . ."

"Yes? I drive you crazy? I make you mad? I make you want to rip all my clothes off? Pick one, Jake."

"All of the above, most definitely," he assured her. "But there's something else. A biggie."

"Spit it out then."

"I love you."

Her own heart tumbled. "Oh, Jake."

"I know. It's a complication."

"It's going to be okay."

"Really?" He shoved his fingers in his hair and looked nearly destroyed. "How?"

"Because I love you back. With all my heart."

He stared at her. "You do?"

Poor, poor baby. "Oh, yes. Very much. You're really not going to sell the Blue Flame?"

"I want you to have it. You should have had it all along."

She took the two pieces of the quitclaim deed back from him, and ripped them into a hundred more, scattering them on the wind. "The only way I want this ranch is to share it with you. Yes, I know you're leaving, and I don't care. I have a big fat loan now. I can help you."

"Callie, no—"

"I'll fly to see you as often as I can."

"You'd come and spend part of your time in San Diego?"

"To be with you, I'd live on the moon."

He looked flummoxed, and a little unsteady, and as if his legs wouldn't hold him any longer, he sank to his knees. "You . . . really love me."

"Yes." She dropped to her knees as well, and cupped his face. "Think you can handle it?"

"I can handle it." He kissed her long and deep, and then pulled back looking very seriously into her eyes. "I have a confession to make. Don't laugh."

"I won't."

"I do love you, and believe me, those words are quite new to my vocabulary, but you're going to have to share me."

"You're not sleeping with your receptionist—

Sorry," she said at his shock. "Too much of the ex-husband today. Go ahead. You love me, and you also love . . ."

He muttered something, and she shook her head. "Sorry, Jake. I couldn't hear you."

"That stupid horse over there. I love that stupid horse." He pointed to Moe.

She bit her lip.

"You promised not to laugh."

"I'm smiling. Quite different from laughing." She hugged him. "Oh, Jake, you're so sweet."

"*Sweet?*"

"You are."

"Well, then, I should tell you, I also love this land. I can't believe it. But I actually want to live here, at least part of the time. I was thinking . . ."

She trailed a finger down his chest. "What?"

"Thinking—" He grabbed her finger. "That maybe I could teach every *other* class of recruits, and be here in between."

She went still. "The best of both worlds?"

"Only if you're in both of those worlds." He brushed her hair away from her face, traced her earlobe with his finger. "What do you think?"

"It won't be easy." She stood up, gave him a hand and pulled him up, too. "I'm bossy. And I like to have things my own way."

A smile tugged at his mouth. "I've noticed. But I have my own bad habits, you know. I can be broody, especially if I don't get sex once a day."

"Hmmm . . ." Her heart surged with such hope and love, it almost hurt. "Then we'd better make sure to sleep together every night."

He stroked her jaw. "That sounds like a commitment."

"I'm not the commitment phobe here, Jake."

His other hand came up, cupping her face. "I find that particular fear has left me."

Her breath caught. "Is that right?"

He looked down at Richard's stone and nodded. "Yeah." He brought her hand up to his mouth. "Do you ever talk to him?"

"Richard? Sometimes."

He touched the stone, then did something he'd never really done before. Talked to his father. "I'm sorry I never told you when you were alive, Dad, because you would have gotten a kick out of this, but you were right. You had it all here." He opened his arms to Callie. "Right here."

She moved right into them, there being no place on earth she'd rather be.

EPILOGUE

Six months later

"I can't believe we're doing this." Jake turned over once, and then again, in a useless attempt at comfort. Max, one of Tiger's soft brown puppies, took advantage of the moment to lick hi12s face. Laughing, he pushed the not-so-little-anymore puppy away.

Callie smiled and stroked the excited puppy. "You promised if I made it through your firefighter training course, you'd try camping again." She spoke patiently, even lovingly, but she had a wide grin on her face, assuring Jake she was enjoying every moment of this.

This being Jake inside a small tent, inside an even smaller sleeping bag with a wild puppy, trying to get comfortable. "I think there're a thousand rocks right beneath me."

"Big baby," she teased.

Back in Arizona after a training session in San Diego, she'd dragged him out here in the Dragoons with far too much glee. With a wicked smile, she picked up Max, set him right outside the tent, attaching his collar to a long lead. "Be good for a few minutes," she said, and zipped the tent shut. Still smiling, she pulled off her sweatshirt. Her T-shirt went next, leaving her in a leopard push-up bra. While Jake's mouth went dry, she shimmied off her jeans.

Her panties matched her bra.

"I charged them," she said a little breathlessly, and climbed into the sleeping bag with him. On top of him.

His hands went on a tour of her body. "I love your Visa."

"Actually, it was yours."

He laughed. "Why don't we just get one Visa together, dedicated to your lingerie issues. I have no problem donating to the cause."

"One Visa?" She eyed him carefully. "That sounds . . . serious."

"Uh-huh." He swept the hair from her face and just lay back soaking up the incredible feeling of having her warm, soft body draped over his. "And while we're at it, why don't we use the same last name?"

She looked at him, her eyes huge. "Are you asking me to marry you?"

He traced her jaw. "How about it, Callie? You're already my lover, my best friend, and most definitely my better half. What do you say you make an honest man out of me and make me a husband as well?"

Her eyes shimmered brilliantly, but her voice, when she spoke, was light with teasing. "I'm not sure. I want a husband who can appreciate the finer points of the life out here—including camping."

"Make you a deal." He rolled with her, until she was tucked beneath him. "We sleep like this, and I'll camp every single night."

"Now there's a deal I just can't pass up." She laughed and rolled again, and they tangled for a while, somehow losing all of Jake's clothes as well, which worked for the both of them.

"So, the future Mrs. Rawlins . . ."

She touched his face. "Yes, Mr. Rawlins?"

"I love you."

"Love you too, Jake."